A British Girl's Guide to Hurricanes and Heartbreak

Also by Laura Taylor Namey

A Cuban Girl's Guide to Tea and Tomorrow
When We Were Them

A British Girl's Guide to Hurricanes and Heartbreak

LAURA TAYLOR NAMEY

Atheneum New York London Toronto Sydney New Delhi

An imprint of Simon & Schuster Children's Publishing Division
1230 Avenue of the Americas, New York, New York 10020
Atheneum logo is a trademark of Simon & Schuster, Inc.
For information about special discounts for bulk purchases, please contact Simon & Schuster Special Sales at 1-866-506-1949 or business@simonandschuster.com.
The Simon & Schuster Speakers Bureau can bring authors to your live event. For more information or to book an event, contact the Simon & Schuster Speakers Bureau at 1-866-248-3049 or visit our website at www.simonspeakers.com.
Interior design by Karyn Lee
The text for this book was set in Celeste OT.
Manufactured in the United States of America
First Edition
10 9 8 7 6 5 4 3 2 1
Library of Congress Cataloging-in-Publication Data
Names: Namey, Laura Taylor, author. | Namey, Laura Taylor. Cuban girl's guide to tea and tomorrow.
Title: A British girl's guide to hurricanes and heartbreak / Laura Taylor Namey.
Description: First edition. | New York : Atheneum Books for Young Readers, [2023] | Audience: Ages 12 and up. | Audience: Grades 7-9. | Summary: Teenage Flora, still reeling from the loss of her mom, leaves England for sunny Miami, where her constant self-doubt about life, including romance, leads her straight into a love triangle.
Identifiers: LCCN 2022034453 (print) | LCCN 2022034454 (ebook) | ISBN 9781665915335 (hardcover) | ISBN 9781665915359 (ebook)
Subjects: CYAC: Grief—Fiction. | Love—Fiction. | Interpersonal relations—Fiction. | British—United States—Fiction. | Miami (Fla.)—Fiction. | LCGFT: Romance fiction. | Novels.
Classification: LCC PZ7.1.N3555 Br 2023 (print) | LCC PZ7.1.N3555 (ebook) | DDC [Fic]—dc23
LC record available at https://lccn.loc.gov/2022034453
LC ebook record available at https://lccn.loc.gov/2022034454

For Kate Elizabeth,
my beautiful and extraordinary daughter

❁

The tree that got hit by lightning
is the one you remember.
—MARTY RUBIN

It's not difficult if you know how.
—EDWARD LEEDSKALNIN

MAY

I hold up okay until Dad plays "Clair de Lune." The piano recording trickles through my house, and dozens of faces bend toward the music. They must be thinking:

Evelyn loved this one.

I heard her play it years ago.

A peaceful song for a woman finally at peace.

Beyond nostalgia and unbreakable sadness, my chest seizes with guilt under the new black shift dress. My toes pinch in these sensible pumps from standing so long over a misted grave site. Standing so long against the living room wall, wedged between family and friends as they share memories of Evelyn Maxwell. My mother.

The stories are lovely. Even I cracked a couple laughs. And I was certain Dad wouldn't—couldn't—speak, but he did. A short bit about their first date when she spilled hot cocoa over both of them and he was already halfway in love.

I thought for sure my older brother wouldn't have managed a speech, the getting-through-it and all. But Orion did just that, with Lila shoring up his side like an iron scaffold. I love her more for it.

Now a cousin says his final words, backed by Debussy. Our

neighbor replaces him next to my mother's black piano but pauses like she's misplaced a thought. "Heavens, we didn't hear from Flora yet." She searches the room, landing on me. "I would never take a turn before you, dear."

Heads swivel, and my face hardens into stone even as my knees collapse. Cotton fills my ears, muffling the buzz of voices. *Flora, yes, Flora. Of course, she should have her say. Flora, Flora, Flora.*

"I . . ." is all I get out. While my mum deserves a thousand memories, I can't stand next to her piano and share. It's not because of the grief of finally losing her to early-onset dementia. It's more and different, and I want to sink beneath the floor.

The gentle urging continues, time ticking against my skull. Sweat beads over my neck as I catch the profiles of friends who came today. I could ask any one of them to stand with me while I speak. But I won't.

If I do, I'll break into bad things. My truth isn't fit for rooms like this.

Before my next thought lands, I'm weaving through our tiny living room and out the front door. I slam it behind me, silencing gasps and murmurs and my name hoisted high with question marks.

With each step, I regret not being able to grab my camera from the bookshelf. To draw strength from its weight and hold it close. I run with only the secret that grays all my memories. Two weeks ago, I ruined the day Mum passed away. And only my camera knows.

Dear Flora,

I'm writing with wonderful news. The Greenly Center's governing board has voted to rename our new common area "Evelyn's Room" in honor of your mother and her years of dedicated service to our establishment. Renovations will be completed in October, and a spectacular event with full media coverage is planned to dedicate the space. As we are a refuge for teenaged girls, we thought there would be no one more fitting to give the tribute speech honoring Evelyn and her philanthropic spirit than her beloved daughter. More details to follow, but please advise.

Sincerely,

Kathleen Morrow

The Greenly Center

ONE

JULY

If that man would quit staring off into nowhere and move two measly steps, my next shot would be perfect. I arm my camera and hover my finger over the shutter button. Waiting. He must sense the impatient tapping of my foot against the pavement because he finally moves along. Now it's perfect.

I passed this row of vintage motorbikes on my way into work. I'd hoped they'd still be parked in the designated bay a few streets over from my family's tea-and-pastry shop when my break time came. The post-drizzle gloom at this time of day makes the best lighting for my photos.

Click, click, click.

I shoot the parts tightly, framing the promise of power and movement. Rain-dotted pipes, rotors, calipers. The gleaming bikes must belong to some kind of club. Millie, our grandfather's restored Triumph Bonneville that Orion took to uni today, would fit right in with all the polished logos and buttery leather. Nothing sounds like these machines; Millie's an angry, growling bitch.

It's only when I pause to check my memory card that the time stamps clue me in. Christ, I'm late. I should've been back finishing strawberry empanadas at Maxwell's twenty minutes ago. It's a miracle Lila didn't text me nineteen and a half minutes ago.

Luckily, I'm not far. I stride along, clutching my Canon DSLR. I bring it nearly everywhere and usually sacrifice my lunch break to shoot around the High Street. When Nan gave me the camera a year ago, she hoped it would become a fun hobby, but it's become my everything. The lens holds some of what I can't carry inside. *Point and shoot. Capture. Refocus.* The black case cages the secrets that stain my fingers like the fruit glazes Lila and I make. Eventually, I'll work through what I've hidden. And then there's the e-mail from Greenly in my box from yesterday—I'll work through that, too. I want to speak this time. To share about Mum. But two months haven't released the vise grip over my tongue, the fog filling my head. I don't know how to do what they're asking.

I stuff the anxiety back where it came from, but my stomach dives for another reason as I round the corner to Jewry Street. The Maxwell's queue is monstrous. I elbow inside past eager customers, tucking away my camera and searching for my apron on a supply shelf. Perplexed, I actually look *myself* over and—*bugger*—I never took it off. My front's stained with strawberry puree, and I must've looked like a walking crime scene out there.

"Sorry! I know, I know, I know," I say to Lila Reyes when she pokes her head out from the kitchen. I pick up a rag and try to look productive.

"Don't worry, amiga," she calls from the back. "I've already got the baker's version of burpees and squat jumps planned for you."

"Of course you bloody do, and I love it!" Give me her annoyance over bland enabling any day. I know what to do with a little piss-off.

Lila enters and lobs a tremendous smirk. She wears a bandanna over the rise of her brown ponytail and a dozen other hats: Cuban-American chef and baker. Miami expat. Le Cordon Bleu graduate. The girl who loves Winchester nearly as much as she loves my brother. And whom I love like a sister.

She's carrying a tray of blueberry scones, which I unload and slide into the dessert case that's replaced our old tea-tasting bar. An appreciative gasp settles across the shop; those pastries will likely sell out in minutes while customers grab bags of their weekly English breakfast and Darjeeling. Partnering with Lila to bring in a pop-up version of her family's Miami Cuban bakery was the best decision Dad's made in years.

We work on refilling trays of Chelsea buns and Cuban butter biscuits when knocking sounds from the pass-through window. On it there's a sign: *Closed, Please Proceed to Our Front Entrance.*

I spring around. Our friend Gordon Wallace is leaning his ruddy face into the glass. "Seriously? Is he going to melt if he stands in the regular queue?"

"Oh, he already tried this shit while you were on your extended break. I shooed him off," Lila says as she runs toward a beeping oven timer.

I stomp over, grab the window latch, and slide. "You!" I point at Gordon, who has the audacity to look affronted. "Yes, *you've* been throwing pebbles against this thing like a ginger Romeo for days."

The pass-through on the exterior side wall was Orion's latest idea to allow customers to step up for a quick snack. Something for Lila alone. Outside, there's a smart awning and chalkboard menu sign. *And* a Gordon angling his torso over the short counter. He's in a checkered shirt, sleeves rolled up. The blues and greens look good against his deep-auburn hair—I'll give him that.

"You can't blame me for enjoying the novelty of your little snack stop." Gordy proceeds to slide the windowpane along the frame, back and forth, with childlike fascination. "Well built, that," he muses. When it's impossible for me to contort my face any further, he stops with a hitched laugh. "Oh, and I want a Chelsea bun. *Please*," he adds, like it's some great thing.

"You're paying with real money and not game pieces?"

"Or you could put it on my tab."

God help me, I step back and grab the bun and even wrap it up neatly. "What tab?" I say as I pass it over. "You usually get your fix free of charge because Lila's nicer than me."

Gordon tears off a bit of the bun. Shoves it in and disintegrates into bliss. "What's that say about you if a girl with South Beach, café cubano, and guayaba in her blood is the nicer one?"

Being both half Venezuelan and a far-removed relative of Lila's, he says the Spanish bits correctly. Lila originally visited Winchester three years ago because her distant cousin and tía of her heart—Gordon's mum—lives here. The Wallaces were the start of why we have Lila at all.

Before I can shoot back something clever, Gordon faces me head-on. "Come on. You're nice enough. A good friend, too."

I bite my lip, tasting the dregs of vanilla balm. "Don't go

too soft on me." Especially after what I've lost. I might shatter. *Don't be too kind; I don't deserve it.*

"Never." He tips his chin. "Well, off I go." He launches into a grand exit show, his movements wonky and overblown as he backs away. All he's missing is a court-jester suit.

"Flora?"

I pivot. While other employees handle the queue, I join Lila over a tablet where she plans out menu items.

"For tomorrow, I'm thinking brioche and levain loaves. Plus cherry-chocolate scones and tres leches cakes. I also feel like doing up some mille-feuille."

A thousand sheets. Lila will handle that delicate French confection similar to a layered napoleon. And I'll help with the rest. "I can start more pastry dough?"

She gives a thumbs-up and scoots off to make herself a cuppa.

Halfway to the kitchen, my heart quits when I lock eyes with an enormous *RAT*! I scream and follow with a round of my choicest words. I left the window open, and a rat's crawled onto the service ledge.

A hundred things happen in the course of three seconds:

The shop queue goes to pieces. (Sorry, everyone.) All of the High Street's surely heard me. And just as Lila rushes over, I peer closer and find that the creature's not moving. With newfound courage mixed with mortification, I grab the disgustingly lifelike and utterly *fake* rat, holding it by the rubber tail. The queue's now laughing. (You're welcome, should I take a sodding bow?)

"Gordon!" I yell out the window.

After years of pranks, Gordon Wallace might as well have

signed his name on this one. Today, he's in for a special kind of payback. I flip around to Lila, already undoing my apron strings. "I know we have work, and I was late, but—"

"Um, hell no. You'd better run, chica," Lila says.

I flash a wicked grin, toss the rat to Lila, and bolt.

The queue parts with gasps and grunts. "Get 'em good. I wouldn't stand for that," one of our regulars calls out as I hit the pavement.

Either Gordy's gained speed along with height and muscle in the last couple years, or he has accomplices. Not a red hair in sight. After a moment of hesitation, I launch myself across the rain-washed street toward the secondhand shop. Owner Victoria's sweeping her entrance. She sees me coming, pausing her task when I skid to a stop.

"Gordon?" she asks, reading my mind. When I nod furiously, she cackles and points with her broom. "Thataway. Took off like a wildcat."

"Thanks, V!"

Of course he'd pick the bustling High Street. Plenty of places to duck into and loads of pedestrians and bikes to dodge. I weave along, leaping puddles and catching enthusiastic echoes of my name as I pass.

"Oi, Flora!"

"She's little but speedy!"

"Someone's done it now!"

Growing up here, I know most everyone. I acknowledge them with a splayed hand or pumped fist.

Two streets in, I lose the band cinching my hair. My tight blond curls are going to swell like proofed dough, soaking up the remnants of drizzle and wind.

On a hunch, I sprint until I reach a stone building with a cobalt-blue door—the architecture firm where Gordon works part-time. *Sonder, Fagan, and Michl* reads the sign hovering over the entrance. I burst through the door, triggering a bell.

Mr. Fagan, founding partner, steps out of my way. "Goodness, miss."

Panting, I will my feet to stop. "Oof, sorry." Left-right-left my gaze flips. I smooth my curls, cringing at the storm-cloud feel. "Did Gordon pop in here just now?"

"Sorry, haven't seen him."

"Right. Thanks anyway," I say, miffed at my gut for being wrong. I take two steps before the admin, Oliver, exits the conference room and flags me.

"Gordy *was* here, maybe twenty minutes ago." Oliver pulls an object from his pocket, hands it over. "Said you might come by, and if so, I'm to give you this."

My mouth drops. I'm holding a golden owl trinket no bigger than a paper clip. A clue—one that's insultingly easy. So Gordon *wants* me to find him? And he not only knew I'd stop here; *he* stopped here first on his way to the tea shop. What the hell is going on?

"Thanks, Ollie. I think." I reach for the doorknob.

Now I'm certain Gordon's expecting me to sprint over to his family's inn, the Owl and Crow—cute, Gordy. And ten quid says Oliver sent a text saying I took the bait. Why not take my *time* and make Gordon think I've given up on revenge? Make him sweat a little?

I change direction and stroll, the golden owl tucked into my fist. I really look where I'm going this time. A hundred uncaptured photos frame themselves, teasing my imagination. I've walked this road since I was a girl. Masked, I could find my way along the grayish pavers and narrow streets. From Primark to Waterstones, to the homemade soap shop Lila and I love to visit.

But the world turning over this street is new each day; life and people change. Only my camera can capture them as they are, or as I want them to be. When I'm shooting photos, people leave me alone. I like that. And they don't know that sometimes I'm not trying to preserve a moment, but to twist the appearances of things. A digital stage where I choose the players, decide who sings and dances and loves. And who lives.

Life is not like that at all.

I take the long route around Winchester Cathedral to the St. Cross neighborhood. My family lives in this part, too, a few minutes away from the Owl and Crow Inn. Gordon's family keeps the grounds of their Georgian bed-and-breakfast tidier than most parks. And Lila's still Gordon's hallway neighbor in the Wallace family's third-story flat, three years after a summer visit turned into her new home.

Rounding the corner, you can't help but notice the towering brick structure. The rose arbor is in full bloom, but not fragrant enough to mask the wily stink of the boy waiting out front.

I halt. We lock eyes, and I'm dreaming up all the ways to—

"Well done, you!" Gordon calls, brandishing a white hand towel. Christ.

Well done? I set my jaw and spring forward, white flag or not. When close enough, I pelt the little owl straight at him; infuriatingly, he catches it.

"Dammit, Wallace," I snarl.

"Wait, wait, wait." He holds out his arms.

"You little—"

"*Wait,* then." He steps into my zone as if it's safe. "If in ten seconds you still want to pummel me with any other objects, I'll be a statue."

"Not just me, you twit. Lila might do you worse because we have work and you tricked me into the middle of a toddler game."

"Had to get you here somehow. You wouldn't have come here first because it's too obvious. Had to plan for that." He wiggles the little owl.

My brows narrow, and once again, I hate that he's right.

"As for Lila, I don't think so." The corner of his mouth crinkles. "You'll see why she gave you the rest of the day off in a minute."

"You're out of seconds."

"I can count, Squiggs." Gordon's nickname for me curls around his tongue like my corkscrew hair that inspired it. He leads me around the inn to the vast garden and guest recreation area.

And . . . *Oh!* The scene in front of me hits all warm and wonderful at first. But guilt rarely works alone. It messes with other, good feelings all the time. Clouds them like this bloated sky. And I don't want to think what I'm thinking as we walk across the lawn, but I can't help it.

Don't be too nice. I don't deserve it.

TWO

A picnic. Gordon set up a surprise picnic—my favorite way to eat any kind of meal. With the upcoming wedding of her sister, Pilar, on the brain, Lila's been joking that my future wedding reception would be a gigantic picnic with finger foods and kicked-off shoes. Gordon's version is a green gingham blanket, and a hamper, and a cute tin container with my favorite bottled fizzy drinks on ice.

My heart cracks, and I feel my face crumple even as guilt pinches inside. "This is so . . . I mean, what exactly *is* this?"

Gordon jostles my arm. "Um, we're celebrating? Did you forget you finished your exams—what, four days ago?"

Forget that? Impossible. Completing the last of the A-level exams I'll need to go on to university only winds the clock ticking over my future that much tighter. *And you're off! Make something of yourself!* Last autumn, when most of my schoolmates were applying to uni, my family had urged me to factor in a gap year before applying; we'd all suspected we were facing Mum's final days, and we were sadly proven right. But . . . now? I have until November to choose a study course and apply for next year, or I'll lose the generous scholarship that my brother worked so hard to secure for me.

Six months ago, Orion nominated me for an eight-thousand-pound scholarship for children of chronically ill parents. I was chosen from loads of applicants. My story. In turn, I must commit to a university program to apply it to. And I'm running out of days.

Four months to lock in what, and even who, I want to be. Easy for some, but when have I ever been the easy one?

A crow squawks, and I snap back to my friend. He's twiddling his fingers as if he's worried he screwed up. *God, Gordon. You're not the one on this lawn who did.* "Look, thanks, mate. A lot," I say, bumping his side. "You going to show me the grub you got to make me forget that prank you just pulled? I'm starved."

He grins, and we arrange ourselves on the blanket. "'Course you are, because you never actually eat on your breaks. Except an energy bar or something dodgy you can shove down while you're taking pictures." He opens the hamper and removes two Bridge Street Tavern takeaway containers. "Is fish and chips enough to keep my head off your platter?"

"Hmmm." I open the lid to fried perfection. Snatch a crispy chip, then another. "Any platter's too small for that inflated mug of yours anyway."

A laugh rockets out. "Fine. I deserved that," he says, sobering enough to blaze a steely trail between our eyes. My throat hitches over a swallow, and I look away.

As one of my oldest friends, Gordon Wallace has always had a bag full of magic tricks to keep me smiling and even laughing. Even recently.

Humor is simply what Gordon does; it's who he is, under
all that ruddy skin that carries enough South America to coax
a tan in summer. He's a next-door prank, a clever trick. The
good kind, though. Gordy's always been the one to get me
home when he found me a little too sloshed, a little too late.

But being friends with this boy is more than that. It's the
crooked bend of his jaw as he hijacks my pot of curry sauce—
again—because he never orders his own. It's his total obsession with the dog-bark text-notification sound no one else I
know uses.

But it's also the way we can just *be*. Merely exist, eating in
our kind of easy, companionable silence.

When we're down to grease stains, Gordon stows our boxes
and rubs his hands together like a ginger grasshopper. With
a magic-show flourish, he pulls a bakery box and his mum's
porcelain serving plate from the hamper.

"So posh," I say, but then my belly flips as he opens the lid
to reveal a dozen assorted petit fours. They're more art than
food. Intricate flowers bloom in pastel colors. "Lila?"

"Who else?" he says, and begins plating the delicate treats.
"I asked her for something over the top. She came through,
yeah?"

The work, the *ask*, suddenly feels like too much. I arc my
hand. "All of this is incredible, but you didn't . . . have to."

"Flora," he says, hurt flickering against his gold-brown eyes.

But I don't deserve beautiful things when I have done such
secret ugly things. *Maybe one day, but not today.* "It's not that
everything isn't lovely."

He exhales. "Listen, this is about more than your exams.
The prank and the special foods—I wanted to do something

just for you. For at least a little bit, did you feel something other than grief?"

"If I admit that, do you think Lila won't put that rat in your shower when you least expect it?"

"No chance she won't," Gordon says as the sky breaks and the rain rudely crashes our picnic. "Oh bugger! Hurry!"

We do, gathering everything from the lawn. Gordon runs ahead into the inn, protecting the precious treats. I dodge the downpour and follow him through the kitchen side door. Being the height of tourist season, the random thumps and chatter of guests echo through the vast property. I brew Maxwell's tea, and Gordy sets up dessert on the gigantic butcher-block island in the middle of the commercial but homey space.

"You get the cherry blossom one, of course," Gordon says, handing me the first petit four in its paper wrapper. I make an indecent face as I taste my favorite lemon raspberry cake under the pink icing.

Gordon goes for one with a daisy and scarfs it down in one bite, which isn't unusual.

I still glare. "Lila's food should be savored. Like a nice wine, or a painting, or a—"

"A kiss."

I nearly spew hot tea on my jumper. "Not what I was going to say."

"It was, though. I know these things."

"What? When have I ever talked to you about kissing?" I press.

Immediately, he says, "Six months ago, for one. Don't tell me you've forgotten that James bloke and his great roving tongue. Which turned into more roving than you'd consented to, the sodding prick."

My memory ticks, and I deflate into a big sigh. "Oh. Too right. He was a sodding prick."

Satisfied, Gordon nods. Makes a sharp angle with his head. "And who did you message with *Help, I'm stuck on a shithole date with an ever-loving arsehole?*"

I grumble out, "You."

He points at me with his next cake. "Yeah. And I raced thirty minutes to that club in Portsmouth."

I soften into the nostalgia. "You did, didn't you? My jump out the loo window was one of my finer performances, too. But still, there was no actual kissing talk."

"There *was*. You were too far into your cups to remember." My brows furrow, but he presses on. "You lowered the seat back and curled up all the way home. I thought I was going to have to carry you in snoring."

"I do not snore."

"Sure, you don't." He dashes out a hand. "Anyway, you went on about his school-dance-level rhythm and cringe lines. And how his tongue was switching between windshield wiper and stand mixer." He laughs, stepping forward. "I almost ran off the fucking road. But then you said he started tinkering with your dress. Which you were *not* having."

"Wow. More bits *are* coming back. Please say I thanked you?"

"Oh, you mumbled it, like, ten times between Portsmouth and your place. Still, the story was a better reward. Lizzie was so entertained, it totally made up for me having to bail."

My next breath skips. "What?" Gordon dated fellow architecture prospect and University of Portsmouth student Lizzie for about ten minutes a while back. "You were on a date?"

He balls up our wrappers, tossing them into the bin across

the kitchen. "Yeah, but not at a show or anything. Just a last-minute hang at Bridge Street."

"Still! You left Lizzie and drove all that way to scrape me off the alley?" When he shrugs, I press on. "Why didn't you tell me to piss off and get an Uber?"

"What if you'd gotten a weird driver? You were sloshed."

I toy with a loose thread on my jumper. "Yeah, but you were *with* Lizzie. Doesn't that mean she gets . . . ?"

"What? Like first dibs on my time? Lizzie went home, but she was safe, okay?" He stops, shaking his head. "I didn't think past your ask for help."

And he came, dropping everything and everyone else. As simple and complicated as that.

My eyes take on a thin sheen at Gordon's revelation. I bob my head aimlessly, my heart stirring like it's been awakened from a long nap. Part of me wants to dare myself to feel something other than regret, but the rest reminds me that so many things I've meant for good have turned sour. *You can't risk any more.*

"Is it really so hard to believe?" Gordon mumbles.

I nearly lose my footing. A thousand conversations I've had with this boy. Now I struggle to pick my way through these few plain words like we're speaking a foreign language. "I . . ."

He steps in front of me. "Did *you* stop to think why you messaged me first?"

"You're my go-to." *This* tumbles straight out, but my mind instantly reaches for a safer spot. "I knew you wouldn't tell Dad, and that you'd find a way to make it better. You turned a rotten night into something fun and even laughable. Like always."

"Like always, huh?" His expression dims. "But not now. It

looks like you're about to cry. And outside, you were clearly bothered about something."

I shrug, conceding; there's no use hiding that fact from this friend. He already understands a lot of what I've been processing since May—that I couldn't speak at Mum's wake, for one. It was Gordon who found me inside the churchyard next to this inn and just held me as I broke down. He took my worst like a fortress. But he still can't know all the things I've buried. No one can.

The message in my inbox is something I can reveal, though. "This came yesterday," I say, handing him my phone.

Gordon scans the e-mail from Kathleen at the Greenly Center. "Wow, this is such a beautiful honor for your mum. Her name on an entire wing?" After I nod, he narrows his gaze and hops onto the island. Pats the space next to him. "This is clearly troubling you, though. Tell me?"

I try to join him, but the butcher-block counter is *just* out of my short-girl hopping range.

"Up you get, Squiggs." He hoists me onto the counter and deposits me at his side. We've sat like this on park benches, and on Millie with him frantically yelling for me to slow down (never), and at pub tables listening to our friend Jules's band.

The lightness of all those days gets to me. My eyes well fully now. And maybe *this* is why I tell him. If I don't, I'll explode. "They want me to deliver this tribute with stories and memories. And I truly want to do this—Mum deserves it. My family does, too, and it would make them proud." After years of me being called out for being late. Irresponsible. Flighty. "But I don't want to fuck this up in front of everyone, and I'm stuck. Blank." I peer up at him, and he takes my hand, eyes like the softest things I can name. "It's like I can't follow through with anything the right way. I mean, look at me! Have I even picked a course though Dad and Orion have tried to 'encourage' me at every second? *No* because I can't decide. Worse, I can't even *see* a future for myself." I shake my head roughly. "What I can't stop seeing is the wake. That day. Literally everyone else spoke, but I ran."

Sweat and heat pool between us, and my tears stream. Gordy finds a tissue (because he always has everything). "Hey. Everyone understood your response. Your grief." He shrugs. "Well, maybe after Lila and I evil-eyed the room to keep quiet before they could get all carried away with gossip. Before I came after you."

He pulls me close, fitting me into the notch between his shoulder and chest, and the rustle of cotton there.

"It's more than not knowing what to say. I don't deserve to give that tribute. To stand up there," I say into his shoulder. There's a bigger truth wrapped around that statement, a bigger failure that would hit like a typhoon and blow the whole roof off this inn. I stomp it back, breathe it elsewhere until my eyelids go lax and my pulse thrums so faintly, I wonder if it's really there at all.

Gordon pulls away, setting his chin. "You are the one they want. Greenly is a home for teen mums who aren't safe with their families. Your mum played piano and brought tea and just listened to the girls, for years. Now they want to listen to you because your voice matters." He points. "*You* are Evelyn Maxwell's daughter."

I nod, my lips curled under. But what does it mean to be that girl? And what am I to do with her?

Gordon feeds me one last petit four with a palm-tree design for Lila's beloved Miami. "You'll figure all this out," he says. "I know you will because you're awesome. And November's still a fair bit away. You'll sort out your uni course and ride that amazing scholarship, too."

"Right," I say, wishing that the good things friends say about you would automatically become true. Wishing that friendship and life worked that way.

He bumps my knee. "There's something . . . else I've been meaning to say. That okay?" Dazed, my mind twirling, I nod. "I've mentioned this before—my degree requiring service and study hours in a place with notable architecture. I've been meaning to set that up, but I put it off so long, I didn't get my first-choice spot in Florida. The program director offered me San Francisco. I've not accepted yet."

"Wow. California?"

"Yeah, but with one word from you, I can easily put it off until after next term. To be honest, I'm leaning that way. It's why I wavered." He squeezes my forearms. "I could stay here and be here for you. And with you. With Jules and the band touring all summer and Lila busy establishing herself at your shop, I didn't want you to be alone." He blinks once, then again. "Actually, I wanted you to be more than not alone, and maybe we . . ."

A roaring pounds between my ears. "Didn't you hear what I just said? That I'm struggling to plan my own future? Now you're asking me to decide yours?"

"It's not that at all. More like . . . God, you really don't know, do you?" he whispers.

My belly flips. I should be able to decipher this—him—

better. The words aren't hard. But somewhere between Gordon and me, they burst into a thousand falling stars with nowhere to land.

He drops his head, speaking to the wooden grain marred with flour and salt. "Even if I had been at a fancy show, I'd have come for you."

A faint whining sound fills the space; I realize it's from me. "I don't know what to say." *Preserve, protect, because it's all turned upside down.* "You just threw a rat into my window."

"You honestly think I'm joking now?"

I swallow hard. "I told you, I don't know what the hell I'm doing with myself."

He hops down. Exhales roughly. "I don't mean to rush you. That's not what this is." His brown eyes are molten. "It's just, before I go, or stay, I wanted to get this out. I swear I wouldn't have said a word if I thought you didn't want, or that I didn't sense you might feel—"

That I might *feel*? When I can't even recognize the word anymore? I've lost my right to look deeper into my feelings.

Sure, my eyes still work. I peek up at Gordon, and he's . . . Okay, he's really fit. He looks good—more than good. I don't know when or how this became so true. The chiseled shape of his jaw and matured set of his mouth, the wider angles and harder planes, the cropped but carefree hair in an artist's palette of deep russet tones.

The problem isn't what I'm seeing; the problem is that I'll hurt him. With all my lies and secrets, I'll hurt him just like I've made a mess of everything else. Lately, that always seems to happen when I try to love and protect myself. Why should Gordon end up any safer?

A truth I *can* admit: I don't know everything that lives in my heart. And I'm terrified that if I take even one deeper look, I'll ruin any good I might find there.

"I'm bad news right now. A disaster," I tell him, my voice mixed with sand. "You're better off keeping your distance. You should go to San Francisco."

Three eternal seconds pass. "That's your answer, then?"

"It's for the best. Go do your program."

"Yeah, I think I will." He whirls around, like he can't bear the sight of me, and strides to the swing door. I'm trembling as he pauses with one palm upon the wood surface, shaking his head. His eyes are rimmed with red. "Forget that bloody rubber rat. Joke's on me this time."

THREE

Before Dad says a word, it's clear he wants to talk about the piano.

A few hours have passed since I came home from the inn. Where Gordon stomped away, and I got what I deserved. I feel a sense of rightness, a morbid satisfaction, about how things ended up. But as the memory of our talk replays, the inside of my head is a throbbing ache.

Dad seems to be dealing with a similar weight. He sits on the leather bench like he's resting loads more than his body. Apparently, it's time to face what he asked us to "think about, just think about" after Mum's part of the Phillip and Evelyn Maxwell Family Trust was read in May. Orion got her engagement ring, and I got her anniversary Cartier watch and gold wedding band. Orion got her first-edition books.

But the piano is the sticky part.

The black Bösendorfer resting against the staircase wall was Mum's from girlhood. She was good at it and tried to get both her children to carry on her gift. We'd given it a go, but all things musical skipped us both.

When the will was read, we'd learned Dad had been keeping a secret of his own. Mum, with her philanthropic heart, wanted her piano to go to hands that would play it—specifically the girls and staff at the Greenly Center.

Dad hadn't told us before then, and he cried that day in May when it came up. He tears up now as he rubs his hand along the matte ebony finish. "I've been putting this off. She was so adamant about her plan, but it's a big ask of us."

"But with the Greenly Center's new common room opening in October, we need to decide," Orion says from his spot on the sofa between Lila and me.

My father looks at us, two blonds and the brunette who unofficially brought us back to a family of four. "I still don't want to go against her. But this piano is a part of her, and I would never rob either one of you of that. That's why I wanted you to think it over." He scrubs his face. "We can always get a secondhand piano to donate to the common room. Not exactly her wish, but the spirit is the same."

"I have been thinking. And talking to Lila about it." Orion scoots forward, bent over his thighs. "The piano was a part of Mum. But the way she cared for others and never missed a week visiting the center—that is the part I'll remember most." His eyes fill, and Lila tucks her face into his shoulder. "That's with me wherever I go. So don't hold it on my account." He nods my way. "While I do like the idea of it being a gift, I still think Flora should have it."

My eyes jerk wide. "You do?" When my brother nods, I go on. "What if I feel the same as you? That I have plenty of heirlooms, and it would feel really good to give something beautiful in her name? Not a substitute, but the thing she truly loved?"

"Okay, yes, that's a lovely sentiment," Dad says. "But this is a big decision, and I want to ensure you've truly considered all the angles. Once given, we can't get it back."

Because according to him, that's something I would do—donate the piano and then try to get it back. I'm the same girl who ran from this very room in May. He probably worries I won't follow through with the tribute speech for the common room, either. And I don't bloody blame him—that's the hell of it. But I still despise the wariness in his eyes.

I pinch my fingers together. "I have thought about it. But that doesn't matter because I'm doomed to be the same as always, right? Flighty, fickle, and rash. Christ, that sounds like a cartoon."

"That's not what I said," Dad stresses. "I'm only double-checking."

Words rush forward, ones that a hundred other sisters and daughters would never say.

I dash my hand toward the piano. "How about double-checking *our* memory? Have you all forgotten the day that Mum couldn't remember how to play 'Clair de Lune' when I asked her? Or that something called 'Clair de Lune' was even a song in existence, never mind that she'd mastered it years ago? It was my favorite!"

After I hummed a few bars that day, Mum suddenly remembered and played the entire piece by heart. But even though she could still play from someplace inside her, she couldn't match the notes to the name of a song or a composer, or to any memory of learning them. And it was terrifying.

"The only thing the piano really played that day was the tune of a terminal diagnosis," I say. "The first sign of what was coming. So, yeah, this piano was a part of her, but it was also part of the worst thing to ever happen to us."

Oh, but that strikes a chord. The air goes chill, and no one speaks for too many seconds.

"I never knew you thought of her piano that way," Orion says softly. "You were so young when she was diagnosed. You had less quality time with her than I did, and I was only thinking it would be a way to keep more of her when . . ." He drops his head.

"When what?" I press. "Say it, then."

"You didn't make it in time to say goodbye."

My lungs deflate in all this truth. And in my greatest lie.

Dad looks up. "It's something I'll never forgive myself for. That I didn't do more to make sure you were able to be there."

Forgive himself? No—that's not it at all. "Dad, it wasn't your fault."

Blame me. I knew what I was doing.

"I've thought that, too, and it keeps coming back to me," Orion says. "If we'd stayed together that day or if Lila and I hadn't stopped by the shop first. Or if we'd all come just a half hour earlier, before the nurse called us, you could've avoided the accident. All the traffic."

There was no accident. No traffic.

"We knew it would be soon," Lila adds softly. "But then her heart rate began to . . ."

Don't go far, the doctor had warned. Stay close.

And ten times more unfitting than picnic celebrations and petit fours are my family's thoughts and feelings about me. Their guilt has no place here.

"Please." I push off the sofa. "I can't stand for you to feel this way." I cross my arms at my chest, pacing toward Dad's wall of photos from his world travels to find unique blends and wares for the shop, and then over to the curio filled with pictures of better days.

"We let you down," Orion says. "And you weren't able to get closure."

A surge—*remorse-regret-rage*—begins at my toes. Heating, rising. "Orion, stop!"

He pauses, sniffling, carrying on as if he doesn't hear me. *As if he doesn't see me.* "The whole time, we were stuck between watching her and watching the clock and not wanting to call or text while you were driving."

I pace with jerky movements inside a mental storm. My feet unsteady, limbs captive under frigid rain. A swirling wind twists up and through, knocking my bones together like wind chimes. Tolling like a great wide bell: *Look what you did. Look, look, look.*

Around and through me grows a cloud, grayed with painful memory, straining against the edges of my skin. It has to blow and break—*I* do. It's the only way they'll really see. It's the only way I can rise above everything these past few years have taken.

I am bigger than this. The disease, the searing loss, has never overpowered me. At ten and twelve, at sixteen and eighteen. I have cried and missed my sweetest mum more than anything, but I have never let dementia win. And I won't let it keep me from being *seen* by the only people I have left.

"All we wanted was you," Orion says. "That moment was never going to be right, but having us all together would've helped. And all because we didn't text you ten minutes sooner."

I find I can't move.

A week before Mum passed, the doctors said it was time to transition her to the hospice ward. I absorbed every warning about staying nearby and followed that first day to her new room, taking it all in. How they try to make these final spaces homey. Floral curtains and a real quilt on the bed. Soothing blue walls and peaceful artwork. Oversized recliners were there for family—for us to eat and sleep . . . waiting.

My heart was in that room.

But my feet began to test fate and took me past the boundaries the doctors mandated in their white coats. I started small and went to Twyford, lining up at the chip stand that serves them steaming hot in a paper funnel. I crept farther some days, to the tops of hills and edges of townships. (You can't tell me what to do. You can't keep me here.)

Every time, I brought my camera.

In a patchwork room, my mum was slipping away, out of my control. I was cursed to bow under frontotemporal dementia and its greedy fingers. (Take everything, won't you?)

But with Nan's birthday gift, I took something back.

My photos were mine alone. I snapped silhouettes of children playing at sunset. A black starling, landing on a rock, stood regal like a queen. I played with macro settings and dove into the pollen-dust centers of flowers, cropping out the dirt around them. I honed in on the grain of a purple petal, not showing the bite a pest had taken from the edge. With my camera I could reframe life. I could manipulate the outlook of my lens universe when the real one had said:

First the piano songs, then the small things of life. Where the sugar goes and "What's our neighbor's name again?"

Then "Who is the blond boy and the younger girl he guards (curly haired, rosy cheeked)?" She will forget she named that girl for the cherry blossom trees in London (so pink, pink, pink). And she will forget what London even is. All the queens and kings, the history of them.

Then she will forget why she is forgetting.

Her limbs won't remember to rest. She will sleep only with medication. You'll tuck her in tight. Your nan will come to help her, and sometimes you.

One morning she will fall and break her ankle. Then she'll leave for Elmwood House. You will visit for years until it's time for you to stay close.

But I didn't stay close. I shot into the world.

Children of dementia are doomed to lose their parents twice. I would lose my mum twice, mind and heartbeat—a double death. One plus one and one times two. And God help me, I decided I would not give disease the satisfaction. I would protect myself, control everything I still could. I would give Flora Maxwell this one bit. All I was saying to myself with that camera around my neck was *You've already done this.* Wasn't the deathbed of being forgotten enough?

But that May morning, disease said no. And when Orion texted, **Flora come now, hurry,** I was not close. That was my first defiance.

My second was in not coming right away. I crumpled to the grass, crying, but then I rose to shape another happier world. I adjusted angles and put my life into the camera between my hands. And then I went to hospice, on my terms, with not a shred of guilt *until* I saw the three faces, the three bodies huddled over the bed, mouthing, *You're too late, too bloody late.*

They looked at me as if I hadn't only missed my goodbye to Mum, but to a dying part of each of them.

And now Orion and Dad are still apologizing and taking on my guilt, my fault? The way I acted was out of my own will, and they can't have it.

I move so quickly, magazines fly off an end table. My spine locks tight, and I hold my hands out like I could part the ocean of anything.

My dad sharpens. "Flora, what the—"

"Stop! I did it on purpose. I chose not to come right away because I didn't want to see her go. I didn't want to be there!"

Lila rises but keeps her distance. "What . . . How, amor?"

"The accident and traffic, I made it all up as an excuse." My movements jerk, hands flailing and heat rising. I flip to Orion. "When you messaged, I wasn't near home like you thought. I was in Allington. And even then, I didn't come straightaway. I took more pictures."

Disbelief. It's written across three faces, and this won't stand, either. I am red and screaming in this room, and they don't even believe me.

I rush to my tote and pull out my camera. "See?" Lila's moved back to the sofa, and I shove the screen into their view, scrolling through the memory card. "Look at the time stamps."

I whip over to Dad; he's still shaking his head aimlessly. I keep talking, trying to explain my truth. The control I needed. The all-consuming guilt that rose in me when I finally entered the room to the sight of Orion, hunched between Lila and Dad. *You weren't here with us. You missed it.* Dad had reached for me with empty, not open, arms. *I needed you, too. I needed my little girl.*

And when I'm done, I brace myself, fisting my hands and planting my feet because I know—I simply *know*—that I have just proven myself to be ten times the flighty, wayward girl they've always seen me as.

My family is going to rage, and I'm ready for it. I wait, my eyes piercing, my blood so thick it curdles. I begin counting down from thirty. Make it to twenty, my heartbeat like a snare drum. I reach fifteen, and ten, and—nothing?

Dad speaks first but doesn't even lift his head from the cage of his hands. "I am so very sorry . . . for you." His words are made from cotton, the softest wool.

Sorry for me?

"Yeah, that you actually thought this, I dunno, charade was okay. God, Pink, *this* was your closure? You lied to us on the day we lost our mum?" Orion uses my nickname, and this is never how it's been when he's dragged me home (too late too far too reckless) from a hundred anywheres. I've always been *Flora Maxwell* then.

And Lila, volcano-force Lila, says, "Oh, amor." So very soft. It burns worse than molten lava. "You know I think of you as a sister . . . and you couldn't come to me."

I'm rooted to the ground, stunned.

When I was ten and Nan had moved in to help with Mum, I overheard her one time. "She's a hurricane, that one," Nan said to Dad as she swept up glass from a vase I'd accidentally broken. But I grew into the label, empowered instead of hurt. Dementia was unmentionably strong, but I learned I could be stronger. I could forge my own way.

And for so many years, temper and fight, a lively shout—even when they were pointed at me—I've understood and respected those. But not the hushed disappointment my family has just dealt. Goose pimples prick my skin; our living room has dropped twenty degrees. My family's faces scroll downward. They can't even stand to look at me.

Coming clean about my actions has only caused more grief around here. The guilt and mistrust I've already been suffering multiplies until I can barely stand myself.

For the next twenty-four hours, I'm not even living. *Existing*'s more the word. I hesitate before sitting on the furniture in my own home, like it's covered in plastic. I walk the streets, and people's stares twist into accusations in my head. Winchester becomes gray in more places than sky and stone. *I'll find a way to hurt this city, too. I have before.*

My insides are turning to ice. And God, I could use some summer, or even a holiday escape from the past year. Just then it hits me. Warmth. Holiday. My plane ticket for Pilar's upcoming wedding in Miami.

Three years ago, after she suffered terrible loss, Lila's parents sent her from Miami to Winchester to heal and cool herself down. My remedy comes in reverse. I need the sun. I could send . . . myself. Since Nan gave me the camera, I've reframed a thousand shots to appear the way I want them to look. Can you reframe an entire life?

I decide I'm going to try, in a place with no footprints of my mistakes along the stony pavement. I need the kind of heat that will burn through the fog around Mum's legacy and the pain I created around her passing. I want to find and settle the good memories I have of her so I can deliver a worthy tribute. And I want to be able to tell the University of Winchester, *I'm Flora Maxwell, and this is what I want to study. This is who I am.*

The plan solidifies, and I move quickly.

I make a phone call, tearing up when I'm welcomed. Then I make one more call to change the date on a British Airways flight for a Cuban family wedding.

I dig out my passport from Dad's office and drag my suitcases down from the attic. I pack a slip dress for the wedding. Sandals and shorts, tank tops, and sundresses come along, too.

As for my family, I can't take any more *me and them* inside the shame and lies I created. While they've barely spoken to me today, I know they'll want to talk soon, and I'm only going to hurt them further. They'll keep twisting my motives and all that's happened in the last two months until I'm wrung out into nothing. It's better this way. Better if I slip away on my own. They deserve a better *me*, and that girl's not here. She's in another frame; I'm already picturing her in that sunrise lighting, the balmy tropical scene.

I pen three heartfelt notes to leave in my place. In two days I'll take a bus ride to Heathrow and a transatlantic flight.

She's a hurricane, my family said. Good, because Miami knows what to do with those.

Dad,
By now you know I've gone and changed my
ticket. I'm sorry I let you down, but I promise
I'm safe and looked after. Please, let me have
this time.

— I love you, Flora

FOUR

MIAMI, FLORIDA

As locations for self-exiles go, this one is the stuff of glossy brochures and maps to better places. And I should've known that barely five minutes after I stepped out of the drenched heat into the Reyes family home, they'd try to feed me.

"You didn't have to do all this." I stab a cubed potato with my fork. "There was food on the plane."

Pilar Reyes looks up from her own portion at the kitchen table. "No, there wasn't."

I crack a smile. The aroma rising from the Cuban chicken stew made with peppers, potatoes, and tangy green olives is intoxicating. Fricasé de pollo. The colors, so vibrant against the ivory bowl, would make a striking still-life photograph.

I shove in another bite, the flavors ripe on my tongue. "You didn't even ask your parents if I could come. You're positive they won't mind having me around?"

"Of course not. It's like you're seven weeks early for the wedding," Pilar says, winking. "Any kind of early is so not Cuban, but whatever. You're family, Flora. Besides, I'm marrying an orthodontist." She pauses, a grin blooming at the mention of her fiancé, Ryan. "Cuban mami rule of all rules: Landing one

of the top three husband choices—you know, medical professional, business mogul, or lawyer—means you can get away
with tons."

"Even harboring fugitives?"

"Don't." Pilar rests her hand over my knuckles. "You all took
in my hermana when she was grieving."

The same girl I can't even face. I reach for the gold chain
Lila gave me that used to hold a precious charm from her
abuela. But it's gone. I left it back in England, unworthy of it,
at least for now. "Lila doesn't even know I'm here yet."

Pili gives me a long look. "The hell she doesn't. But I won't
share anything when she calls until you're ready to talk to her
yourself, sister or not. I promise."

"Is *that* Cuban?" I ask. "Some unwritten code?"

"No. It's friendship."

Friendship. I've earned a failing mark there, circled in
bright red. Abashed, I turn back to my food, but faces still
appear, framed inside the last moments I had of them before
Heathrow. There's Lila and Orion, asleep on the sofa, Netflix
streaming on the TV. And Gordon's bowed head as he left the
inn kitchen and didn't look back. (Not once, like he always
does. That one last check, that final wink. Not once—)

Stop! I scream into my inner void. My body joins in as I slam
my fork down, rattling the bowl and my end of the kitchen
table. "Sorry." I inhale-exhale roughly. "I'm a little messy."

Understatement, meet Miami, Florida.

Pilar tips her glass dismissively. A wedge of lime wings off
the side. "Jet lag's no joke." She takes a long sip but manages to
maintain eye contact like a stalking leopard. "Plus, everything
else."

Pili won't ask outright why I've come last-minute. That's rarely the way in this home. Instead, I'm welcomed and fed exceptionally well, which is this family's trapdoor into the hidden truth of anyone.

I shake my head. "I work plain and clear. If you want to know what I did, just ask. I'm not a slice of pan cubano that needs buttering, ¿tú sabes?"

Pili nods appreciatively. "Ay, niña, qué bueno el acento." If she's at all offended, I can't find it anywhere in the wide set of her brown eyes. She rises to place the fricasé into the freezer. "And as for plain and clear," she continues, and shuts the door, "meddling is more Lila's style. I work with numbers and invoices all day. And now wedding disasters, apparently." I raise a brow, and she says, "Our photographer just backed out because of a family emergency in Mexico. He got his partner to fill in, but Ryan and I want a modern, journalistic feel. This other guy's vibe is more traditional, and by that I mean totally dated."

My nose scrunches up. Though I brought my camera, it's useless for Pili's problem. It's nowhere good enough to capture a grand wedding, and neither am I. Photography is something I keep close to myself. "I'm sorry. You've worked so hard to make everything perfect."

"We tried," she says. "And now it's too late to get anyone else. My hermana . . . Well, she says not to settle and to keep bugging vendors. But I'm tired."

I nod, conceding. But I don't miss the shadowed haunt that passes over Pili's face when she says the word *hermana*. *You miss her so much.*

"I can't even *look* at a freezer without picturing your sister," I offer. This kind person has given me her home in the middle of busy wedding prep. *Come,* she said. And I don't have anything to give her but a little bit of Lila.

"Why's that?" Pili returns to her seat, interlacing her fingers.

"The day after my mum went into hospice, Lila started cooking." I toy with a pair of Hummel figurines just like my nan has (saltshaker boy and black-pepper girl meet in a kiss). And I close my eyes into the story of my kitchen counters filled with plasticware and countless ingredients, steam and oil seeping into the floorboards.

"I don't know what else to do," Lila had said back then, pulling me close when I confronted her about the obscene amount of food. "Let me keep you all fed."

Let me love you. This is what she really meant.

I helped a bit, but she didn't stop. She kept cooking for days after I untied my apron and picked up my camera. Lila filled our freezer, and I filled my memory card.

"Bah—I rarely used to cry," Pilar says when I pause. "Lately, I can't stop. Has to be the wedding." She thrusts out her palms. "I swear I'm not pregnant."

"If you were, Lila would know and would have already told me. But as for the freezer, there's more. We'd been eating those meals since May, and it never seemed to make a dent, like she'd cast a spell. A couple weeks back, I defrosted a container of what I *thought* was Bolognese. I even cooked up some pasta."

Pili drains the last of her drink, picking up on my cringe. "Oh no. Lila never labels anything."

"Exactly. Which is why we ate picadillo with rigatoni instead of rice."

Pilar snorts out a laugh, but a weird burst of self-consciousness hits me.

"I dunno, it seemed a lot funnier then. It's like my radar's off, like everything else. I keep ruining relationships when I'm just trying to figure out where I'm going. You know, learning to trust myself to choose all those 'next things' without screwing up what I already have. So, again, thanks for giving me a place to get away." I glance upward and meet a kind but knowing face. Mine drops in self-deprecation, realizing I spilled more than I meant to. The nostalgic room where Lila cooked for years, the comfort food—the Reyes *everything* got to me after all.

Pili gives a smirk. "Don't be too quick to thank me. You'll get only a couple days to adjust before Mami gives you her Flora-Do List. Fair warning, vacuuming will be on it. She likes to see lots of lines in the carpet." Pili moves her arm back and forth like she's hoovering.

"It's fine. I knew what I was getting into."

I did not, in fact, know what I was getting into. Three days later I'm in the driver's seat of Elisa's Honda minivan. She's up in front. Pilar's in back, texting Ryan as we run errands and I sit for another kind of exam. Even though I drive Dad's car all the time. Even though I'm the only one in this van who can pilot a motorbike, and extremely well. But I really would like to explore Miami on my own, so I force my tongue to stay put.

It's not that Señora Reyes doubts my driving ability. She

doubts my ability to stay on the correct side of the street, which is the wrong one in Winchester, as she pointed out repeatedly.

"You might start off okay, cariño. But it's easy to forget after some time," she offered as we set out around local streets. "You know the . . . ahh, sí, the muscle memory? The mind thinks *left* on its own. Before you know it, you turn the wrong way and you're in big trouble."

A problem I know like an old friend. But I promised to be extra alert.

And then Elisa said that talking on my mobile or playing the music too loud would surely ruin my focus.

And I, stifling a giggle while catching Pili's silent amusement in the rearview mirror, said I wouldn't dare.

Now I'm directed into the posh Coral Gables neighborhood toward our final destination. Here, oak trees bend and touch from opposite sides of the road, casting sunlit diamond shapes into their leafy tunnel. Some trees in England do this, too, but that's the end of similarities between my real home and my holiday house. In Miami everything is flatter and laced with humidity. Even the color green is different here—brighter somehow? There are a thousand new shades to discover.

"No, Mami, remember the craft fair isn't at Douglas Park like last time," Pili calls from the back. "It's at Salvadore Park."

"Er," I say. "Do I keep on this street?"

Elisa ignores me and flips up her oversized tortoise shades, bending around. "Ay, Pilar, siempre el tiki." She pantomimes some rapid-fire texting thumbs. "If you weren't doing the kissy talk to Ryan, we could have gone the right way earlier."

Pili throws up a hand. "What, do we need passports to get to Salvadore from here?"

"A ring on her finger and now she's a comedian aparte de ser novia," Elisa mutters.

"Like this ring isn't your wildest dream, Mami. Whatever, okay?" Pili leans forward. "Flora, just turn left at the next stoplight."

I do as she says and follow our new route, noting that this mum-and-daughter duo are now chattering gleefully about the custom wedding favors we're going to pick up from a craft-fair vendor. The good mood doubles as I pull into a lucky spot along the pavement. This place looks so . . . happy. Food trucks line the perimeter, and rows of tents and booths cover the park grounds, some with misters to fight the thick humidity.

"Ay, the favors, Florecita. Just wait," Elisa says as we hop from the van. She crosses her hands over her heart. "We brought one of Abuela Lydia's lace doilies, and Lupe was able to paint the design onto three hundred miniature picture frames."

Pili leans in as I loop my camera strap around my neck. "Which makes them extra Cuban. We love a doily. Abuela would've put one under my pink baby ass if Mami would've let her."

"Pilar, ya!" Elisa scoffs. "The frames will grace every table in honor of Abuelita." Her large green eyes, the corners of her mouth droop, like she's tasting all the bittersweet. But then she jostles my shoulder gently. "Go explore on your own and take pictures. Lupe talks on and on forever, ¿tú sabes?"

"Right," I say, grateful. Beyond the bright colors and shapes, the shady clusters of oak trees are begging for some camera time. Before I set off, Elisa presses a ten-dollar note into my hand "for ice cream or a hot dog."

Time slows around me; this is such a motherly move. By the time I look up to tell Elisa that I can use my own money, the Reyeses are already halfway across the grass. I pocket the note as a tinge of guilt comes. These ten dollars feel like a million considering all they've already done.

Finally alone and not driving, I reach for my mobile and scan my messages: nothing from Orion or Dad. Not a peep from Lila. Zero bits from Gordon, either off to or in San Francisco. I'm not too surprised about Gordon. But the rest usually chase after me even when I tell them not to bother. Not this time, though. No one is acting like I've expected lately.

The only avatar in my recent queue is the same one that popped up yesterday—my brilliant musician friend, Jules. And her messages streamed in all at once.

Jules: I stopped home from a canceled tour stop. Flora Maxwell, what did you do?

Jules: Your family's not saying a bloody word

Jules: Was it me? Did I screw something up?

That last one stung. And I hoped one general response would hit all targets.

Me: I know, I'm so sorry, friend, but I need a break and some time. Promise I'm okay and safe

But Jules's immediate response hit me in the gut.

Jules: You are a walking Olivia Rodrigo song. You left a whirlwind and this better be worth it. Love you, and peace, friend

Peace. Do I even remember what that feels like?

Arming my camera comes the closest. I adjust settings once for the afternoon light, then shoot freely, capturing striped awnings and rainbow-shaded balloons and wondering if you can imprint the salty-sweet aroma of kettle corn onto a memory card.

Rounding a corner, I come across a booth. *Tea Leaf Readings.* An older woman with a graying black plait and floral caftan sits, shaded. I lower my camera as her stare bores deep into mine, angling too much into the space I take up. Even when I glance away, she won't stop. *What, lady, are you trying to find some telling symbols on my face? Keep your bloody feelers off me,* I want to yell out. But before I spew a word, a young couple steps in front of me, blocking the connection. The eerie moment vanishes, but my heartbeat holds on tight. I glance around nervously; Elisa and Pili still haven't texted or come for me yet.

I stow my camera, willing my annoyance to cool as I stroll past some of the vendors. The goods are pretty and well crafted, but nothing makes me want to stop . . . until I approach a section of artwork mounted on trifold display walls. I scan pastel watercolors and whimsical oil miniatures and cheeky comic-style scenes. It's then that I reach a section of framed photographs. My eyes want to look everywhere at once, over tropical flowers and insects in macro like I've shot them at home. Lifestyle scenes peer down the colorful Miami Beach coastline from high above.

One photo stands out, though, calling me over like something kindred. Here, a night sky in steely blue-black hosts a stormy cloud mass, grayed at the watery horizon, billowing up into shimmery whites and rosy tones. The photographer snapped the photo just as a lightning bolt strikes through the middle, sizzling in neon pink.

She's a hurricane, that one.

The childhood moment when Nan christened me with this nickname rushes in. It was a pile-on day of learning I wasn't invited to a schoolmate's party, and impossible maths, and Mum changing so quickly. My needs were often postponed like I was the smallest being in the entire world. But that afternoon I accidentally knocked over a vase, and glass shattered everywhere. Nan came running and hugged me tight, and for a few minutes looked right at me and listened. The breaking brought her close. My family used the word *hurricane*, and I made it my own.

It's true that the past weeks have pooled a heavy dose of shame into my nickname, which I'd always thought of as something cool and strong. But this photo shows another side of this force, and of me.

I might even call it beautiful. And more than a tropical storm over a Miami landscape, I see a self-portrait. Good or bad, right or wrong, I'm somewhere inside this frame. *I* could be the pink force striking, the gray mass waiting, not only to break loose over everything that hurts, but to be what it was made to be, and destined to do.

Whatever that is.

I glance at the price—only twenty-five dollars? The signature scrawled onto the white matting is mostly illegible. I make out an *S* followed by an *M* and *N*. Investigating further, I note that the booth is selling works from many different places and artists. I locate a sign identifying this photo group. Hand-lettering reads *Studio Marín*.

Of course I'm buying it. Lately, I've been wavering and stressing over every decision, but this purchase doesn't even feel like one. It's only a photo, but I can't shake the notion that having this bit of lightning with me in Miami is part of the spark I need to move forward.

FIVE

Later at the Reyes home, I'm cross-legged on my bed as I unwrap my gift to myself. Shortly after I made the storm photo purchase, Elisa and Pili found me but only casually asked about the item in my shopping bag. The two Reyeses were *consumed* by their hand-painted frames (which did look lovely all stacked up in the large box). That left little attention to give to *my* framed photo.

But now it gets center stage in the bedroom Elisa gave me—Abuela Lydia's old room with its buttercream walls and daisy-print quilt. A rose scent lingers like the air is garden-dipped.

As I remove the last bit of Bubble Wrap, the whip-snap of lightning bursts from the frame into my imagination. *Studio Marín.* The name has stuck to the back of my mind all day. Something more than curiosity has me typing the words into my search engine: *Studio Marín Miami.* The pull is similar to when you hear a new song that reaches right out from the radio and clamps around your chest. I play those on repeat and Google the artists to learn more about the music that made me feel so much.

That's exactly how this pink-lightning-and-gradient-cloud photo works, stirring that same part of me who saw a bit of herself on that craft-show wall. A photographer is another kind of artist, and I want to know about this one, too.

As Google spins, search links identify Studio Marín as a family-owned commercial photo studio. From the home page, the website splits into another section dedicated solely to Marín Photo. A map location perks up all my insides; both the studio and photography divisions share the same address in Coral Gables. An area I know well enough after my driving lesson. All the hits point toward the owner, Sebastián Marín, and the black-and-white photo accompanying his bio. A wide forehead tops thick eyebrows and full, coiffed hair.

A click on the Marín Photo site places me into a stunning gallery showcase. His work is the definition of style and elegance. Pages of the most beautiful wedding and event photos flood my vision. I scan on through links to newspaper and wedding magazine articles, and blurbs from prominent citizens. No storm or landscape photos exist here, just dozens of beautifully staged events.

I glance at my storm photo with its garbled matting signature. The studio wall tag plus the S and M and N surely peg this as Sebastián's work.

Loafers clomp down the hall, and as Pili's dad passes by, I call out, "Señor Reyes?"

He pivots and crosses my threshold, clucking his tongue. "It's Alan, chica."

Which I'm still not used to. "Er, Alan," I try. "Have you heard of Marín Photo, or Sebastián Marín?"

"Ay, Sebastián," he says, gently correcting my pronunciation. *Seh-bahs-TYAN.*

I give it another go and earn his thumbs-up. "And yes, I know of him. His family comes from Manzanillo, the same part of Cuba as mine. He's one of the most famous event photographers. Many of the brides Elisa does her grandest cakes for try to book him for their weddings. He also runs a commercial studio."

I hold up the frame. "I bought this today, and it's supposed to be one of his."

Alan cranes his neck. "Qué bueno. I would hold on to that one."

I'm planning on it. "Did you try to get him for Pili's wedding? She seems so unhappy with her new photographer."

"Sebastián books more than a year in advance. I didn't want to get Pili's hopes up by even suggesting him." He gives a little wave and backs toward the hall.

After Alan leaves, I rise to change out of the gray crop top I wore to the craft fair. I might sit outside later, and long sleeves are a must to keep my skin from becoming an insect appetizer.

I step up to the double-wide dresser to grab a thin cotton shirt. Elisa left a small grouping of her mother's mementos, or recuerdos, on one side. I haven't paid them much attention beyond leaving them undisturbed while I stored my perfume and a few hair accessories on the other end. Yet spending the day with the mum and daughter who are so connected to the woman who owned these items leads me to investigate them closer.

I take time to study a crystal frame with Abuela holding

Pilar and Lila as children. Then a larger photo of her grinning with a teenaged Elisa and Gordon's mum, Cate—distant cousins and the best of friends. Lastly, I swirl my finger over a rosary coiled on a trinket tray, and across a heart-shaped porcelain box with a tiny chip on the edge. It feels sacred and I don't dare open it.

Laid out under everything is an oval lace doily. It tickles the space between my ribs now that I understand its significance to this family. The sensation doubles when I think of my own mementos of my mum.

They're on my bookshelf at home, and it only strikes me now that I didn't pack even one to bring along. Fine, yes, I was torn and upended, scrambling to get to Miami. But the ugly truth? The daughter who is supposed to give a tribute speech to her mum has barely thrown a glance at that memorial shelf for months. Right now, that oversight feels unbearable.

I pinch my eyes shut, trying to go there in my head, trying to make this right from four thousand miles away.

My mind lands on an item that might seem mundane to anyone but me. A pink gumball, the kind that's too large for anyone to chew. Memory rushes in now, of me at seven leaving Waitrose with my mum. An ordinary shopping day, that was. But for the first time, Mum let me put a coin inside the bright, exciting gumball machine. Green came out, but I so wanted a pink one. And here's the part that sticks, the reason I placed an identical gumball on my shelf a couple years back. Instead of telling me to be satisfied, Mum pulled another coin that day. And another. White, yellow, orange—all the colors bounced out. Even when she ran out of coins and had to trade in a five-pound note, she wouldn't quit. Not until minutes later, when we cheered as a perfect pink gumball fell into my little hands.

Eleven years ago, my mother let me do something frivolous but deliciously fun. And I felt . . . special. I felt worthy of the time Mum likely didn't have. Instead of being practical, she let me be perfectly useless and do something just because I asked. I was special.

I haven't been able to sit inside a good memory of her for so long—the "before" space has been bitter and sharp (because of disease), and then too guilt-ridden (because of me). Since May I've felt more shamed than special. But now this small part of us is soft and shaded pink . . . and okay.

The corners of my eyes fill, and I bend around; I have something to add to this dresser display after all. Another pink item I bought with money that could've gone to something practical, too. Like a song that keeps playing in my mind, I need to know more about this storm photo. Tomorrow I must go to Studio Marín to find the man who captured this piece of my heart. The artist who snared this part of my memory inside a hurricane cloud with a pink lightning strike.

I grab the photo and lean it on the dresser behind Abuela's recuerdos, hoping it's okay to rest my memory here. Hoping this grandmother welcomes my storm next to her glass and porcelain treasures, even though I'm so good at breaking things.

The next afternoon I score the van for the short drive into Coral Gables. I snag a nearby parking space and wind around to the front of a structure soaked in the same pure white as

Maxwell's but with boxy, contemporary lines. Stenciled block letters spell out *Studio Marín*, and a bronze placard reads:

Marín Photo
Sebastián Marín, Photographer

A hum of activity surrounds the building. People slip through the door dressed in black, tugging along photo equipment in both directions.

There's a short lull as I reach the entrance, and a thought rushes in. *Why am I here?* Yesterday's notion seems so much less clear twenty-four hours later. It's good to crave information and be drawn to something. But I didn't call ahead. Like usual, I didn't come here bringing any kind of plan along with my curiosity.

My friend Jules pops into my head and tells that thought to sod off. *If you act like you belong, people think you belong.* Jules lives by this rule, and it once got us backstage to meet Frightened Rabbit in Soho. All it took were some fake lanyard badges and important-looking clipboards, courtesy of her forethought.

I hope I'm half as good at this game alone. At least I'm wearing the right colors. My black crop top skims over baggy jeans with well-placed rips. White platform sandals. Renewed, I straighten all the spine I have and deftly arrange all the boobs I don't under the stretchy top and glide into the studio.

Steps inside the frigid space, my eyes bug out over white walls filled with enormous photos. I pass dozens of framed brides in minimal gowns that must cost the max. Then diverse bodies in cocktail dresses and suits on yachts and ornate rooftops.

What I don't find are any storm photographs. Not a single cloud or lightning bolt. This jolts me back into the rest of the gallery, which is also a receiving room. Two employees dressed in black hover over a Lucite console. A white-brick partition backs their work space. I wind through the growing crowd and catch the attention of one of the clerks in a minidress and patent Doc Martens.

"Pardon me. Is Sebastián Marín here?" I ask.

The clerk's nose—rose-gold piercing and all—scrunches up, and the look coming my way is one of *Whothehellareyou?*

Is there a code word? Hand signal mimicking some sort of winged creature? *Flora, act like you sodding belong.* Right. I flutter my eyelids in total boredom. "Señor Marín," I repeat, using the intel from Alan Reyes. "I'm here to see him. Is he available?"

The other, redheaded clerk clicks off her phone. "If you're here for his portrait workshop, all those spaces were reserved online. This one's a closed event, as we have live models."

My hopes evaporate. Sure, I could loiter for a while to simply get a look at the renowned artist, but what's that going to accomplish? I feel like wasted time itself in ripped jeans, which fits perfectly with everything else in my life. I pivot halfway to thank the assistant for her time—

"Well, well. Blond, fair, and shorter stature it is. So you *did* show up after all? Typical. Like they ever fucking update us."

Sorry, what? The words directed toward me are attached to the voice of someone called Armando, whose white name tag glares against another all-black outfit.

"You're Quinn, right?"

"Flora."

"Whatever." Armando waves his hand dismissively. "Glad the shits and hurls passed enough for you to come."

Excuse me, shits and hurls? I'm now a vacuous stare in ripped jeans. "I . . . er" is all I manage.

As Armando brushes past me, the redhead strides around the console. "Why didn't you say you were from Palladium? Señor Marín is never your school's contact." Thumb to the chest. "That's me. Luna."

"Um, of course. Nice meeting you," I say as the universe clicks into place. Somehow this crew thinks *I'm* one of the class models.

Luna adds, "We've never gotten a British girl before."

Two more clerks appear in a heated rush.

"Oye, they've already started in the loft," one in baggy Dickies calls.

"And with that *hair*, ay qué paquete, they'll need the full hour to get her even close to camera ready," says another aide in a black jumpsuit grasping a tablet.

My hand clamps around my curls. Eyeballs flame. I envision my transformation before I strike: hand on cocked hip, pursed lips. I'm nowhere near the height of the model they think I am, but I *am* louder. I'm about to serve this black-suited crew with a tirade spiced with a few British swear words since they're so bloody taken with the novelty of my homeland. I plant my feet, draw in a gust, and in three, two, one . . . utterly fizzle. I exhale it all.

In reality I'm too flustered to put on my own pink lightning show. I'm a glow stick at best. So I just stand here as the group encircles me, pointing, noting my every flaw and feature.

Hello, Jules, I need you! How can I act like I belong if I don't fully get what I'm supposed to do? But . . . there is one other angle that comes to mind. If I play along and somehow manage to fill in for this model who's likely home suffering from acute bowel discomfort, I'll get more than a few seconds with Sebastián Marín. I might be in the same room with him for an hour.

"Um, sorry, but this is my first time doing this." Whatever this is. "Could you go over the details?"

Armando heaves an affronted sigh. "Luna-boo, can you handle that? And we need her *yesterday*." He turns to the assistants. "With me, please. Setup time, just the way he likes it. Haribo gummies or don't bother, and *only* the guacamole-flavored Takis, and if I see even one ice cube in that entire studio . . ." He trails off as the trio exits.

Luna draws closer. "Sure, hon. This is a two-hour advanced workshop with Señor Marín and his crew."

"And I'm to . . ."

"Wow, you are new. Striking, though, and you've got a good street vibe." Luna stops and uses hand motions to direct someone behind me. "There's a student team from Paul Mitchell doing hair and makeup. Then you'll be led into the studio for the class with the other two models. They've told you about compensation?"

"Not everything."

"Per the Palladium agreement, you'll receive five edited headshots from tonight compiled by Señor Marín himself. I need an e-mail, or I can forward them to your contact at—"

"I'd like them sent to me, thank you." I rattle off my e-mail address and sign a waiver. I guess I'm Miami's newest model.

My surprise situation proves far more interesting than my original evening plans to rewatch *Derry Girls* with the spiders taking residence in my room. We've reached an understanding, the four of us. They may stay if they keep away from my bed.

In the next forty-five minutes, two cosmetology students do something straight out of a sorcerer's handbook with my appearance. They'll also stand by for the class to touch up our looks.

By *our*, I mean myself and the two *actual* models. Over sprays and serums, I learn Binh is Vietnamese, and their biggest dream is a gig in a Fendi print-ad campaign. And Nerea is from Spain, eighteen, and bloody incandescent and runway ready (black-swan hair, circus-stilt legs).

Then there's Flora, who barely clears one hundred fifty-two centimeters, knows shit about modeling, and would simply like to figure out a life plan and study course before her clock strikes *too-late*.

This thought goes to mist as I follow Binh and Nerea from the loft. Extra quickly, on Armando's frantic cue.

When he throws open the studio doors, the *wow* of it all slams against my chest. While getting primped, I learned Studio Marín is one of the top photo studios in Florida. Commercials are shot here, as well as print work for the latest trainers Gordon's saving up for. The vast space, covered in pale wood, can transform into anything a designer envisions. One side is filled with industrial windows for natural daytime light. An opposite wall forms an enormous white curve shape, creating a blank backdrop for fashion shoots. So far my experience with photography stops at one entry-level camera, a school class, and my own way of framing the world. This room is all that spun out into an entire galaxy.

I snap back to the scene. The twelve students are already in place, unpacking gear and looking us over. I try to wipe the stunned-deer flash from my eyes. *Act like you belong, love.*

Luna directs us to a small nook, where a banquet table offers three kinds of waters and Italian fizzy drinks. There's a cheese platter and a large bowl with green crisps. The guacamole Takis? Another crystal bowl is filled with gummy bears.

"Between shots, you're welcome to refreshments," Luna says. "Questions?" Her offer's lost as a collective gasp bursts through the room. The door's swung open, and a tall man strides in. Clapping ensues from the students.

Armando and Luna skitter across, flanking each side of the gentleman. But I am confusion renewed. The photographer walking over to greet the students looks like he took his website image and submerged it into a lake of chaos. He's rocking an orange floral shirt worn untucked over rumpled tan chinos. Brown Birkenstocks. And the sleek, graying dark hair has exploded in all directions like the cloud in my photo. *This?* This is the photographer that socialites and dignitaries fight over?

Inside my next blink, he's approaching. I won't ask him now about my pink lightning; it wouldn't be proper. I'm technically working, too.

Somehow, I make out a broad smile underneath the beard. "Bienvenidos a todos," he says to his models in a liquid baritone. "Qué bueno. Such a lovely group."

Our greetings are swallowed up by none other than Armando, who resembles a warning label for over-caffeination as he guides Sebastián to the food table. Some sort of strange telepathy ensues in which Señor Marín merely directs his eyeball toward the various selections and Armando fills a plate. Gummy bears, guacamole crisps, cubes of white cheeses, a five-finger pour of sparkling water.

The photographer carries his snacks over to the students. Is he actually going to teach with guacamole dust on his fingers? I can't look away.

A large monitor powers on with a thumbnail gallery of studio shots, and Sebastián begins by saying that he and his assistants will be sharing techniques for getting the most out of their subjects. The students gulp down the tips like parched desert dwellers.

After some minutes, movement snags my attention as the main door opens again. A person appears, also dressed in head-to-toe black.

Armando mutters, "Of course he's late," to Luna, then scurries across the room, escorting the figure out of the darkened entrance.

Light wades over the duo, slowly revealing shades of an older teen, likely about my age. When one of the spots catches him in full bloom, it lights him glorious. *Well, hello, you.*

The guy stands a head taller than Armando, with light brown skin and dark hair that's shaved close to the sides and playfully mussed on top. Wide, carved cheekbones and eagle-wing brows. A tiny split in his chin. A grayscale tattoo tracks along his left forearm. His thin black tee keeps nothing ridged and toned underneath a secret.

As my eyes (hopefully discreetly) carry on, Armando's all hand motions, rattling away.

But the guy pays the uptight studio manager little to no attention. He scans the room, including the models, landing on my face for a split second. Then pulls out his phone.

"Who's that?" I whisper to Nerea. "He's the first person I've seen who ignores Armando and gets away with it."

"Because he's royalty around here." She has to bend to reach my ear level. "That's Baz. Sebastián's son."

SIX

I have zero time to indulge my father-son curiosity before I'm whisked off to my first posing area. The students split into three groups, with instructors rotating between them as they work on directing and shooting the three models. One of which is me, stood as tall as possible against the harsh white of the ski-slope wall.

Baz is working with Binh's group, and Luna's is shooting Nerea as she poses gracefully on a velvet chaise. Sebastián is with my group of four and their armed cameras.

"Your job is to capture a subject's heart by way of their eyes," he tells them. "To guide them, patiently, until the precise moment when the eyes reflect what is in the heart." My cheeks flame under the layers of makeup as he steps up to me with his own camera. "This is the core idea of authenticity within photography. Pero, what is not given freely, you *must* coax."

I give a little snort—authenticity? Sure, this man is brilliant, and I'm certain his methods are why he has all . . . *this*. But they're not mine. I rarely use the camera his way. My life has felt too authentic for years. There, disease is real, and it *takes.* Memory. Mothers. Shame and mistakes and grief—God, they're so real, they're bloody everywhere. No, my camera craves an escape that lets me breathe. A better frame. A brighter filter.

But I shake it off. *You're not here for your camera; you're here for a storm photo.*

And I am. Until even that plan gets a reframe.

It's actually Sebastián himself who inspires my new idea. As he captures me, click by snap, something Pili said about her replacement photographer jumps into the frame: Lila wouldn't give up or settle. Added to that, the esteemed Señor Marín turns out to be much more approachable than any of his staff. He's patient and kind as he demonstrates how to shoot someone a little shorter (moi). But I want something far bigger. Forget wait lists or impossibilities—this man needs to photograph Pilar's wedding. I'm here and he's here, so why not ask?

At worst, he could simply say no. If his staff falls into a tizz, I'll just escape again. I've gotten practiced. All I have to do now is stay through class. To not be discovered as a fraud.

That thought barely dissolves before Baz steps up and whispers into his father's ear.

The older man nods, then addresses the group. "Forgive me, por favor. I must step away briefly. Baz will fill in for me."

I glance across the room; another studio aide has taken over Baz's group.

"Hey, everyone," Baz says as he reaches for a black stool. "We're going to work on the classic headshot now. No props, no frills." He spears a look my way. "Just a face. Take a quick break, and then we'll get started."

The group hits the snack table, and Baz strides across the smooth white backdrop. He arranges the stool to his liking and motions me over.

I sit. Unlike Nerea, my legs fall too short to reach the floor. The foot perch it is—and what about my hands? Here I also get my first clear view of Baz's grayscale tattoo. A tree is etched into his left arm with such grit and detail, I can almost smell the sap. Feel the bony edges inked sharp enough to break skin. The exposed root ball webs across his wrist, clawlike.

He leans in, smelling more like a citrus grove than a forest. "I'm impressed," he says. "Most crashers don't make it this far into class before they're booted out the side door. You're center stage on our stool."

My insides ice over. This is not good. "What?"

"You're not Quinn." His voice is his father's Miami Cuban but kicked up a few notes into tenor range.

I jolt my torso from an undignified slump. *Act like you belong.* "Of course not. I'm Flora and filling in because Quinn's feeling a bit poorly. Armando's totally aware of—what was it he said? Her case of the shits and hurls." I watch, waiting for the crassness to land. It barely digs a crease at the edge of his cheeks, and I'm trying to hate that, and maybe even him and his too-cool presumptuousness. But I also like a person who can stand a little muck. So here we are.

"You're not a model, either," he notes.

"Not all models are tall."

He barks a laugh. "Sí, chica. Pero all Palladium models can pose on cue while napping behind their 'smizes,' and that has not been the case for you. You have to overthink to move your body."

He's been watching me?

Baz closes in, spearmint breath puffing between us as he directs me to shift sideways while angling my face frontward. He wants my shoulders back, arms skimming my sides, then tells me to pop my elbows out a hair. So I pop.

"Hold, please."

Beneath my posed frame, my heartbeat races. Is he setting me up just to throw me into the alleyway when everyone returns?

Baz backs away and juts the posh Fuji camera up from his neck strap. *Click, click, click.* He checks the screen and adjusts the studio lighting. "So, Flora from London?"

"From London plus about an hour train ride. That puts you in Winchester."

"Nice. But you can give up the charade. Are you doing a blog piece on the studio?" Baz's mouth tilts sideways. "Or did someone from Encuentro Photo hire you? They've been up my papi's ass for months now, and I wouldn't put it past them to send a decoy."

Twin flames strike hot in the center of my eyes. "You actually think I'm faking being English?"

"No, you're faking being a model, and I want to know why you're here."

There is no way I'm going for truth now. *I came because your papi shot a storm and I followed down the rabbit hole of it like Alice. Oh, and can he work my friend's wedding because she deserves all the good things?*

"You should ask Luna" is what I really offer, my voice rising. "She obviously found me good enough for hair and makeup. And even Armando—"

"Tranquila, Flora. I've changed my mind. I'm not kicking

you out, but it was a close call," he says on a chuckle.

I dash out my arm. "Which means I'm supposed to thank you, then? For your gracious . . . er, grace?"

"No, you're supposed to play headshot model for another forty-five minutes." He signals Armando to send the group back from their break. "I figure these students won't always be shooting pros like Nerea and Binh. You're good for the mix."

My face pulls tight. "Because, naturally, they need to learn to shoot mere mortals. The plain and drudgingly regular, such as myself."

As the students return, Baz leans in once more. "Do you always twist people's words so they end up slapping you across the face?"

He's already feet away when my mind replies, *Well, yeah. That's precisely what I do.* And if you really want to knock me off a perfectly fine stool, tell me something sweet and good that I haven't earned. Then I'll really twist it 'round until it's grown spikes to hurt us both.

I hate that my eyes glaze; at once the makeup artist appears with a dust of powder and another swipe of pink tint. A spritz for a curl that's made a run for it.

When she leaves, my own words are still messy and unfixed. I pinch my lips into a line to hold them back, then ease up, turning my head sideways toward the door.

Click, click, click. Baz shoots again.

At the end of class, Baz bolted straightaway, but not before expertly guiding students in posing me with micro corrections so precise, they brought on a dull headache. And not before his "Goodnight, Flora from sixty miles southwest of London."

I'd choked back something passable while musing on the fact that either Baz is as skilled at geography as he is at lens work, or he'd looked up Winchester between directing students. Which is not *un*interesting.

What's downright irritating is Armando hovering nearby, foot pattering as I sort out my belongings. "You know you can leave now," he adds.

"Mm-hmm," I say, and *oops*, did I drop my bag and now need to repack the spilled contents? Shame.

He grumbles as I chase after a lip gloss, eyeing my target. Sebastián's still debriefing with Luna at the far side of the studio. I only need sixty seconds. And I will have them.

"May I make a takeaway snack plate? I didn't want to crease my makeup before." This is only for stalling purposes, mind. Elisa would hardly approve. Munching Takis crisps whilst driving is a fast pass to distraction.

His sigh is so full of hot air, it could float. "Whatever. Fine."

I grin, piling up my plate. "Mmm. I quite fancy that cheese as well. Manchego?"

He rolls his eyes and says, "Asiago. Naturally, all cheeses must be white," as Luna exits the studio. This is it. *Go, Flora, go.*

"Toodles," I toss to Armando, and scamper away.

As predicted, I intersect the boss as he reaches the studio foyer where all of *this* began.

"Señor Marín?" I call, sidling up before I'm invited.

He turns. "Ah, Flora." He peers down at my filled plate. "¿Tienes hambre, chica?"

I feel a blush. "A little, I suppose. The guacamole Takis are really the only flavor worth eating."

He brushes this off. "I like them all. I just tell my assistants those things. The extra fiddling they do keeps them out of my way, ¿tú sabes?"

A laugh bubbles up fierce in my belly, but I keep it there.

"How may I help you?"

Well, this is the most pleasant spot in my whole evening so far. Now for step one. "I wanted to say how wonderful it is that you give these workshops. I was only posing, but I could tell how much the students appreciated it."

"Oh, that is very kind. I hope you will be happy with the headshots. I wish I could teach more often, but my schedule does not allow it. Baz does most of our student liaison work. He'll be teaching a class tomorrow night on editing."

My ears ping, but I move on to step two, heart pounding so hard, it cracks. "Forgive me for the request, but I was always taught to shoot your shot, and I don't mean with a camera."

His eyes darken slightly. "It's about a wedding, no?"

He must get this all day. My breath hitches but I carry on. "Honestly, yes. A Cuban woman—my friend—from West Miami just lost her photographer and has always admired your work. I'm aware of your bookings and the wait list. More, I was hoping for a lucky chance. It's the first Saturday of September."

He softens. "You should always, as you say, shoot your shot. But I am afraid I cannot help. It's true that I'm booked out every available weekend for about eighteen months now."

His kindness almost makes the disappointment worse. I would've taken haughty sneers and *How dare you even approach me?* arrogance and met it head-on with a raised jaw and all the pride I've stored in this fake model frame. I know what to do with that.

The thought fades as a storm moves in over everything else. The real one that brought me here. "Wait," I say, and set my plate on the console. "I bought one of your framed pieces yesterday. The one of the lightning bolt in this incredible neon pink."

He narrows his vision. "Lo siento, pero I do not have such a photo up for sale in any gallery."

"No, not a gallery. From an art booth at a craft fair."

Sebastián looks like I switched to French or Russian. "I assure you, this fair is not selling my authentic work—"

"They're selling mine, Papi. I took that photo."

I turn and find Baz. Wait, Baz?

He steps up to his father. "Go home. Mami said you've got fifteen minutes or she's eating without you."

"Ay. Good luck, my dear," Sebastián says, and exits.

"You?" is all I can say.

"Armando texted that I left one of my Nikons." He snuffs out a laugh. "He's useful enough sometimes. So here I am, and to my surprise a fake model from England is not only asking my father to do the impossible"—I guess he means the wedding—"but then going on about a photograph that wasn't even supposed to be sold at that fair."

"I'm so confused. Yours was in the Studio Marín section."

He nods. "Yeah, with Luna's and Armando's work. All our studio aides are emerging photographers, and they were asked to submit pieces for the Salvadore Park showcase."

This morning I took a picture of, well, his picture. I reach for my mobile and expand it in my photo app. "I read this as your father's work. *S. Marín.*"

"That's not an *S.* My teachers always got after me for my shitty cursive. It says *B. Marín.*"

I squint. Sodding right, it does.

"I gave three storm shots to Armando to put up in our consultation room. But he accidentally mixed them into the fair lot." He gives a flat shrug. "I let it go, but he still thinks I'm pissed, which is why he's been acting like an overattentive puppy around me lately." He holds out his hand. "Sebastián Marín Junior."

Oh. *Oh.* Baz is short for—of course. I accept the hand. "Flora Maxwell. Not a model."

He releases me. "A storm chaser?"

She's a hurricane, that one. "Not yesterday. I was in the right place at the right time. I didn't even notice the other two, just the one with the pink. I had to have it."

"Thanks for that." He gives a fleeting smile. "Okay, so this picture is why you really came here and ended up in our class."

"I just wanted to know more. The origin. How you even got this shot precisely at that moment."

"Patience, the right gear, and tons of snacks. Plus Papi's friend, who's a real storm chaser. He's invited me out a couple times." Baz pulls out his phone and clicks onto his Instagram page. The first thing I notice is that @BazMarin_Photography is verified, with eighty thousand followers. Wow. Then he lets me scroll, and I can't keep my mouth from hanging open like the non-model I am.

I thumb through and find least a dozen more storm shots exploding over his feed. Cloud and lightning arrays are expertly captured, with the wind pulling trees and majestic waves curling under bulbous storm cells. And then, there it is. My pink-lightning photo, with ten thousand likes. I read the caption: *Tropical lightning storm over the Everglades.* The date pegs the shot at the second week of May of this year and, God. *Oh holy God.*

I almost lose my footing. Baz took this photo the day after Mum went into hospice. He shot a storm and a furious pink bolt while I was playing one in person around England. Shooting far and not staying close. Defying, striking back.

A thousand emotions rip through my bones, and I can't shake the feeling that this photo means *someone* saw me that week, whether it was God, or the universe, or even Mum herself.

At once, it all melds—the pink gumball in my room, in my memory. The pink lightning bolt striking like a bright, electric prelude to a final realm. And swirling around it all, the fact that this photo was put up by mistake. It wasn't supposed to be there. Or was it?

I can't contain all of this at once. I can't even speak.

"Flora?" Baz says.

How could I possibly explain? *Get it together.* "Sorry." I breathe in short puffs. *In, out, in, out.* "Just a long day." I scroll on and flip the haunting image away, noting that his photo wall is more than storms. It's life. Incredible composition and vision eat up the screen. Baz's portraits exude passion and angst and impeccable elegance.

"Your work is stunning. Your father taught you?"

Another smile, this one looser. "Yeah, as soon as he could, and thanks. I spent years assisting and editing for him until I learned enough to teach."

I find more on his page. Parties, tuxedos and gowns. Cakes and dance floors and flower-strewn walkways in grassy parks. And my solution is so clear, it reflects everything in Prismacolor. "You—you could shoot my friend's wedding!"

I throw out a short recap of Pili's debacle, ending with "She's part owner of Panadería La Paloma."

Baz lights up. "I love that place. The best Cuban bakery in Miami."

I light up, too. "Yes, exactly. So you'll do it? You'll shoot her wedding?"

"No."

"No?"

"Sorry, but I can't help."

"Oh . . . you're booked for September, too, like your father."

Baz squints a tad, shaking his head. "I'm not booked. I don't do weddings."

Air rushes out in a defeated burst. "You mean, you're unable?"

"Um, no. I've shot dozens with Papi." He sighs, almost pained. "But now I only do branding, portraits, and some lifestyle work. I'm studying photojournalism, too. No weddings." He seals it with a casual shrug.

And I am not having it. "But it would be just this once. She'll pay your rate, I'm sure."

"You're still here? Seriously?" Armando scurries into the showroom, bearing one Nikon camera.

He plunks it into Baz's hands and halts, entirely too close to my nose. "You were supposed to leave after class."

"Now hold on!" I yell, right as Baz says, "Calm down, bro."

Armando pays neither of us any mind. "I'm on a red-eye to LA in two hours. Want me to throw her in the hold for the good of all Miami?"

"Excuse me?" I spit out as the rest happens so fast—Baz shaking his head and Armando reaching out but not getting very far because—

"Anything you lay on me, you'd better be keen on losing!" I blare.

Pointer finger out, he walk-pushes me toward the door. "This is you, leaving Baz alone. Do you know how busy he is?"

"This is me, *gladly* leaving, you sodding oaf," I say, clomping backward. "And for your information, Señor Marín Junior isn't all that busy. Check his September calendar." I whisk open the door. "I hope they serve only yellow and moldy cheese varieties on your flight! And that they give you extra ice cubes!"

The door smacks shut in my face.

SEVEN

Naturally, I return to Studio Marín the next evening, but not without reinforcements. Namely, a large white box and a printed-out ticket.

> *Class: Photo Editing for Beginners, 7 p.m.,*
> *Studio Marín*
> *Instructor: Sebastián Marín Jr. (Baz) with*
> *Luna Pasquale assisting*
> *Materials: Device equipped with Photoshop*
> *and Lightroom, and three images to edit. A*
> *portrait, a landscape, a macro shot.*

Tonight, I waltz into the foyer with zero interference. If Armando hadn't shown up with his snooty pointer finger, I'm almost positive I could've won Baz over last night.

"I was surprised to see you on the roster. I didn't know you were a photographer," Luna says as she checks off my name.

"Thought I'd give it a go," I say, because it's easy. Am I a photographer? Am I anything (real, long-term, serious) I can truly name for sure? Not yet.

I leave that piece of uncertainty in the foyer and follow signs to a large conference room. Six long tables face a large monitor, and other students are already setting up. Time for step one of my persuasion plan.

Bakery boxes naturally command attention. A roomful of it snaps over me as I set a large one on a console table. "Hello, everyone. Tonight's refreshments are provided by Panadería La Paloma." I undo the lid as the scent of butter and mouth-watering fillings clouds the room, having something Cuban to say about the dregs of lemon-pine cleaner and someone's woodsy perfume. The pastries win.

And my plan is working so far; grateful students attack the box of pastelitos de guayaba like starved wolves. I also brought a dozen cheese rolls, recalling that Ryan once said he fell in love with Pilar over one of these sweet, flaky pastries. I need someone to fall in love with an idea.

With my trap sprung, I return to my seat to set up my laptop. As my editing programs load, a stream of chatter starts up behind me in Spanish, which is nothing unusual around here. What is, though, are a few key words that slip out between pastry-munching. *That box. Lila. Panadería. England.*

I freeze and tune my ears.

"The La Paloma bakers were talking about it. My sister works there, and I went to high school with Lilita. Ay, pobrecita," the girl says before going back to full Spanish in a stream so fast, I struggle to keep up. What about poor Lila? And Pili didn't say anything about any baker gossip over there.

I narrow my focus and draw upon the three years of

Spanish lessons I had whilst kneading dough and dusting chocolate back in England. And when I really cue in and piece words together, I wish I hadn't bothered.

I've been going there for years.

Lila and Orion missed their trip.

Can you believe that?

Lila works so hard, and now she can't have a break.

Oh. Oh God. I now remember that Lila and Orion had been planning a weekend away to Paris. And I left her and Maxwell's with no notice. Of course she had to stay home to regroup.

Lila was working with some girl in England. Her friend, too. And she just left her. So ungrateful. What friend would do that?

It's my blood that reacts first, rising from an agitated simmer to a fierce boil the more words I pull from these people. My fingers clamp together, sweat trickling down my back. And it keeps on.

England or no, she's Estrellita forever.

The OG, right?

And now she can't even take a little break with su novio?

Orion was probably going to propose to Lila. And now this chica ruined it all.

Irresponsible . . . rude . . . the nerve of that fulana de tal.

That is completely and entirely it. I slam down my fist, earning every stare in the conference room, swiveling around to the three students behind me. "I'm the fulana, all right? ¡Soy yo!"

I'm shaking now, but that's never stopped me.

"I'm the ungrateful friend and bakery assistant who left

Lila in the lurch. That's right. Yo hablo español. Who do you think taught me?"

The chisme crew (as Lila would say) is a trio of full-moon eyes and mouths stuck wide.

"Maybe you all should know what's really going on. That way, you don't have to speculate."

My eyes fog, and I'm lost inside the blaring words. It's all I can think about. All I know how to do.

I arc my hand like a tidal wave. "You can blame me all you want for hurting one of Miami's finest, because I deserve it. But your info is suspect. Orion is my brother, and no, he wasn't going to propose, and won't until he gets out of school. I mean, Lila won't let him until then, okay, so you can all skip the call to Dadeland Bridal to bet on whether she'll pick a mermaid or ball-gown style."

The breathy outbursts that fill the space make it seem like I've dashed a few dreams. Seriously? Do these people follow Lila like a member of some Miami royal family?

"So there's no confusion," I carry on, but softer, "yes, I created a shitstorm back in England, and I—"

My words snap away when footsteps and laughter echo from the hallway. The door creaks open. It's Baz, with Luna trailing behind.

"Er, so now you know. Good, then," I sputter helplessly, spinning around. Even though no one says another word, my pulse is a fiery hammer, my pits as damp as this entire city. Did I just do what I think I did?

It's fine, it's fine, it's fine, I repeat like a classroom drill until I almost believe it. I gulp down half the water I brought along and finally try to remember why the hell I actually came here. Thank Christ, Baz didn't witness the last five minutes.

The photographer-slash-instructor in question deposits a gear bag, and it takes him a count of four to notice me, a hint of confusion shading his face when Luna pegs me as the sugar benefactor. *Do I eat a pastry or smush it into this annoying girl's curls?* That's the vibe he's flinging, and he doesn't even know the half of it.

"Cool," he says. "Save me a guava cheese, and welcome to photo editing."

Bloody fucking welcome, indeed. I answer with a demure wave and go back to sorting my photo library.

Mercifully, he starts the class immediately, and I can't deny how fresh Baz's content seems. He shares a five-point cheat sheet that would make any artist better and loads of other tips and tricks. I take note, even though I feel I've managed just fine with my camera so far. It does what I need it to do.

But I *am* here. So I drag out an old macro flower shot to work on (a large yellow rose dusted with raindrops). I can't even look at a large chunk of my recent photos—the hundreds of curated images I took last spring. I doubt Baz has any tips on Photoshopping the doubt and shame from your entire life.

Before my thoughts spiral, I catch them. Digging my thumbnails into the pads of my fingertips, letting the pinch snap me back to my greater goal. I'm here for Pilar.

The class moves on; Luna drifts around the student tables, assisting as Baz touches up raw footage on the monitor. All goes smoothly until it's time to work on portrait editing.

"You might recognize the headshot I'll be using for our demo," Baz announces. "I had another planned, but I think I'll use this one instead. Not only does the subject have excellent taste in Cuban baked goods, but she also makes an interesting model."

After a click, there I am, blown up hugely for all to ogle. It's the shot Baz captured where I'm gazing with eyelids at half-mast, head tilted away as if the camera's called me out. Or caught me lying.

The nerve.

I sense everyone's gazes and shoot back a collective glare. *Yes, it's bloody me—again! Now move along.*

I flag Luna as she passes by. "Really? Of all the shots he could've used?" Is this the universe's payback for my little overshare an hour ago?

She bends down. "Sorry, hon. You signed that waiver."

Seething, I find Baz simultaneously fiddling with his computer and darting furtive glances my way as if he's awaiting my reaction.

It takes a miracle not to give him the one he deserves. Unfortunately, my reacting parts have already overextended their welcome around here. All I can do is put every bit of pissed-off into my eyes.

He's right in my sight line, a dark sort of amusement teasing his mouth. "I know a good shot when I see one. But I'll show you how to make it great." Baz steps forward, zips up his features, and carries on with his tips to make me look even better in that black cap-sleeved top, perched on a stool, gazing off-center.

And damn it all to hell, the final product is not entirely unpretty.

At the end of the session, Baz barely deserves the last guava cheese pastelito in my grease-stained box. "Thanks for the class. Really good stuff," I say, pulling a napkin and fetching it for him anyway.

He shuts his laptop screen and takes the pastry. Bites. Makes an indecent noise that rumbles through my own belly and spills a few flaky crumbs down the front of his navy-blue tee. But unlike Gordon, he paces himself. "Last night you play model and tonight, photographer?"

"I just thought an enrichment class would be, er—"

"Enriching?" His laugh's half dark, half goofy. "Okay, sure, Flora. You forget I have a Cuban mother and lots of tías. I know these tactics well."

"What tactics?"

"The sneaking-in, then lying low like you're just another potted plant in the corner. Classic observation tactic, usually used for chisme-collection purposes. A skilled Cuban must've trained you well."

"You know nothing about me. I never sneak." And I didn't lie low. He really did miss my drama-show opening act. "And anytime I have to make a secret escape, like out some dingy pub window, it's because someone's been an unforgivable twat and I'm simply trying to protect myself." Immediately, I feel the redness creep in, and why do I do these things?

"That sounds like a good story. But don't try to deny your obvious food priming to get me to shoot your friend's wedding." Another hearty bite. "You think I haven't spent nineteen years being manipulated through my stomach?"

Crap, crap, crap. Adjust, adjust, adjust. "I'm friends with the La Paloma owners. They rarely enter any new room without some sort of food offering."

"That, I believe." He eats a larger chunk from the pastelito, then surrenders the rest on the table, which Gordon would never. "But before you ask again, my answer hasn't changed. I don't do weddings."

"You mean you *won't*," I snarl, which I should temper for the good of my cause. But I can't seem to locate my softer parts.

"Yo, Baz, don't say I didn't warn you," Luna calls from across the room. She approaches with a tablet.

"What now?" Baz asks.

"Didn't you check your messages?" she asks. "Your papi switched to texting me when you didn't respond."

"I was *teaching*!" He pulls a phone from his back pocket, and it pings relentlessly when he powers it on.

"If *teaching* means using my face as target practice," I add, because I'm still here. And I don't hate it when Luna gives a muffled snicker.

"Your face ended up more than fine," Baz deadpans. "But I have bigger issues."

"Yeah, you do," Luna notes, amused. I like her uniform tonight. A black leather jacket flares over a long tank dress that's simple but cool and striking against her red hair.

"One peaceful, drama-free summer. Was that too much to ask?" Baz says. "Now I have to slink around and be 'too busy' for everything. And I'd change my number, but they know where I live, carajo." He starts texting furiously.

"That sounds ominous," I say, still in total darkness.

Luna digs around in the bakery box and finds a stray cheese-roll corner. Pops it in. "Since Baz used your photo with no warning, I figure you deserve a little dirt on your teacher."

"Seems fair," I say, finding I quite like this Luna girl.

Baz, still texting, bats her away like a fruit fly.

"Good. So, there's this family the Maríns are pretty close with. The Acostas. The father is a well-known Miami producer, and one of his daughters is a rising fashion photographer. She also shoots bloggers, and her Instagram's, like, stunning. Sebastián trained her, which rarely happens."

I flash a slow-moving grin. "I think I can follow the clues to where this is going."

"Uh-huh. The abridged version goes like this: two scheming Cuban mothers and two protective, well-meaning fathers, plus two nineteen-year-old media heirs who would add the right kind of attention to both businesses if they're together."

"But Baz objects, I take it?"

"Yes, Baz objects." He looks up from his screen, brow strained with annoyance. "Kelly is great, but she's not into me, which my family doesn't buy no matter what I say. Forget the good optics if we get together. Mami's got this, I dunno, brujería gut feeling about us. Basically, she's convinced Kelly and I are endgame, and Señora Acosta is the second biggest fan of this idea. But I'm not looking for anything beyond casual. I set up my own shots, if you catch my drift."

"Excuse me, but you have set up zero shots in, like, a year, which is partly why a heart-shaped target is painted on your back, bro." Luna grins. "And for even more fun, Baz shows up a lot in the society pages around here, and the combo of talent and looks adds to the chatter."

"Shut up, Luna," he says with no trace of bile, squinting over his screen.

"Nah, I'm good," she says. "Anyway, the Acosta family returned early from Costa Rica. They live abroad most summers, which has helped before to manage all the scheming. Kelly dated this dude for a solid year, and Baz's mom almost threw a party when they broke up last spring. So now Señorita Acosta is back and single, and Baz's summer just got a lot more complicated." Luna leans in. "It's funny."

"It's not," he says.

"*And* . . . we're not done because of the even more pressing issue, which is what Señor Marín was texting about. Next week there's this huge charity gala for Canvas Miami, in the Design District. Amazing organization benefiting school art programs and community enrichment."

I pretend to know what all of this is, nodding along.

"Studio Marín is a major sponsor," Luna says. "Both Baz and his papi are donating experiences for the silent auction. They buy two tables each year, and the entire staff gets to come."

"The Acostas are taking four seats as our guests," Baz says on a grumble. "I can't bail. I'm this year's emcee."

"Um, here's an idea. Why not get with Kelly and have her help calm down your mums?" I'm a pro at these matters.

"Not that simple," Baz drones. "Kelly's been around a lot training with Papi, but we aren't that close. I have no clue how she'd react, and I can't risk her going back to her family or her friends with anything fishy. Our studio gets tons of referrals from the Acostas. But there's a big media project we're partnering on, like, in five minutes. Papi wants to keep the peace, so I've been told to 'go along with things.' I'm stuck in the middle and also single and available, which is the Cuban version of desperately seeking—"

"Wait," Luna notes. She cocks out one hip. "What if you weren't, though?" When Baz frowns quizzically, Luna carries on. "What if you're the one dating someone now? Kelly's convinced enough, the two mamis chill because it's obviously not the right time, and the two señores keep working on their project."

"You mean Photoshop a girlfriend into my life?" he says.

Luna rolls her eyes. "Get someone to play along at the Canvas gala, plus a few other places. All it takes is some blog or Instagram shots of you and her—done. And you get to stay an artist recluse."

"Hey!"

"You love it. Anyway, I can ask someone at Palladium," Luna says, and turns to me. "Do you have any friends there?"

It's clear that Baz is keeping his mouth shut about my modeling ruse, so I'm certainly not going to out myself. "When I said I was new, I meant the actual color green, and I won't be working with Palladium any longer. It's not for me," I add, as this part is entirely true. "Plus, no offense, but this sounds like something that would fit right into some Netflix film about fake dating. Those usually end in disaster in real life."

"Wait, back up. I'm not asking anyone from Palladium. Totally iffy." Baz scrubs a hand down his face, covering up a low grumble. "You forget how much people talk around here. I get the wrong volunteer or 'friend of a friend,' and all of South Beach catches on, and my scheme gets back to Papi and Señor Acosta. No bueno."

After Baz put my portrait on display, it's been satisfying witnessing him squirm a bit. I bend to tighten the laces on my Docs, lifting up to find Luna and Baz staring me down. Then signaling each other in some indecipherable facial code. "What?"

"You could do it," Baz says.

"She could so do it." From Luna.

I lose all language.

"Hear me out," Luna says, entirely too giddy. "You're new and from England, which cuts out the 'Which Miami socialite is Baz hooking up with?' talk." Her face shades. "Oh wait, are you dating anyone for real?"

"Not even close." I pretzel my arms. "But I just said you've got a fake-dating disaster in the making, and now you want me to star in it?" I've faked enough the last few days. I'm here to find who I am for real, not to get wrapped up in yet another detour going nowhere.

"It doesn't have to be that way," Baz says. "Luna's right. No one knows you around here."

"That's not true. I'm a guest of the Reyes family, the owners of La Paloma. That place is chisme ground zero. Do not ask me how I know."

"We'll be extra careful." He dashes out a hand. "Please, Flora, I could really use your help. You'd just be a quick stand-in."

My skin heats red. "I'm not a date for hire, Baz. If someone asks me to an event, it's because they want me there, for *me*. Not my British novelty, or my skill in playing adoring girlfriend. Not my face that might fit in with your Miami charity-gala crowd." If there's one thing I've kept intact across continents, it's this small part of my self-respect. "Again, amazing class, but goodnight."

I spin to grab my laptop tote, resisting even a single look back. My steps into the hall are strong, each pace full of rightness that for the first time in a long, long time, I stood up for myself in a good way. I stood for something admirable.

The feeling lingers, stretching long into the foyer where it crashes into the brick wall, shattering over the stained concrete floor.

Oh no. Oh bloody hell.

I halt and pivot and can't believe I'm doing this. I can't believe it's come to this. But it turns out I didn't need class crashing or pastries; the only thing my persuasion plan needed was Flora Maxwell herself. Back in that room, coming off my outburst *plus* the irritation of Baz showcasing my unedited face, I forgot my goal, the whole reason I came back to Studio Marín. I totally missed the way to shake these unbreakable walls from an entirely different angle.

Still, I don't crawl back into the conference room with any puppy tail between my legs. No, I walk proudly, as catwalk ready as this fake model gets, nearly running headfirst into Baz.

We trade *oomph*s and I add a *sorry*.

"Forget something?" he asks.

I land two steps away. "I'll go with you to the gala, and any other places we need to be seen. I'll do it."

"You will?" He blinks twice, and do I detect an exhale of relief?

"On one condition," I state. "The first Saturday of September, for the rate of their current photographer, you shoot the wedding ceremony and reception of Pilar Reyes and Ryan Vega." My heartbeat's a soft drizzle. I officially have nothing left to lose.

His face is unreadable, a perfect unaffected pose. Then "Fine. But just so we're clear, the Reyeses will not parade my involvement in the wedding around town. No one will tag me in anything on Instagram. And you won't tell a soul. If it leaks, I'm gonna get a hundred more asks."

Reality snaps into focus. *He agreed.* Baz Marín is going to capture Pili's wedding with all his artistic skill. I fight the urge to jump like a schoolgirl. "Mum's the word, I swear. And no tagging—understood. Because you don't do weddings."

"Nope. And you don't play fake girlfriend at charity events."

I smile. "Never. And just so *we're* clear, our agreement includes hand holding, dancing, and being seen at beaches and cafés. No snogging in alleyways or anything scandalous that might end up as a hot topic on society blogs."

He holds up both hands. "That wasn't in the plan. So, novios?"

We shake on it, but my gaze tracks over his other arm. At the base of his tree tattoo, near the root ball, lies a Cuban flag I missed before. It's worn threadbare, edges torn to near shreds. I want to ask what it means. It's something a girlfriend would know.

Dear Lila,

I don't know what to say. The way I left things, and us, is not how I wanted it to be. But I can't face anyone here right now. Especially you. I'm truly sorry. And please don't worry. I'm safe while I try to work everything out. But I might not ring for a while.

— I love you, Flora

EIGHT

Salted French butter and La Paloma Cuban bread wait on the kitchen table beside my Flora-Do List. I've become one with the list since showing up here. Previous tasks range from running the Hoover and mopping the kitchen, to addressing invitations for bridal events. Simple enough, and it keeps me busy.

Today, the list has only one item. I sip cafecito instead of tea and listen to a yellow bird announce morning at the window (once, then again in case I didn't get the hint). And I laugh wryly over the two scrawled words. So much easier than crying over them. Easier than letting my gut twinge with apprehension over something I used to do without thinking, like blinking. Aren't the most familiar, dependable people the hardest to come back to when you've done something hurtful?

> *Florecita*
> 1. *Call Lila.*

Honestly, I'm not surprised after what went down last night. Miami should provide reinforcement gear for these situations. I knew the Reyes bunch would be thrilled over my surprise wedding photographer announcement. But I'd totally underestimated the sheer magnitude of their excitement, which funneled into a relentless interrogation. Armed with only my wits, I did my best. Questions shot from everyone, including Ryan, who joined in on Pilar's phone.

I chose my words carefully, such as *editing class* and *Studio Marín*. I dropped the name *Baz* and showed his Instagram page, ending on the word *favor*. That's how I'd framed the fact that I'd be attending Miami's social event of the summer, keeping all the other agreement details a secret. Me being invited to one party was nothing close to a big deal, right?

Ha—wrong times a thousand. I might as well have been announcing my own engagement, the way they carried on. But the celebrating soon died down into one person, one name. A candle flame, blown out with a single wish. *Lila.*

"It's too late to call her," Pili mused after Ryan hung up.

"Too early in England, también. Mañana," Alan said. He looked at Elisa who looked at Pili who looked back at her father, and then I just knew.

"You all think *I* should be the one to call her," I said more than I asked.

"Claro, chica. You made it happen. Ay, she'll be so proud," Elisa said, cinching me tight over a word I haven't felt about myself in so long. I wanted the pride to last far beyond the hug.

But now tomorrow is today, and my cafecito is down to dregs. It's time. I haven't flaked on a Flora-Do List item yet, which is new for a person known for her flaking tendencies.

I clean up breakfast and grab my laptop. I was going to

contact Lila anyway—truly, I was. At least, sometime this week. Nearly ten days is an eternity between two girls who are three years apart but usually linked together like paper dolls. Often, there's a certain blond boy wedged between us. (I need to call Orion, too. And Dad.)

Naturally, I procrastinate, which is a close cousin to flaking. My laptop rests open on the living room coffee table. It wasn't on the list, but I do a few rounds with a duster, fluff throw pillows, and straighten the crocheted throw blankets I suspect Elisa tosses over sofa arms for every reason but warmth. Miami already *is* warmth.

There's one feature here, however, that I don't even approach. A honey-brown upright piano stands against the far wall, smaller than the one Mum willed to the Greenly Center.

Though I still feel the pinch of running away from Mum's piano, from a room with "Clair de Lune" trilling from ivory keys, it's not like I hate all pianos now. But they're unnerving, dredging up the sort of memories I never ask for. The kind I'd never put in a tribute speech. I take two steps toward the wall. The upright's lid is closed over the keys, and the bench is pushed in, leaving no room to slide onto the seat. Not one Reyes ever plays or talks about this instrument.

My phone dings and my heartbeat skips. It would be just like Lila to contact me right when I'm gearing up to finally call.

Instead, my lock screen flashes a certain number with a Miami area code. I swipe to read the whole message. **Good morning, your friendly neighborhood fake boyfriend here. Just getting a stream started because that's what people do when they're dating**

I'm smiling and don't fight it as I type back, Wait, who is this again? Jonah? Adam? Julio?

His reply comes in seconds. Haha, nice. I'll be sending more details about the gala next week. Have a great day. It's Baz btw

Ahh, NOW I remember. Thanks for clearing that up, and good day to you too, I send. After fifteen seconds, his reply doesn't come, which is the correct move. I hate it when people keep messaging drawn-out nonsense because neither person knows when to stop. Ten points to the fake boyfriend for stopping.

I let out an airy sigh. Lila is my *real* friend, and I owe both of us something better than another minute of stalling. I drop my phone into my dressing gown pocket and power on my laptop to open FaceTime.

Peeking through caged fingers, I get my first glimpse of Lila as the app pings to life. It's afternoon in Winchester. She's in her bedroom at the Owl and Crow, right next door to Gordon, if he hasn't already left for California. I'm itching to ask, but how is that the first thing I need to say to this person?

For too long, no one says anything at all. Expressionless. Silent. These two words rarely hang around Lila Reyes, but here we are. It's my move. "Hiya. So, before I share some good news, I wanted to say that I'm—"

"Stop." She holds out her palm until it masks the entire screen. "Don't say you're sorry again, Flora. I read your note."

My mouth hangs open. So we're doing this part first. "Okay." It's not okay. Slowly, I reveal myself. "You missed your Paris trip with Orion. I forgot when I, er, left. And I'm so—" Her face goes sharp. "Right. I hope you can reschedule."

"We'll go in a couple weeks. I had to rearrange shit and get Marjorie to up her hours." She drags Orion's old gray cable knit cardigan around her shoulders. Seeing her throw it on now knocks against my chest because it's her biggest comfort item. "Before you ask, yes, she's doing fine with me in the kitchen."

Lila's shrug lands a little too relaxed, her coral lips pulled into a bent smile I don't understand.

"I cannot believe you got someone from Studio Marín to shoot the wedding. Let alone el jefe's son," she adds, perkier. "I told Pilar to fight for better, but you were the one who locked it up."

Just like you would've done, I want to say, but something else looms bigger. "Your mum told you?"

"And Pili. Group call about an hour ago."

I give a snort. *Call Lila,* the only item Elisa wrote on my list, and, God, this family. I want to slow-clap the entire crew. I'm right where they want me, but I can't fault them. I'm right where I should've been days ago.

Lila angles her head oddly, clearing her throat. "The news did soften my irritation over a few interesting texts I got earlier this morning."

My oxygen supply quits. It's been less than twenty-four hours! There's no way—

"Before my first cafecito"—she pauses to wave her phone and skim the screen—"I find out from a couple La Paloma bakers I chat with that it's good I'm, quote, 'sticking to my guns' about my future. And that not marrying too young is a wise choice."

As if spilling my overshare from Baz's class wasn't enough, the bakers took it and added their opinions? Forget pink; I'm as red as blood. Goddamn photographer sister of an employee with a big mouth. *Hell, goddamn Flora Maxwell with a colossal mouth.*

I hold up both palms. "I'm really so very sorry, so please don't tell me not to be. It was such a mess. These students were talking about you being left in the lurch, and Orion, and me, but they didn't know it was me, and I couldn't stand it. I had to shut them down. But I didn't think it would get back to you."

"Oh, I'm sure you didn't. Welcome to Miami," she deadpans. "I've probably thwarted the bridal-lace dreams of all of West Dade and its surrounding areas by now."

No, no, no. "I ran my mouth and fucked up."

"Yeah, you did, and it was a shit move," she says in the British manner that's part of her new world. Our world. But finally, here are some words I deserve.

I nod into them like something known and needed.

"I trusted you. All those things we've said over dough— they're ours, okay? Pull something like that again, and I *will* show up at your bedside the next morning. ¿Me entiendes?"

I bob my head. "Sí, claro . . ." Hermana? Amiga? I don't know what to add.

"Wow, Flora." She exhales a drift. "I mean . . ."

"I know, believe me. I keep messing up the good things." I dash my eyes before they spill, and reach for water. My throat's parched along with all the rest of me. "That's why I actually left, you know?"

"Here's what I know. You've just gone through a time when you could've asked for anything you needed."

But I didn't ask. I didn't *want* to ask. I needed to act. I stretch my vision long and wide, daring to truly look at Lila. If my camera were close, if I shot her quick and unaware, I could post the photo as the perfect demonstration of a single emotion: disappointment. "We're not all-the-way okay, are we? Not just about my gossip flub. About . . . before."

"You didn't even try to let me understand. You hid everything and lied." Her words end in a clipped sigh. "I would blame you more if I didn't get that *you're* not all-the-way okay. That comes first, right?"

I blow out a gust. And yes, I'm on a razor wire with this friend, but we're still standing. "What about my brother? He hasn't called. And I know I told him not to, but he never listens to that sort of—"

"Because he can't, Flora."

I swallow a lump.

"He just can't right now. So this is me speaking from the middle, okay?" Lila stresses. "Everything about the piano and you leaving that way set him back. Losing your mum hurt him worse than he's let on, and he's not been himself. Give him time?"

"Yeah. I will," I spurt as the guilt falls darker. "But please tell him I'm sorry."

This whole time I figured Orion would be rolling his eyes at me and my escape. But I cracked his heart instead.

Give him time echoes once and again. I take a fortifying breath. "I'll do better, and I'll figure out where I'm going," I tell a girl who *owns* that concept.

Staring at Lila Reyes—someone who knows exactly what she wants, and who she is—I feel my throat clog with frustration. She's slaying her new gig partnering with Dad and Orion at Maxwell's, adding her amazing food to our quality tea service. But we have big plans to open more shops, starting in London. Our new brand is tea and select baked goods with a French influence, a Cuban touch, and worldwide flair. Dad constantly reminds me that I can have a place in the expansion, too; I just need to settle on an angle. I could study marketing or business management, like Ri. Maybe hospitality. Hell, I could even go to culinary arts school like Lila and really be a partner in the Maxwell's food division she's heading up, as more than an assistant.

Why is it so hard to choose a direction? Part of it is that I've lost the ability to trust any of my own decisions. But there's another gap here, one I can't name. It's a Polaroid I shake and shake, but no answers materialize on the paper.

"Flora?" Lila says, and I climb up and back into the moment, having been in the bad place for so long, she's noticed.

"Sorry," I say. "I'm here."

"In my home." She leans forward as if she's trying to place herself into my space, the childhood living room she left.

My curiosity suddenly piqued, I turn the screen to the far wall. "That piano. I didn't ask about it the last time I was here."

"It was Abuela's." Lila's tentative smile is the best part of my day so far. "Mami and Papi, Pilar—none of us can play a note. I don't have to tell you why Mami kept it. You're in Abuela's room, no? With some of her other recuerdos?"

"Yeah." I think of Baz's storm photo that I propped up to start my own altar. "Was she good at playing? Abuela Lydia?"

Lila laughs. "God, no. Not anywhere close to your mum. Abuelita was downright terrible. But she loved it and kept the piano because it was fun and beautiful." She glances upward. "Mami keeps it because Abuela was, too."

Fun and beautiful. My thoughts fill with pink gumballs, with albums packed with photos of a blond-haired angel, laughing and holding her small children. Grinning at her husband in faraway cities. Something shifts and clears then. Maybe I can think of Mum's Greenly Center speech as a collection of snapshots, instead of pages of words that keep taunting that I've lost the right to speak them. In my hands, the camera has always meant control. Taking something back.

The idea settles like it's right, and I've felt that so rarely lately. It's the brightest sunlight, the most cooling mist. My Miami exile might be helping after all. Or it's Lila, a girl who's never really left this city. She shared her abuela's memory, and it's given me a way to sort out my mum's.

"Thank you," I say. Again, it feels too simple.

"For what? Last I checked, I wasn't the one who saved the wedding photos." She snorts. "You do know you probably canceled out your good deed by setting off the West Miami chisme chain. Like, karma-wise?" When I cringe, her head bobs in a slow, knowing nod. "Still. What did I do?"

"Three months after you left Winchester, you came back to us."

"Oh. That's all?" Lila's chin crumples as she thumbs her cheeks. "Hey, I need to run. Can you hug my hermana for me?"

I nod and wait two beats before I say, "If you hug my brother for me."

NINE

Two days later I'm the one in the back of Elisa's minivan. Emotions are so high, this Honda is going to blow, and it won't be because of my doing for once. It's all because of a dress.

Ryan's mum is waiting for us in front of Dadeland Bridal for this tremendous occasion, as I've been told. Pilar's wedding gown is ready for her final fitting. Knowing this family, I packed extra tissues from the box in the guest bath, which is housed in the oddest knitted cover in grays and blues. Why a tissue box needs a cardigan, I have no idea.

My first steps inside the shop include a head rush of floral potpourri mixed with a dozen competing perfumes. Racks bow under the weight of plump gowns. Dadeland offers a funhouse array of mirrors, and deep-blue carpet covers the presentation area. We crowd together, waiting. And when we get the signal that Pilar is ready to come out, I open FaceTime on my phone to bring in Winchester and the maid of honor.

"Any minute now," I tell Lila. "I want you to see how she looks walking in. So hold tight."

"Wait. Flora."

I switch the screen to face me.

"Thanks again for what you did," she says, and though the connection from Miami to Winchester is perfectly clear, a certain static remains between us. "I looked up Baz's work, and *wow*. I know there's more than what you and Mami told me. I know you did *something*."

I nod, conceding. "But nothing dodgy. I promise, Lila." *You can trust me,* I add silently, out of habit. Lately, my trust hasn't been worth all that much. But I'm trying.

A flash of white fabric signals Pilar, and I flip the screen back to capture her graceful entrance. The two mamis are instantly wrecked. (What's going to happen on the actual day?) And I'm right there with tissues. The bride is perfect in a strapless gown in the frothiest organza, like the pastry confections she rules over. A thin, jeweled sash circles her waist.

The Dadeland staff wears all black like the Studio Marín team. Two sales associates tug the bodice and unfurl the skirt into a billowy parachute. And for the final touch, they top Pili's updo with a simple tiara and flowing veil. I bring Lila close so she can blow kisses to her sister.

For a time, I exist inside this bubble of love and family, chuffed to be included. But even this level of glee and emotion can't last all day. Eventually, Lila goes back to work and the mothers check on their own gown orders at the counter. Pilar moves to shoe options, testing out various satin numbers with plenty of staff opinions flying everywhere.

Elisa sidles up, her signature tuberose–and–lime-blossom scent trailing behind. "Por Díos, this day," she says, and the flip from musing to mischief across her face is so fast, I almost miss it. "I am guessing it will not be Lila's turn on that platform for a while, according to her La Paloma friends. Ay, even Pili and I didn't know about some of those details about her and Orion."

My stomach drops. I'm going to need a dozen boxes of cardigan tissues. "You heard?" I whisper. "Pili, too?" What I did at the editing class. What I said.

"Oh sí, but those bakers are already onto another bit of chisme. There was a walk-in cooler . . . incident," Elisa says, pausing to flip her manicured hand. "With one of the fry cooks and a girl on the pastry line who is engaged to another man." She winks. "Pero you did not hear it from me."

My laugh coughs its way out, but the easy humor is mixed with too much regret and bundled nerves. A really fun combo, that. I sober and tell her, "I'm so sorry if I embarrassed your family. Lila was pissed. And I wouldn't blame you if you sent me home early."

"So you want to leave us, mija?" Elisa asks pointedly.

"Not at all. It's just . . ." I trail off into nothing. I didn't expect her to take this route.

"Mm-hmm," she says. "How about this? Next time . . . eh—"

"Next time, *don't*?" I supply, and she shrugs. "It got out of control so fast. Or I did. Their facts were wrong, and I was trying to make it stop. But I just got louder and went further than I meant."

Elisa braces my shoulders. "We are a loud family, cariño, with big feelings. And it is good for you to be loud and strong and big, too. Powerful."

My chest blooms. She gets me, heart and hurricane.

"Pero, here is the thing. Before we get loud, we stop and look ahead to see how and where our loud will land. And what it might do there."

My head droops toward the carpet, and just as her words take shape, the clerk runs in from the stockroom.

"Óigame, señora," she says, waving a sheet. "Everything is fine, and your gown is coming in next week. You should schedule your alterations."

Elisa kisses the top of my head and strides away, and Pili waves me over. I approach the platform. Beveled mirrors reflect everything.

"Yup, still here. After I chose the shoes," Pili says, "I told Maria and Leti I wanted to hang out a little longer in my dress."

"Well, you only get to enjoy it for one day. Maybe you could wear it to a La Paloma staff meeting after?"

We share a laugh, and she models her "something blue" robin's egg–shaded heels. When zero words about my chisme overshare come out, I relax over wedding chatter and silly poses and fake bridal prances.

But the moment turns when she invites me up onto the platform. I'm level with the mirrors and this "maybe" part of my future. It's a part that hasn't hit until now; I've never had a big enough nudge to think about it. This one is as large as ten yards of bridal chiffon.

Who will sit on a sofa and cry over me if I'm ever dressed in white and fussed over? I hope to have my nan there. But never have I wished more for a camera with a lens that could merge the *here* and *gone* on these kinds of days. The thought burrows so deep, I have to click it away.

I turn to Pilar and remember that there's another gown to figure out. "So, you know I'm going to Canvas Miami, and when I looked up last year's event, I saw all the posh outfits." I tug at my faded denim shorts and blue swingy top. "I've got this sort of stuff, and I packed something for your wedding, but even that's not right. Any ideas where I should—"

"You're going to Canvas Miami, chica?"

I pivot to find Maria and Leti, as well as Elisa. How did I miss them with all these mirrors?

"Sí, ella va con Baz Marín," Elisa says. "Tú sabes, el hijo de Sebastián Marín."

"Ay, qué bueno. It's a date, no? Lucky girl."

"More of a last-minute invitation. A sort of date, I suppose." I exhale roughly and quit before I draw more questions. "But I don't have anything to wear yet."

The consultants "consult" in a language of furtive looks and hand motions. "We will help," Leti says at length.

They'll help? I'm fake-dating Baz, not eloping. "Thank you for the offer, but I'm not sure you have the sort of dress I need."

Maria is already coaxing me down the platform with spiky red nails. "We have a lot more than wedding gowns." She eyes me carefully. "Okay." Another angle. "Aha." She makes me turn. "Do not worry. Wait here, and we will bring our choices to a room."

The consultants scurry off, with Elisa tagging along, and I *wasn't* worried—five minutes ago! I send a *sodding help me already* glare at Pilar.

She hops down the best she can in her own gown. "I know this place is a little extra. But it's going to be fine. Those two found my dream dress in thirty minutes."

I whisper closely. "I can't show up to Canvas Miami in Disney Princess tulle. And if they bring anything with a bow that's twice the size of my arse . . ."

Another associate comes by with pink drinks in crystal flutes. Apparently, dress shoppers get such things. And why the hell not? I suck down the lemonade spritz.

Pili nudges me a few minutes later. "Leti's waving you back. I told you they were quick."

Elisa returns to the sofa for my fashion show, excitement oozing all around her. I plunk the empty flute on a tray and go off to meet my dress demise.

In my life, when I'm clearly proven wrong, I have no problem admitting it. This is one of those times. I, Flora Maxwell from Winchester, Hampshire, England, was wrong.

Surrounded by loads of sparkles and finery, I'm in the gigantic fitting room next to Pili as she changes out of her gown. The Dadeland ladies brought me four formals from their ready-to-wear rack. Options one through three were like bad warm-up acts. But the fourth dress is a star.

"You haven't cussed in either Spanish or English in two minutes," Pili calls from next door. "Tell meeee!"

"This one is actually quite nice," I say.

There's a rustle. "I don't care if your titties are out. I'm coming in."

I snort as Pili barges through the curtain and gives a squeal.

"Look at you, bella!"

Dress number four is crafted entirely of blooms from thick appliqué lace in a delicate blush shade. The hem falls midcalf, and dainty straps creep over my shoulders. The entire look is see-through in a good way. A short underlayer covers all the important bits.

Pilar grabs my arm. "Come on. You know Mami is beyond impatient out there."

In seconds, I'm the girl on the podium, with Elisa snapping pics with her phone, nearly vibrating as Leti and Maria fiddle and a seamstress pins the too-long straps.

Maria croons, "Her figure in this, and that beautiful skin. Ay, qué hermosa."

And Leti says, "We've tried this dress on so many, but it was waiting for Flora. Como una English rose. We knew, verdad? We knew it was this one."

"Gita can shorten the straps, and we will deliver it, steamed, with Pili's gown."

My head's a twister. I haven't even looked at the price. I search for tags bearing the worst news ever.

Elisa steps up, clasping her warm hand into mine. "I already asked, okay, nena? This is my gift for you."

I break a little inside. She can't be so nice, so kind, after she's already taken me in with more baggage than two suit-cases. After I made her daughter the next stop on the West Miami gossip train.

"Flora," Elisa says, "I know what you are thinking, and we can put all that in la basura, okay?"

I nod. "But I . . . and I'm sure this dress . . ."

"*This* makes me happy. Pilar bought her own gown. And I hardly get to shop with Lila anymore."

My throat burns, and as she squeezes my hand tighter, the feeling changes around us. My fingers don't make a fist that fights back—my move, so often. Our linked hands are a safety net instead. *Okay,* I tell myself as my mind flashes back to a scene that's now so clear, it really could be a photograph. *Let her.* Let her be kind, like another mum spending too many coins, going for pink. Calling me special.

"Thank you so much," I tell her. "I love it."

After Dadeland, Elisa drops me off at home, sparing me and my growling stomach from part two of wedding errands. The backs of my thighs rip from the leather seats when I hop out. My insides were torn apart, too, then put back together with a child's glue job. Shaky and uneven. I need a minute, and lunch.

I reach the driveway right as Miami's daily bout of rain barges through, surprising me with a ropy waterfall. I usually sense it coming. I skitter under the porch and use my key. I'll never get over the wonder of how good the air-conditioning still feels even when I'm coming in from a storm.

I set the dead bolt and realize that I'm not alone. This I sense perfectly, and it's weird because Alan's filling in for Pili at La Paloma all day.

"Hiya?" I call out. "Who's there?"

No answer.

Light floods from the kitchen, and a blue sweatshirt drapes over a chair in the living room. I vaguely recognize the black logo on the sleeve.

Wait, I'm thinking, but it's too late. I've already reached the archway, and the lump in my stomach shoots up into my throat.

"Gordon?"

One blink, another, and he's still there, leaning on the

Reyeses' countertop and eating the last few bites of a cheese-burger. Midchew, he sees me and yanks out his earbuds, tip-ping his chin.

To which I'm rendered frozen—in Miami, no less. But my eyes carry on. Gordon looks rumpled and worn; a stubbly shadow not part of his usual fit pricks his jaw.

He springs off the edge of the counter. Adjusts the band festival T-shirt he got on a trip we made to see Jules. One rou-tinely pulled from the laundry basket if it passes the smell test. He rakes a hand through his hair, ruffling the mix of auburn and russet tones. And that's all there is. We never go this long being silent.

I don't know why his tongue's stuck, but for me, there's so much old noise, like the aching rasp when I cried on his shoul-der. The echo of his questions pushing me into unsure places. Our goodbye words. Maybe he's hearing them, too.

We hold our silence until a loud bong sounds through it, and us. The grandfather clock in the other room chiming half past two is like a starting gun at a race. I dash through the gate, and we're off.

"This is hardly San Francisco."

"It's not supposed to be. But I got no sleep on the plane, so you could probably convince me otherwise."

"What are you doing here?"

His eyes bug out. "What are *you* doing here?"

My head angles away, but he gets right up to me, arms crossed. And that won't do, so I move, too, jaw set as tight as it goes.

"You're supposed to be in California." Doing the program I told him to do, clearing him out from my path into safety.

"My plans changed." Gordon snuffs out a wisp of air. "You couldn't have known. It's not like you texted me."

"You haven't texted me, either, so . . ." There's a point here, I'm sure.

"Not my safest move after the way we parted, I thought."

The burning's back, slicking my throat, clawing into my sinuses. I'm the one who told him to leave, but Gordon and I are more complicated than one sticky conversation. I feel the pulse of his stare, eyeing me from head to toe.

"You're hungry," he says plainly. "Your forehead goes all tense and strained when you're underfed. Plus, I can see you pining over my Wendy's grub like some secret lover."

I scoff, wanting to stomp on his shoe and cry and laugh and throw something. Why am I having *all* the feelings all at once with him lately? "I've come from a big emotional wedding morning with more tears than snacks. There was sparkling lemonade, but that's all."

"Well, here." Gordon rolls down the top of the greasy white takeaway bag, revealing a pile of chips. "We can't argue properly otherwise. I could sleep for three days, and you're about to pass out."

I accept the bag. "Right. Thanks." I bite into one of the chips, and it's suddenly all I need.

I've already knocked out about ten when Gordon rinses his hands and reaches into a drawer for a hand towel.

"You seem to know your way around," I note.

He hangs the towel on a cabinet pull. "It's not my first visit. And by the way, my reason for being here has nothing to do with badgering you. I heard you last time, Flora."

"What? When did I say that?"

"It was implied. Message received. I'm not on any recon mission from your family, either." He tosses our rubbish into the bin. "I went dark, hiking for a few days with some mates. I come back to Winchester to find you'd left the way you did." He dashes out his hand. "I've always known you've had guts. But God, Flora, you don't do anything by halves, do you? I shouldn't have been so surprised."

"That's on you. Bitchy and predictable, as you've said."

"Now who's shoving words into mouths?"

"Someone has to. I still don't know why you're here. I, at least, gave the Reyeses some warning. Asked if I could come."

"So did I! Or my mum did, rather." At my blank face, Gordon rattles his head. "I suppose I should back up a bit. Someone dropped out, and a spot in that architectural internship in Key West opened up. It's the one I originally wanted."

The memory clicks into place. He *did* say Florida was his first choice, but that bit was swept away with an entire conversation I've been trying to forget.

"Anyway," Gordon continues, "I'll be spending a month in the Keys joining a group on a grant-funded project to restore some important structures. I have a little carpentry experience, but I'll learn a lot more here. There's a block of flats set up for interns, and I was gonna head there straightaway after landing. It all starts up on Monday."

Now it's clear. "But your mum wasn't having it. A long drive after that flight."

"On a bloody *two-lane* road over water, no less. Which is why she called Elisa sometime—yesterday or two days back—hell, what is time? Alan hid a key. I'm surprised no one told you."

"I'm not. I brought home a huge surprise for Pilar's wedding. The excitement may have overshadowed your news. Then today, her wedding-gown fitting was loads bigger than anything."

"Ahhh." He rubs at his eyes, but the wilt and redness linger. "I need a nap. I can't control the next thing out of my mouth, so it's best I quit."

"Hmmph. That's never been my way."

"Quitting or bowing out—no. But escaping's another thing, yeah?" He shakes his head. "Hey, it's fine. I won't jumble up whatever you're doing. Pretend I'm not here." He strides past me but turns before reaching the carpet. "I'll likely be off before you wake. So I guess it's goodbye, Flora. Again."

Goodbye? I'm clearly missing the *good* part. No matter what he intended, he's jumbled me up in every way I know. I march to the fruit bowl and grab an apple, biting into the crisp flesh. Gordon didn't leave his irritating nerve in England back with my mistakes. He brought a double dose, sliding in last minute—internship or not. And then calling me out for not sharing my plan after the way he left me at the inn? What was I supposed to say? The way I felt after he walked off was a huge part of the reason I took the quickest flight out.

I polish off the apple and glance out the window as I toss the core. The rain's stopped, nearly as quickly as it began. Inside I'm catching buckets.

TEN

Two hours later, after chores, I finally buck myself up to ring Dad. Not only has the notion been niggling me for days; sharing a particular memory with him might be the safest way to close the space between us. I hope. In the manner of plaster-ripping and cliffside jumps into water, I tap his icon on my phone.

We're connected, but there's a long pause before Dad says, "Flora. Well." My nerves double down at the blandness of his tone. The quietness of it. The Reyes crew came home briefly but went out again, Gordon's still asleep, and I'm on the back-porch step overlooking a potted-plant garden.

I inhale a rush of post-rain. "Yeah, it's me and—"

"Well, miss, I suppose you got—"

"Dad, wait. Please." I squeeze my eyelids together. "I know you want to go at me, and I deserve it. But can I say something first?"

"Fine, then."

Another exhale. "This is strange, but hear me out. I was thinking of that time you missed a few dentist appointments.

And by a few, I mean, like, seven or eight years' worth. And the longer you put it off, the worse the fear became that something was wrong. But instead of that feeling pushing you to go, you put it off even longer. That is, until the almond brittle Nan sent."

He fills my break with a messy sigh. "You don't ring for nearly two weeks, and now you're talking about *my* mess-ups?"

"No. I mean—yes—I mean, there's a point here. Just hold on. When you bit into that brittle, you got the worst pain. Had to rush in for an emergency procedure." My eyes well at the corners. "That's been me, okay? At first, I didn't want to speak to anyone. But as the days went on and I got settled, not calling became like you putting off the dentist."

"You were afraid," he says. "And then more afraid of my reaction the longer you went."

"Yeah. But I found a bag of brittle in the Reyeses' pantry, and it made me think of your tooth saga. Basically, I don't want to let things go so long, I get hit with that level of pain. So today, I stopped waiting and rang."

"I do understand, but I was hoping this was about my e-mail."

"What e-mail?"

He sighs, long and loud, and I know I've screwed up again. "Responsible people check their messages, Flora. I forwarded it last night."

Tingles shoot around my palms, and I fumble with my phone. "I, er, haven't looked yet today. Wait, Dad."

"Christ, I'll save you the trouble. You never contacted Mr. Everly about the mentorship at Stonefield Media. You know, the one I begged and pleaded to secure for you?"

"Oh God." The tingles sharpen into daggers. Weeks ago, Dad had gone through loads of trouble to get me into a digital marketing and advertising firm a couple afternoons a week to see if I might like to explore that field for my uni study course. I was supposed to set up a consult. "I'm sorry. I let it slip with traveling and everything."

"You do know Mr. Everly turned down another prospective student? Because I vouched for you. And now it got back to him that you never followed through with his admin."

I swallow a lump. "I'll contact them today. I'll fix it."

"It's too late now. Everly's no longer interested. I had to . . ." My father stops, his voice thickening. "I had to bloody use your mum's passing as an excuse for your lapse."

My eyes fill, and I don't have to work to imagine anything. Guilt and shame flash from the clearest full-color photograph. "I messed up."

"Royally. I doubt they'll ever work with us again. Your brother had to deliver a sodding crate of tea to Stonefield for their conference. A peace offering."

"Orion," I muse, thinking of more than his inconvenience or lost profits. Just him.

"Yes, your *brother*. The one who was heartbroken to wake to a measly *note*."

In hindsight, the notes I thought were just enough proved nowhere near enough. "Lila said not to call. To give him time."

"Wise. He needs to process. Lila's in the middle, trying to support both him and you."

"How can I make it better?"

"Oh, I dunno, you could come home?" he says dryly.

I hitch a gnarled breath. The Miami escape I chose to repair myself is ripping hearts in England. "I have to see this through. Dad, please, you saw what happened. I was only going to hurt you and Orion and everyone even more. I had to break that and start over for my own mental health. I'm sorry that's only causing more hurt."

"That's the hell of it, isn't it?" There's a short pause. "Speaking of mental health, you're aware I've been talking to a counselor for some time now. I brought up that night with the piano," he continues. "We both feel it's best you see someone, too."

Everything goes tight—my grip on the phone case, the space between my shoulder blades. And I understand Dad's request. But what's a psychologist going to tell me? That I need to face my past and my loss? I've faced that trauma so often, I've named it a hundred times over. Reframed it into a hundred photos.

And I've coped, too, by overcoming things my way. That's my strategy, the one that keeps a little bit of leftover fight so close. It slips out easily when I'm nervous and frustrated, like now, reddening my words, sharpening their edges.

"I hear you. I get it," I stress. "And I'll figure out a way to reach Orion. But I haven't changed my mind about Miami."

"Miami is not the same as therapy."

"I *know*, and I'll go. But right now I need a place to regroup to write a speech for Mum that she deserves. And to figure out what I'm doing next."

"I'm glad you mentioned that because Ri and I found a spot for Maxwell's London. It will take some time, but you're a part of this. Since deadlines have been a problem, do I also need to remind you that your scholarship disappears next year if you don't, quote, 'figure out what you're doing next' with your course of study? With so many of our investments tied up in our expansion, we can't be lax with these kinds of funds!"

I exhale roughly. The fact that it was Orion who secured that money for me needles deeper into the strain between us. "Let me stay in Miami until the wedding to sort it all out?"

For too long he doesn't respond. Three tiny lizards creep by, and colorful birds flutter over for a turn at the hanging feeder.

"Only until then," Dad says at last. "But I expect you to check in more."

"I will. I promise."

Dad ends the call with a fleeting "love you," adding nothing like *okay* or *all right* to my promise. As if he's not sure he can trust my word to be solid yet. I can't blame him.

I'm belly-down on the bed after dinner, watching Netflix on my laptop, when a strange *tap, tap, tap* sounds through my room. It's my conscience for all I know, plaguing me out loud this time.

What if Orion never forgives you?

Are a few weeks of this heat worth the endless winter of that?

Bugger. I duck my head under my pillow to smother my own noise. It's not like Orion to not want to talk. He's an empath, a solid rock. For now I can only hope he comes around, because I can't bear to lose the bond between us.

The *tap, tap, tap* comes again, louder. It's clearly from the window, not my imagination.

I trot over and yank the venetian-blind cord with a *ziiiipppp*, revealing the late-night tapper. Gordon in a black tee and athletic shorts. He gives me a sheepish wave behind the glass. Christ.

I slide open the frame, leaving the screen between us. "I'm afraid to ask at this point."

"Hiya," Gordon chirps from the side yard next to my bedroom.

"Sleepwalking?" I ask to the top of his head. "Your latest circus trick?"

"Hey—" He stretches up on his toes, grumbling. "This won't do. You're too high." Gordon looks left, perking up. "Wait," he says, and drags over a stepladder. He wings it open and climbs up. "There we go. I woke up and went for a walk. And after some thinking, I ended up here."

"Okaaay." I drag out the word. "But why not come to my door like, I dunno, a non–cat burglar?"

"You don't fancy cats."

Which is true. *"Gordon."*

"Right. Look, I need to say some things." He scratches his chin, now clean-shaven. "I saw your light, and this window reminded me of the one at Maxwell's."

I fold my arms over the sill. "The one where I screech at you while you get your morning pastry?"

His grin sparks through the dark night, orbiting us both. I've missed it. I've missed him.

"Something like that. Say, can you remove this?" He pokes at the mesh screen.

"And let in all the bugs?"

Gordon points. "They'll make food, or friends, for that spider you've got crawling up the wall. Just there," he adds when I crane my neck.

"That's Penelope," I tell him with great dignity. "She's a resident along with George and Consuelo. They're around somewhere. But they know not to wander into my bed or it's—" I pause and pantomime a throat cut across my neck.

"And they mind your rules, these highly trained spiders?"

I hold out my arms, free of bites. "I'm going with yes, and if not, I don't want to know." I find his eyes, the twinkling amusement. "Maybe I felt like not destroying something for once, and I—"

"Flora." The air thins between us, and the way he says my name sends the entire window space into shadow. "I need to apologize."

I feel my pulse quickening. The streak of sweat fingering down my back. "You do?"

"Yeah, for earlier. The jet lag got to me, and I was a right arse."

"You did share your chips, so there's that. And I wasn't exactly flinging rainbows at you."

His shoulders rise into a shrug. "No. But I was too much on edge to try my usual tactics when you're hungry-grumpy."

"In all fairness, it's hard to sing 'Tiny Dancer' off-key whilst you're stuffing your face with a cheeseburger," I point out.

He wrinkles his nose before gathering a long breath. "I guess I was afraid, seeing you again. It's no excuse, but it didn't help that I'm a little anxious about the internship as well. I didn't make this clear before, but there's another reason I picked Florida as my first choice, besides the architecture."

"What's that?"

He sweeps his hand. "My mum was mostly raised here, largely by the woman who used to live in your room. But I don't always talk about being half Venezuelan with Cuban blood, too. I'm a white ginger Brit with the last name Wallace.

Most people don't get two hints of Latino from that. From me."

"Doesn't mean it's not there."

A half smile. "Right. So when Key West was one of the program options, ninety miles from Cuba at that, I wanted to explore that space."

"I hope you find something . . . more. Now that you're here alone, I mean, without your mum." I find myself watching my words in a way Gordon and I never have. But that was before the inn. Before I pushed him away and he pushed back. "Hopefully you're not too alone. You did bring your drawing kit?" I ask quietly. This stuff is safer.

"Always," he says with ease. "I've drawn Key West cottages. And some from around here as well. But it's time for some new ones."

Homes, he means, sketched at his drafting table from fine colored pencils and incredible skill. For years Gordon's filled his Owl and Crow bedroom with drawings of houses in all architectural styles. Walking around his room is like strolling the world all mashed together into one four-walled neighborhood.

"If you see any wonky-colored, offbeat structures and get inspired, maybe I'll finally get a Wallace original," I tell him.

One hand to his heart. "They're rare and priceless."

I let out a faint gasp. "Except you drew one for Lila after two months, and I've known you since we were kids."

"It was her eighteenth birthday! When we all thought she was leaving England for good." He pauses as if he's rewinding his own words, lips compressing into a pout. "I never knew you fancied having one of your own."

"What? Why?"

"Maybe it's in my head, but I didn't think you felt that

strongly about them either way. Which is totally fine."

This is feeling less fine by the minute. "No, I mean, I know I've goaded you for drawing really typical structures and nothing more unique. But I love those houses. All of them."

"Yeah?" he asks, and his surprise stabs a little. Have I really made him feel otherwise? We're off-center, and it might take more than a stepladder to even us out, but I thought he knew.

"Yeah, Gordy . . ." I cut my thought short and try to unlatch the screen. "You're right, this is annoying." A click tells me I've unhooked a part of it. I pull, he pushes, and we manage to remove the panel.

Gordon sets the screen on the ground. "No creepy-crawlies will get past me." He bends over the frame, filling the space. He smells like home, and his hair is still damp from a shower, glistening in the yellow lamplight.

I swallow hard; he needs to know what I apparently haven't said enough. "Your work is beautiful, and you're going to be a fabulous architect. You'll do great in Key West, too. I know it."

"That means loads," he says. "Thanks."

"And it's cool that you get to trace your mum's footsteps," I add. "Except the salsa-dancing ones, because we all know how that'll end up."

"Rude!" Keeping up with the rude theme, a winged *something* hovers between us, and Gordon shows off some impressive reaction-time skills. *Splat!*

We break into laughter. I hand over a tissue, and something long held cracks enough to slip free. "It's my turn to explain, I suppose. Since we weren't texting." He tosses the tissue and motions for me to go on. "Every part of my life lost hold and crashed together. I have some huge choices to make in the coming weeks. I came here with nothing except my camera, hoping the new scenery would help me see clearly. There was too much chaos and regret at home."

"I understand. But your family's been worried even knowing you were safe. Worried about what's going on inside of you. And Lila—"

"I know how I treated her. And everyone." I edge back and use the space to breathe before what's next. What I owe him. "You as well. I didn't mean to be so . . . harsh."

"Hey, no, I—"

"Wait, you didn't eat" slips out, my attention snapping to the dark shadows still winged under his eyes. This is a hungry Gordon if I've ever seen one.

He takes a second to catch up. "Er, not since the burger," he says. "But before we get onto that—"

I glare pointedly. "No *anything*. We both saw what happened earlier before you shoved Wendy's chips into *my* mouth. Plus, skipping a meal is like high treason in this house. If Elisa finds out you left for a walk without proper nourishment, she's going to go off."

"This is true." His mouth crinkles in amusement before his gaze tracks up to the evening sky on his side of the window, then down again. It's a slow, steady motion that looks like he's trying to leave something there, high above and galaxies away.

Gordy's back now, his ginger mug centered in the window opening. I'd need a viewfinder into his brain to know what all that was about. "Any leftovers?" is all he asks. "I can fend for myself."

"I'll do you one better. Wait here on bug watch." I dash out and into the kitchen, returning with a foil packet from the fridge.

He eyes me quizzically and then spouts the biggest Gordon grin as he unwraps two slices of Elisa's homemade pizza. That's more like it. "Here you are, feeding me through windows, just like home." He takes a hearty bite, nodding through it. "Perfect. Who needs heat?"

Not him, like always. Gordon Wallace, king of cold pizza.

He tips his late supper at me, exhales. Looks a little bit everywhere at once, with the same buzz of uneasiness about him that I noticed earlier. Too soon, it becomes weird that he's eating pizza in my bedroom window and not saying anything. What happened to our companionable silence?

"So . . . ," I try.

He tucks the remaining slice into the foil. "Right. It's late, and you and the spiders probably want to get back to your show." A toothless smile. "I'll be off tomorrow, you know, early. So I guess I'll see you when I see you?"

My heart rate jitters like I've been running, which rarely happens unless there's a shoe sale or something's on fire. It's like I can't catch up to all we've said here, and that's not typical of Gordon and me. We're usually running at the same pace or trying to best each other at some game. I don't know the rules to this one. "Hold up," I say, grasping for any words that work. "You'll check in? When you get settled?"

"Count on it." He springs off the ladder and does one of his cheesy dance moves. He makes it three steps before dashing back and hoisting the screen back up. "Here. To keep out the bad stuff."

I help fit the panel and click it into place.

Our eyes lock despite the height gap and the wiry mesh between us. "I hope you find what you need here." He gives a little wave. "Be well, Squiggs."

"Be well, Gordy," I echo as he trots away, probably to slink through the front door and into Lila's old room. I close the rest of this Miami night away, shutting the glass, lowering the blinds.

My legs wobble like a baby animal's as I spin around. That's when I see the strange bit of sparkly gold resting on my comforter. I rush over and grab the tiny brass owl figurine—the one I pelted at Gordon. From my palm shoot images of the silly rubber rat, and our picnic, and all that came after. He must've thrown it through the window while I was getting his pizza. He brought this all the way from Winchester. Something from home.

I stride to Abuela Lydia's dresser. On the opposite side from all her treasures, Baz's lightning photo from the week my mum passed slants against the wall. I turn the little golden owl in my palm and, after a quick thought, rest it in front of the glass-covered frame. I guess I'm building my own set of recuerdos. This one, a memento of one singular time when I knew exactly where I was supposed to go.

ELEVEN

Something is off. I'm on the back patio the next morning, shooting the stephanotis vine Elisa's growing in a huge pot. The tiny white flowers will go into Pilar's wedding bouquet, and neither mum nor daughter can speak of this without tearing up. There's something sweet and calming about the little blooms.

But today, the images filling my memory card don't match what I'm framing. I've checked my settings, shot from different angles, and *no*. Something is clearly off.

I dart back into my bedroom, and after transferring my recent shots onto my laptop, I find the same issue present on all my pictures from the craft fair. I hadn't checked them carefully until now—too caught up in everything with Studio Marín and Baz.

Baz. The name glows brighter than any flashbulb inside my head. Of *course* Baz. I pull up our text stream.

Me: Does being your fake date also mean access to your camera help?

Baz: Sure. Among other benefits

My belly gurgles, but I also haven't eaten yet. Either way, I tell it to sod off.

Me: My Canon is acting dodgy. Or it's haunted. I'm getting this weird, triangular plane of light photobombing all my shots

Baz: Hmm. As much as I dig the idea of haunting, I think I might know what's up. Send me 3 pics

I do, pasting them into my next message. Not fifteen seconds later, he replies.

Baz: Yup. Your shutter is damaged and needs pro help

I pick up the Canon. After Gordon's window apology, after the golden owl and the prickly emotions still between us, I armed my camera straight from bed this morning. I always do when I'm more shaken than settled. And now my trusted go-to is broken? My next message is ringed with dread.

Me: Pro help sounds expensive

Baz: Yeah, it could be. We know a guy and get special rates, which makes me sound like a Mafia kingpin, but we don't trust our equipment to just anyone. He's back next week. I'm going over with some gear, so I'll drop yours off for a look

I exhale in relief.

Me: Wow, thank you

Baz: I'd be a shitty fake boyfriend otherwise. I'll grab it when I grab you for the gala

Baz: Um

Baz: That came out wrong. Promise 😉 En serio. No I mean it

I'm grinning when we sign off, even though I have to live without my camera for God knows how long. The idea makes *me* feel overexposed. Too vulnerable, like I'm in a fantasy film and a key piece of my armor has been stolen away. At least the hurricane I keep inside will never break.

I pad out into the hall. Barrel through the cracked-open bathroom door. "Bloody hell!"

Gordon's brushing his teeth. Why is he still here?

"I'm so sorry," I blurt out. "I thought the house was empty." And, Christ, I'm wearing a sleep tank and shorts from the nothing-left-to-the-imagination collection and no bra. I jerk my dressing gown closed, cheeks flaming.

Gordon, respectable in joggers, spits, and I find myself half looking away for no reason. Have we ever brushed our teeth in front of each other? After a rinse and towel-off, he grins. "Nah, I didn't bother to close the door. Already had a shower and such." When I continue to impersonate a mannequin, he adds, "Yeah, so I was set to head out this morning, but Elisa talked to Mum and found out I'd booked a hotel for tonight before move-in tomorrow."

I give a breathy laugh. "Say no more."

"It does save me some quid. Plus, it's really festive in Lila's old room. Kind of floral-smelling and lacy? Is that a word?"

"Could be the dried rosebuds for the reception," I say. And we're still here in the cramped bath with its cardigan tissue-box holder and fluffy blue toilet-seat cover that looks like a Muppet crime scene. Add Gordon's white T-shirt to the mix—tight across toned abs—and where the hell did my own toothbrush go? "Er . . ."

"Oh here." He plucks my toothbrush holder from the medicine cabinet. "I didn't want any of my sprays to get on there. Used your toothpaste, too. Nice cinnamon flavor, that."

My face wrinkles up, but that's all he gets. I let it go.

"Hey, so," Gordon says, "I'm dying to visit Coral Castle again. Have you heard of it?" When I shake my head, he adds, "No spoilers, but it's an incredible place. Want to come along since I'm here all day?" He hooks one hand around the edge of the counter. "Just like our weekend adventures at home."

"You mean where I never know where the hell we're going, and I might need a flotation device or bug repellent or motion-sickness tablets or all of the above?"

He laughs through a shrug. "Maybe just your saddest Spotify playlist this time?" Before I can ask why, he's off.

"All yours. We'll grab donuts on the way" echoes down the hall.

As we near Coral Castle, Gordon reveals that the attraction is more museum than castle and best described as an outdoor sculpture garden. The part that makes Gordon's fingers twiddle over the steering wheel is that all the carvings were fashioned by one man entirely out of the gray oolitic limestone that's native to the area and embedded with fossilized coral. That was enough to snap my attention away from the mind-blowing powdered donuts we'd grabbed twenty minutes outside Miami.

By the time he pulls his rental into the car park, my curiosity is revved. Coral Castle is just *right there* off the highway, tucked behind a nondescript hedgerow fence. No royal fanfare here, but tell that to Gordon as he yanks me from the passenger seat and into the ticket queue. Like an impatient toddler.

"I know, sorry," he says to my side-eye. "But I haven't been here in years." He nods toward a few of the larger oolite sculptures that peek over the entrance barrier. "This place is a scientific and engineering wonder and should not be possible. It shouldn't exist."

This gets me. I pivot, facing my friend as he stretches to peer over the queue, hands stuffed into his shorts pockets. Have I forgotten how it feels to be excited about something like this? Like him? Next week I'll be attending an epic event with Baz. But it's not a calendar square I've circled in red and decorated with hearts and stars. It's my end of a bargain. I can't remember the last thing I truly looked forward to.

Is that strange? The sensation creeps across my skin. "Thank you," I say without thinking. His lit-up Gordon face dims for a moment as his brow narrows in confusion. "I mean, I had nothing cool like this to do today."

And your happiness is so simple. Pure like a child with a circus balloon. I want that, too, but don't know how to find it. So for now, maybe I can borrow some of yours?

I start by following his eager steps toward the gated entrance. A sign inlaid into a stony arch greets visitors: *You Will Be Seeing Unusual Accomplishment.*

From what Gordon hinted, I believe it. I reach instinctively across my chest for my camera. Ugh—right. My camera is back at home, damaged. I pull out my phone instead and— "No! Bugger, I'm so daft!"

"Like in general or . . . ?"

Glaring, I flash the screen, which is currently showing 10 percent battery life. "I grabbed it off the dresser when *someone* was yelling down the hall that we needed to get on the road. Didn't even check." And last night, there was a window and a golden owl, and I'd neglected to charge it.

"I have a cable in the car," he says. "Why didn't you plug it in?"

"Donuts, Gordon. Donuts. I was totally waylaid by sugar and fried dough. So really this is all your fault."

"Sure, Squiggs. We'll go with that. At least Alan was spot-on about that recommendation."

One more glare at my phone. "The sign promised that we're about to encounter amazing sights, and I can't even spare the battery for one shot."

"I have another option. You usually take pictures of everything, and good on you." Gordon nudges my arm; it's our turn to enter. "But how about you just experience this place? I purposely didn't ask for self-tour headsets because I know the history. We don't need anything more than my geek-out research. You can simply enjoy it."

"Hmm. Sure," I say, dubious but willing to humor him. I never visit museums or tourist attractions without documenting . . . something. And now he wants me to do the opposite and *like* it? We move into a large courtyard paved with reddish gravel. The huge freestanding sculptures are accented with willowy palms, shrubs, and succulents.

"You just need to be wowed a little. How about this? All these structures were moved and carved by one Latvian immigrant called Edward Leedskalnin, over the course of twenty-eight years," Gordon says, gesturing through the space. "There's a quarry just outside the wall, and we'll get to see all his equipment, which is surprisingly little. He had no help or modern machinery and used only basic, rudimentary tools to mine the rocks."

My mouth goes slack; I'd forgotten what it's like to let Gordon tell you a story. He speaks slower, shifting dynamics and savoring each phrase in a way he never does with pastries or pizza.

"Oh, and here's maybe the most important bit," he says as

we approach tables and rocking chairs, chaises and L-shaped beds, all carved from the pocked, speckled limestone. "This whole place was because of a girl."

Our eyes lock for a single beat before he shifts away, gesturing broadly.

"You can imagine my love for this place. And my respect for it, and Edward, after studying building and design."

I'm still stuck ten seconds in the past. "Wait, Gordon, this bloke spent twenty-eight years building all this for one girl?" When he nods, I let out a relenting sigh. He's won this time and knows it. "Please tell me the whole story. And I won't say another word about my camera."

His grin flashes white against all the stony gray. "It all started in Latvia. Good ol' Ed came from a family of mason workers, and he only had a few years of formal schooling," Gordon begins, touring me around the weighty sculptures. "At twenty-six, he was set to marry a sixteen-year-old girl called Agnes, and he was utterly gone for her. But the day before the wedding, Agnes rejected him. Left him heartbroken."

We've stopped at a large oval rock shaped like a pond stone with a dipped basin carved out of the center. It's full of rainwater because this is Florida. "Living in wedding central, it's hard to imagine Pili doing that to Ryan."

"Even if she did, I'd bet anything Ryan wouldn't react as eccentrically as Edward did," Gordon notes. "He came to Florida because he fell ill, and the humid weather helped his recovery. He truly believed that Agnes would have a change of heart and follow him here. He wanted to build something for her, like a surprise for when she arrived. A castle of her own."

"Most guys go with jewelry or flowers, not . . ." I pause,

craning my neck. "Is that table shaped like the state of Florida?" We sidle up to the whimsical table set with chairs all around.

"Sure is. I wanted to see if you'd notice." Gordon winks. "I'm sure he planned a hundred banquets in his head. You'd have to do something with your mind whilst working for decades." He squints, moving around the structure, investigating the curved planes. "But here's the part that always gets me, and most people. Even today, engineers and scientists can't figure out how Edward moved and cut some of these pieces from the quarry without diamond saws and cranes. They've tried, and no one can replicate his technique. Like, the rock's so porous, it should've crumbled during much of his work."

"So one man comes here ages ago and stumps all the top brains of the modern era."

"Basically." Gordon shakes his head in wonder. "Edward only said he understood the laws of weight and leverage, which scientists later related to the mystery of how the Egyptian pyramids were built. People would sneak over here at night while he worked to try to discover his method. He'd always climb up to that wall and shine lights in their faces, yelling that he'd resume working when they left."

I bark out a laugh. "Sounds like something I would do. Those nosy snoops."

"Yeah, but a few did catch him. There's a firsthand account of some teenagers covertly witnessing him manipulating a triangular device when moving gigantic rocks, like he was harnessing magnetic current. They reported the stones simply levitating. He allegedly used some sort of reverse magnetism to lift them. They weigh thousands of pounds."

Chills skitter down my arms, and I suddenly want to look

everywhere. My baffled wonder only increases when Gordon shows me the inside of Edward's towerlike living quarters and the part of the museum housing his rusty, deceptively simple tools. Saws, chisels, levers, and chain-and-pulley systems are all on display.

Yet the initial frustration I felt over the impossibility of what I'm seeing bumps aside for plenty of awe and enchantment. Especially when we tour the celestial section of the garden with pillars showcasing suspended planets—including a perfectly ringed Saturn—and two huge crescent moons. He built a galaxy for his love.

"Okay, maybe there *was* some weird magnetism or ancient secret at play," I muse. "But I think I'm good not knowing everything. Like, it's simply cool that he left this for all of us to see."

"Oh, so you're just enjoying it, yeah? Experiencing it?" Gordon asks with too much cheek, bending his words up a half octave. "Without taking a single picture?"

"Bugger off, Gordy." We stop at a heart-shaped table with a built-in centerpiece planter filled with green ferns. I run my hand over the rough, toothy rock.

"So this here is rather nice," Gordon chimes. "I read that he meant the heart to be a permanent valentine. Maybe so he'd never be guilty of forgetting the holiday."

I nod and volley my look from the table to my friend. "How does the story end? Tell me about Agnes and her finding out about all this."

He steps closer, blinking once, then again. "Well, here's the thing. She never came. She never even saw it."

"Really?" Tiny sparks flit across my skin again. I recall

Gordon this morning, suggesting my saddest Spotify play-list would be fit for this place. "How incredibly depressing. I mean, I suppose she never asked him to do all this. To devote his entire life making all these creations for her."

"No," Gordon says, "she never asked. And after studying this place, I think the building of it helped him. Gave him a purpose." He runs a hand through his hair. "Other times I feel it completely did him in."

I stare at the stony heart and think that, sometimes, there are passions we devote our lives to that do both at once. I'd actually welcome one of those.

Gordon pivots, breaking my muse as he urges me along toward another section. "This is the final part. And despite all the magical elements, I think it's the weirdest thing here. Check out that sign."

I step up to read the green plaque. "'The Repentance Corner.'" We're at an alcove, sort of like a small portico. Tucked inside, a bench faces two long keyhole shapes cut out of the opposite wall, like windows. "This reminds me of a church confessional."

Gordon holds up one finger, runs around, and pokes his head through the top part of one of the holes. "Hiya."

"Wait, it's another kind of repentance." I make a rough gasp. "He made a bloody medieval stockade."

"That's the theory," Gordon says. He remains on the exterior side of the wall, teasing his head through the round opening. "Perhaps Ed had a barbaric side. Like he expected to have children and could put them in here for a bit if they misbehaved."

"If that's true, I don't feel so bad that he remained alone." I sit on the stone bench; the air inside the shady alcove is cooler.

Lighter. Gordon examines some of the angles and cuts with the kind of engineering interest I can't bring to this place. Soon, he's back, staring at me through the keyhole opening as if it's an old-world replica of the night before. Of us on opposite sides of my bedroom window.

He draws a long breath. "Since this is the Repentance Corner, I've got a confession of my own. I was going to say this last night before you brought me the pizza. It's actually the second reason I came to your window after my walk. I tried, but then . . . didn't."

His mouth pulls into a half smile that feels inward, like it's meant for himself, but it stirs a dozen small places up and down my body. My throat closes.

"Can I say it now?" he asks. "It's been a bother, and I don't want to drag it along to Key West."

What could be so touchy that he'd lost his nerve over it during his first go? I nod, motioning him to continue.

"Back home at the inn, I overstepped, and I was selfish." Gordon splays both hands, pressing from forehead to chin. "That day of your picnic, you bare your soul and admit something that's hurtful and stressful, and I go and make it about me."

If one of South Florida's many flying creatures comes through here, there's a landing spot with a welcome sign: my gaping mouth.

He sighs roughly. "It was a shit move. I was caught up in all these emotions, and I had no right to put you on the spot."

"You . . . didn't?"

"Of course not. And I'm truly sorry. I thought a lot about that—our talk—whilst hiking and over the last couple weeks.

I want you to know that I am, er, totally cool. Over it and done."

Miami is on hurricane watch this time of year, but they don't tell you about the earthquakes. This one shakes me from the inside out, rattling the rock-solid space around Gordon and me. And I can't even articulate why. "Um. Okay?"

"You look confused," he says.

"No—*no*." Yes, so much yes. "I'm taking it all in." My lip quivers, and I can't make it stop, and I can't simply cover my mouth with my hand because he'll ask about it.

"Good," he says, offering a bland smile that's missing its signature gleam. "I hope we can go back to before, to being the best of friends." He releases himself from the stockade and creeps around, joining me on the bench. "I'll be working in Key West, but we get a couple Fridays off, so I might come into Miami those weekends. We can hang and hit up some fun spots like we used to?"

Like we used to. A clean slate and a fresh start like all those clichés that are so common, they should feel known and comforting. But they don't—at least not yet. I nod at him anyway.

And as we sit in the shade awhile longer, I realize that if I'd brought a camera after all, I could frame an entire reel of two old friends who appear *totally normal* and *all better*. I could make us look that way. Even though the words we said are still chiseled deep into the stony, impossible place we've carved out for ourselves.

TWELVE

The next week is so packed with Flora-Do List items, my uneasiness at Coral Castle dissolves into busyness. Between helping Elisa organize her cake shop, attending a bridesmaids' lunch, and assisting Pili with wedding stuff (I mean *actually* stuffing sugared almonds into tiny doily wrappers, for one), it feels like minutes instead of days between my saying goodbye to Gordon and opening the door to Baz.

Now that it's the night of the charity gala, Baz is here, and it takes real effort to debug my eyes. His charcoal suit molds to his frame, sporting a subtle check design. It looks . . . artistic? He's paired it with gray patent loafers, a crisp white shirt, and a tie with a few bits of blue. He steps in, grinning into a customary cheek kiss, leaving a trail of sharp green citrus. "Wow," he says. "When you play decoy, you don't go halfway."

"I'm staying with two women who don't understand 'halfway.'" I ruffle the skirt of my dress, now altered to perfection.

Baz smiles. "They did you proud."

Minutes later we're off. "You didn't say we'd be taking Cher's Jeep from *Clueless*," I note as he helps me into the Wrangler with gray leather seats. My damaged camera is tucked into the back for repair.

"Hey, white cars rule around here. Keeps you from getting extra crispy." He buzzes around and starts the engine, easing away. "I'll admit, I was nervous about the pickup. I had a really good opener worked out."

"Trust me, the universe was kind," I tell him. It's a miracle that all three Reyes family members were summoned from the house before he arrived. "But I've been fielding demands for pictures for an hour."

"You picked the right fake partner for that."

All of a sudden too much awareness of my current situation skitters through my belly. I'm about to waltz into a major event with a teen influencer. I'm way outside my impostor ability. "What did your parents say when, *poof,* you're bringing a date?"

"Well," he says through a laugh, "you can thank Pablo Neruda for Mami's reaction. That's right, the poet." The light turns green. "Luna didn't mention this part to you. When I was born, Mami received a gift from a venerable member of the Cuban community. A framed copy of Neruda's 'Oda al tiempo.'"

"Ode to Time?" I translate.

"Yup. The poem's about how time moves forward, but it's also fixed and tied to fate. Like, time will do its will and leave its mark on us, and we can't stop that. She hung the gift in my room, and later, when I started up with photography like Papi, she felt even more like the poem was prophetic about me. And that this viejita who gave it to her had known . . . *something.* Essentially, I stop time with every picture I take. But time still wins and goes on anyway."

"Yeah, it does," I muse, stopping my *thoughts* before they go to dark places. "But how does that relate to our fake dating?"

"Mami claims she had a 'special feeling' as soon as she met Kelly, and she's convinced it will be our time one day. Worse, Kelly's mom is right behind her. And me bringing you simply means my time with Kelly is delayed. It's not today, but some unknown tomorrow. She'll see you as the girl who's with me *now*."

"Ahh, so I'm temporary and not a threat to her endgame dream. I just have to be convincing enough for a bit."

"Right. Just long enough to get Papi and Señor Acosta established in their media collab. It's a huge opportunity." He sends me an off-color look. "No pressure."

Then why are my hands clamming up? "Hmmph. To be more convincing, shouldn't we coordinate our stories? At least our meet-cute?"

"I hate that term, but good idea," Baz says as he accelerates along the interstate on-ramp. "It's best to stick to as much truth as possible, no?"

Except what's true between Baz and me is another muddied thing. "All right. We met at the studio when I subbed in for a model?"

"And hit it off right away," he provides.

"So we went for a coffee."

Baz shakes his head, his fingertips tapping along the wheel. "That won't work. I can't stand it and everyone knows. We went to a boba place."

"*You* suggested boba and found out later that I only tolerated the stuff because I was so smitten and all."

"Smitten, is it?" Baz nods appreciatively, preening a little.

"Please. You know you look good. Apparently, a large portion of Miami feels that way."

"There's a difference between how *everyone* views you and, you know, the ones who matter." A piercing stare.

He's faking, right? I mean, he's just extra good at this ruse already? "Yes, there's a *difference*." Flustered about being flustered, I roll my eyes. "So, as I was saying, my family owns a tea shop in Winchester, and iced teas are not the usual. I know boba is popular, but I can't get into it."

"My flub keeps it real. I can't always get it right with dates."

I sit up against the gray leather, squaring my shoulders. "You might only rarely get it right with me any given day."

"Oh, okay now, chica," Baz says, dangling his hand. "I have to learn more about your tea place."

"When I learn more about your tree tattoo," I counter.

He stiffens imperceptibly. "We're a new item. Makes sense that I haven't told you everything about me." At my conceding shrug he adds, "But maybe we cover some basic facts?"

He goes first, and I learn he has one older sister called Selena who attends NYU and is studying art in Florence for the summer. He's left-handed. And there's his private Miami university and study in photojournalism.

I take my turn as we near the event space. The Design District unfolds, vibrant and bold with muraled structures, galleries, and posh joints to eat and shop. And it's now that I choose to tell him about Mum because everything else about me currently arrows back to her.

Sometimes it quiets entire rooms, this revelation. Here it summons a hush that whites out the engine noise and the strains of an indie radio tune. "I figured a date would know straightaway," I add after summarizing the major bits.

At a traffic light he faces me. "I'm so sorry, Flora. I can't imagine."

"Thank you." I exhale a cleansing breath. "I didn't mean to kill the party mood."

"I capture real life every day." This part comes out in all sincerity before he brightens, turning into the valet zone. "Ruining party moods is what Armando is for."

"Why would you even—"

"I know, and lo siento. I made sure he's not sitting at our table." Baz shoots me a grin before winding around to help me out.

"Does he know? Does anyone? About our . . . ?"

"No one but Luna, and she's a vault." Baz juts one arm around my back and aims his next words close into my ear. "So we're clear, is this kind of stuff cool? Touching you?"

"Sure. It won't look natural if you appear too hesitant to hold my hand or go in for a peck."

"Bueno," he says, webbing our fingers together, the air already dampening the skin between us. "Let's do this."

The Canvas Miami gala thrums with energy. Laughter and joyous greetings crowd the space as cameras flash over cars pulling up to what Baz said is one of Miami's most unique venues. The multi-floor Moore Building was originally a 1921 furniture store. Today, the structure gleams in a renovated Art Deco style with a curved arch at the entrance and decorative molding details.

As we close in, I'm hit with a rumble of anxiety. "Can you give me a last-minute primer on what's next?" I gesture toward the swarm.

"Totally. There's a standard step-and-repeat posing wall just inside the entrance. I usually do it alone, but tonight we'll pose as a couple. It's best to keep your body forward, one hip out." He smiles. "But turn your torso into me, as I'll be gazing adoringly at you."

I chortle a bit. "Like the decoy duo we are."

My words and everything else are lost as Baz guides me into the Moore Building. Instantly, I spy an enormous art installation strung between the rails of the open atrium, four floors high.

"Amazing, isn't it?" Baz says of the white web of a structure that resembles stretched putty. "It's called *Elastika*, and the legendary Iraqi architect Zaha Hadid designed it."

The word *architect* spins a circle. I can't help but wonder what Gordon's doing this Saturday night, in Key West, while I'm four hours away with another kind of artist.

"Our turn," Baz says, and nudges me forward.

We reach a step-and-repeat backdrop covered with the Canvas Miami logo and sponsor names. At the center we stop, and Baz pulls me in under a relentless stream of light and flash. I remember his cues and try to act naturally as photographers call for us to shift or turn. While I'm moving on borrowed instinct, Baz is a natural. All I have to do is keep up. Until—

"Some with the lovely lady alone, please?" the line of photographers calls.

Oh God, they mean me.

"You've got this, Florecita." Baz steps out of camera range.

I so do not have . . . this. Still, I try my hardest to buck up, catching Baz at the corner of my vison covertly demonstrating how I should pose. I follow and clamp my hand on my hip, one foot forward, shoulders back, neck as swanlike as it goes, until I hear a "Thank you, dear."

Baz is right there with an obligatory forehead kiss; I can almost taste the stares of onlookers. "Nice work."

I huff, unconvinced. "For the first few, I felt like a lost farm animal. Thanks for the pantomime guide, by the way."

"No prob, and don't worry. They'll only put the best ones online."

With the photo wall done, I finally take in the event in all its stylized glory. Round tables pop with centerpieces mixing sculpted media and bold flowers, and a band at the head plays something salsa adjacent. Baz leads me up to the next open floor, where impressive student artwork is on display. And the third level is home to the biggest part of the fundraiser, the silent auction.

"Hey, I know that guy," I quip as we pass Baz's entry and headshot: a two-hour photo shoot with Baz Marín of Marín Photo and Studio Marín. Opening bid: one thousand dollars.

"Do you ever get curious about how much you're going for?" I ask.

"The whole night," he deadpans. "It's like *The Bachelorette*, silent auction edition. But hey, good cause."

With very good prizes. We stroll through offerings for pro-athlete experiences, vacations, and spa packages. At the end, there's a large black-and-white photo of Sebastián. I point to the polished image. "Your dad looked rather different at the class compared to his website bio."

"Yeah," Baz says over a chuckle. "He's in this phase where he likes to reinvent himself. He took Mami to Hawaii and came back on this tropical-but-make-it-lazy kick."

"Ahh, that's it exactly."

"He keeps the website really classic and never shows up to jobs in anything distracting." I feel the intensity of Baz's stare before I meet it. "A big history rides behind everything you might see on the outside. That part never changes."

"Would a decoy date know about it?"

His eyes skim over the scraggly tree peeking out from under his shirt cuff. "Eventually" is all he says, as if that history is carved into his skin as indelibly as his tattoo.

The next moments rush by like I'm on the train with the countryside blurring past my nose. We arrive at the two Studio Marín tables. They're in prime view of the band, but *my* view is eclipsed by Baz's mother, Iva, elegant in a cream jumpsuit, nut-brown hair pinned back into a twist. Sebastián is up, too, black-suited and marginally trimmed compared to last time.

"We are so happy to have you join us, Flora," he says sincerely.

Iva nods, deftly whisking her gaze over me. "Claro. And mi hijo is full of last-minute surprises, no?"

I arrange my smile with a touch of demure. *Act like you belong.* "Thank you so much for having me. The event is brilliant."

As Baz pulls out my chair, I catch Luna with her boyfriend at the staff table. She gives a wink of approval. I return it, grateful Armando is chatting to a server and hasn't noticed me.

"The Acostas like to make an entrance," Baz says, gesturing to the four empty seats.

As if on cue, a Black family of four struts through the room, sporting posh evening wear and expert grooming. The Maríns are up again with hearty greetings. I catch Luna observing the two Acosta daughters, one of whom is my decoy mark.

This sister duo makes quite an entrance simply by breathing. They're beautiful, with long-legged bodies arranged into clingy dresses. Kelly's center-parted hair is smoothed and glossed, threaded with highlights. Iva tracks her like a mystery-novel detective. Fitting, as she's devised her own story about this girl's future.

Meanwhile, unwilling love interest Baz goes in for friendly cheek kisses but clamps a hold on my arm at the same time. "Hey, Kelly, this is Flora." He squeezes and draws me up as I go in for a handshake with his red-dressed "friend."

Play the part, sell the ruse. I flash a wide grin. "So nice to meet you."

I don't miss Kelly's sideswipe glance at Baz before she kindly, if a little blandly, returns my greeting. "Yeah, you too. This is Leonie. My sister."

White-dress Leonie is wearing the smoky eye and cat liner duo of my dreams. (Pilar helped with my makeup, and I'm decent, but this is a wow.)

"Hi," she chirps. "I like your dress."

My "thank you" is lost as the adults return, and a waiter serves the most artistic salad I've ever seen, composed of edible flowers and delicate greens. A large baguette goes right on the table. I recognize it as pain d'epi, something Lila perfected at Le Cordon Bleu. The bread resembles a wheat shaft, and guests can pull off one of the tear-shaped sections.

As we eat, Baz makes sure to deal out plenty of smoldering looks and check-ins. *Would I like another mocktail? More water? Is the state of the world generally to my liking?* And

I know it's all for show, but I'm convinced Baz would make someone a fine real boyfriend. Zero percent of our interactions go unnoticed by our tablemates.

So yes, by the time the dinner course arrives, I'm quite aware that I'm the one to watch around here. Baz usually attends this event alone. Not with a blond Brit newcomer.

The scrutiny makes each bite of my lobster tail squiggle down my throat. Of course it's Lila who ends up saving me again. It happens when Baz casually mentions I'm a close friend of the esteemed owners of Panadería La Paloma.

"Lila Reyes has been dating my brother, Orion, for three years," I say, *without* adding a bloody word about their status or future engagement. Oh, I'm well onto myself tonight. For backup, I'm eating loads of the amazing pain d'epi to keep my mouth stuffed shut.

"Ahh, Lila! Our very own Estrellita." Señora Acosta beams over Lila's Miami nickname. At my nod, a hand smacks over her heart. "We love La Paloma."

The adults reminisce about their favorite Cuban pastries, asking if I know how to make them. I'm proud to nod my way through the comments, and I detail a few favorites.

"Óyeme, Flora, can you find out La Paloma's secret recipe for the little mango mousse domes?" Iva asks. "Mine never come out the same."

"Mami," Baz warns. "It's a secret for a reason."

This is as far as he gets before an attendant wearing an earpiece appears, tapping Baz on the shoulder and waving him to the front.

"The program is starting." He tucks a stray curl behind my ear. "You'll be fine."

Minutes after he scoots off, I try to set aside my anxiety about being left alone under the reverberating scrutiny and enjoy the presentation. But my attention span is a Ping-Pong ball:

• A heartwarming video documents art students who have gone on to use their Canvas Miami scholarships to study worldwide. *(Iva Marín paying more attention to me than to her emcee son. Me, leaning in to whisper that I'll try to get her the mango mousse recipe. Her light-show smile.)*

• Another video shows two children talking about the roving art bus that visited their school. *(The Studio Marín staff table. Armando with a glare that's equal parts boredom and haughtiness. Me, sitting up proudly and biting my tongue instead of sticking it out.)*

• Baz steps up again, unmistakably comfortable in front of the mic as he outlines the goals of the organization and encourages guests to visit the silent auction. *(Kelly on my right swinging from Baz's every word like a circus trapeze. Leonie watching me watch everyone.)*

Blessedly, the presentation ends, and as my fake date moves off for interviews and photos, I scoot elsewhere, too. I feel like picked-over fruit at the market. Plus, all that French bread I ate brought on an overconsumption of water, which has made a good wee the next thing that must happen.

A few moments after, I use the powder-room mirror for a lippy touch-up. I don't always like what I see in mirrors; my insides tend to spill out and dull the reflection. But tonight, yeah, I'm doing okay. The thought rearranges, bringing me back to when I slipped into this dress at home, the last of

Gordon's presence still clouding the hallway bath. Tonight, I'm still Squiggs, but a refined version. My earrings, lent by Elisa because the pearl clusters suited my look just right. My hair, set by Pilar into a retro style.

I tug at one of the blond spirals; it springs back into place, jolting a memory that's been hiding underneath. My mum used to do this at the mirror with my hair. I swear I can hear my little-girl giggles.

I didn't realize this fully until now—how much of my mother my hair still holds. Curls like mine can be hard to care for. But Mum showed me early on how to manage them.

It's been years since those days, but I repeat her same steps every morning. I likely will forever. And what's perfect about this memory, this image, is that it's one that I haven't messed up. Despite all I've done, this one is blond and young and giggly. And as sweet as a pink gumball.

I glance at the wall clock; I can hang out inside this feeling for a few more minutes. So far, I've been the good kind of alone in here. I use the solitude to pull out my mobile, scanning my message inbox. Both Lila and Jules checked in earlier, but it's too late now to reply.

Four texts each came in from Elisa and Pili. I'm grinning, shaking my head in mirth as I dump us into a group chat and respond with: Yes, I'm quite positive Baz is not "un sinvergüenza," hair and makeup holding up brilliantly, and the event is lovely

When I land on Gordon's name, I stop scrolling. We haven't messaged in days, probably because of everything new in Key West. But weeks ago, when I left Winchester,

Gordon and I let ourselves drift apart. Even though I'm still a bit shaky over our talk, he did try to bring us back to usual and normal again. And a five-day span without a single *what's up* is the opposite of our normal. There's no window between us, but this gigantic mirror says it's my turn to reach out. I expand his message screen.

Me: Hiya, checking in for proof of life

I get my powder and lippy repacked before the three talking dots poof into words.

Gordon: Hey you! Sorry, been busy getting settled. Just back from the gym

I decide to have a little fun.

Me: How do I know it's really you and not one of your flat-mates with your phone?

Gordon sends a selfie of him wearing a sports singlet that shows off his arms. Behind him a balcony view drops off into a Key West streetscape.

Me: Nice, but some kidnapper could have snapped that photo days ago

Gordon: So true. At this moment, THE REAL GORDON could be chained to a drafting table for ransom. You should ask something that only he would know

I've got a good one.

Me: At Win-Fest, when I was 14, what animal did I want to take home from that stall offering rescue adoptions?

Gordon: Black cat with that white circle bit on its face

Me: Wrong! It was the tan dachshund/Chihuahua mix. Now unhand Gordon Wallace immediately. He knows I don't fancy cats

Gordon: He knows you've only ever fancied one cat. The black one at Win-Fest with the perfect white circle over its mouth so it looked like it was always surprised

Me: Excuse me but that dog! I was going to name him Tiny

Gordon: This kind of questioning only works when you actually remember the correct answer to your query

I expel one of those really aghast sounds into the screen, as if he could hear it. Then another message pops up.

Gordon: I remember the dog. But we left to get some chips and came back around to the stall. You saw the cat the second time, said any cat that could draw a perfect surprised circle over its mouth was a magic cat. And magic cats were different than regular cats. And you thought of course you needed a magic cat. But your dad said NO PETS of any sort

Well, shit. Reading the text, the image of that black creature with the white marking emerges like a shaken Polaroid.

Me: Hiya Real Gordon. You got me there

Gordon: No worries, we both know what happens when you eat chips. Rest of world = vanished

Fizzy tingles skitter across my back—must be leftovers from window ledges and him shifting us "back into our normal lane." That's how I explain it.

Gordon: Don't I get a selfie?

I don't have anywhere near the brain capacity to explain the details of my Saturday-night situation. I scramble and find a nondescript portion of blue wall. No fancy blush lace in this photo, either. I shoot and send a *proof of life* caption.

Gordon: You look posh, Squiggs. One of those Pili-Flora spa nights where you paint each other's nails and sip bubbly drinks?

My laugh zings out.

Me: That's what you think girls do when they hang? You forgot pillow fights and ringing cute guys anonymously and hanging up after they answer

Gordon: You texted me, not rang. And you didn't hang up

I am no longer in need of a blush touch-up. Exit. Get out *now*. I manage to recover well enough to tell him I need to run and we'll chat soon.

"So you didn't go missing."

I jump at the sudden voice and the reflection of Kelly Acosta behind me.

THIRTEEN

I pivot as acid shoots through my stomach. Kelly's even more stunning in the bright loo lighting.

"Baz was asking where you were," she says when my tongue refuses to move. She struts up to the counter and opens a gold clutch. "I told him here, unless he was being a total cabrón and you bailed."

Goddamn the trill of nervous laughter that skitters out between my lips. "Not at all. He's fine." *Sell it, Flora.* "More than fine. I drank too much water, and I'm known for having this pea-sized bladder and, well, when nature calls . . ." Mortified, I trail off.

Did I just use the word *bladder*?

"I like your Instagram," I add, and she looks across at me quizzically, and I want to crawl down one of these drains. I. Like. Your. Instagram?

"Thanks." She pulls out a lipstick and barely has to look in the mirror to achieve a perfect swipe. "Baz told you about me?"

I clear my throat and snap my clutch shut. I am better than this. "I asked who'd be sitting with us tonight, and he told me about your family. And your work in fashion photography. I had a look and followed you immediately."

"Cool, and thanks. It's fun." Kelly's mouth quirks a little, and I wonder if she's going to question me about Baz, or worse, *meandBaz*. I sneak out an exhale when she continues with "I usually shoot friends or local bloggers, and I've done some street-style looks from our travels." She caps the lippy and fixes the buckle on sky-high stilettos that would spell out *p-a-i-n* instead of *s-h-o-e* on my feet.

"I'm from an area outside London. If you're into street style, that's the place to go."

Kelly dashes out her arm, a trio of thin golden bangles chiming. "Claro. My papi did a job there when I was younger. I'm dying to go back to shoot."

I bristle inside at the way she's eyeing me, her cat-slope eyes boring like enhanced laser beams, head to toe. "Is that Self-Portrait?" she asks, and *what?* "Your dress," she clarifies. "Is that the designer?"

I relax, but only marginally, and don't know what else to do but turn and lift my hair, shrugging. And I can't help but wonder what Baz would say if he walked in to see Kelly peeking under the edge of my bodice. But here we are.

"I knew it!" she says, chuffed with herself.

"You want to work professionally someday? Shooting campaigns?"

"Absolutely. And Leonie wants to be a makeup artist, for runway and print. For now, we have fun on social media building up our names."

Well. Her idea of fun on social media translates to a verification check and a six-digit follower count. "Really cool, yeah."

"My dad and Baz's are partnering on a TV pitch," she adds. "He must've told you about *that*, right?"

"Er, not all that much yet."

"Hmm." She fixes a stray hair. "It's a reality show. I'm going to beg to be involved because I know it'll be huge. Like, Netflix huge."

Netflix. The home of on-screen fake dating. The ruse pokes from the inside out, and I tease a glance at the door. "Well, I'd better get back before Baz thinks I really did take him for a sniveling, um, cabrón and dashed off."

"Nah, he's one of the good ones," she says quietly. "You're lucky."

I leave Kelly there with that, noting her off-center smile, and hooded brown eyes that would show up melancholy blue in any selfie tonight. Two distinct things come to mind. Much of the act I'm supposed to be putting on is for Kelly's benefit (and that of a huge network deal, apparently). But I quite like her, more than I thought I would. And savvy, sharp Baz is as clueless as his Jeep about Kelly. She is very much into him.

That lingering realization outlasts the floral scent of the bathroom soap and makes it slightly awkward when I meet up with my fake date at our table. But I decide to keep all hunches about Kelly's feelings to myself. "Nice job up there," I tell him instead. "And I had an interesting chat in the loo with a certain someone."

Baz glances around and offers a hand. "Not here. Can you talk and dance at the same time?"

I cast a wary eye across the room. The band has moved to a soft ballad, and guests are paired on the ample space lit into a dreamy purple tone. "I'm not sure I can *dance* and dance at the same time."

He wiggles his hand. "Do I look like I care?"

I grab it. "Fine. Only because I have intel."

We carve a space of our own near the band. "So it's a false stereotype that Cubans have really good moves?" I ask.

He sends me a long look, which dissolves into a laugh. "Wait until we make a salsa club one of our to-be-seen spots. My mami taught me that young. But, as a whole, yes. You owe me a false British stereotype now."

"That we all have bad teeth." I flash my gleaming, straight set, and Baz makes a noise like a game-show buzzer.

"Okay, so your intel?"

"Kelly wants to get involved with your fathers' TV project."

His brow line jerks upward. "I . . . did not know that. It's a reality show about Miami influencers and bloggers, so that tracks. But now her involvement just adds another layer of . . ."

"Of me needing to sell our dating deal even more." I shoot a wry look over his wink. "You can't say I'm not earning every shot you take of Pilar and Ryan."

"Nope. You're acing it."

I exhale a scrap of tension. "You never said *why* you're so against shooting weddings."

The first strains of an acoustic duet of Taylor Swift's "Exile" begin. "The drama, for one," Baz says. "Helping Papi for years, I've seen it all. Drunk relatives, feuds, attitudes like you wouldn't believe. Emotions are high, and some of that's to be expected." He tips his chin. "But more, it's about me, making a stand about my work and brand. Exactly how I want that to be, and how I want to come across. Dreaming and working toward an amazing future is a privilege. I don't take it for granted."

On my next step, it's as if the floor drops out from under my feet. Leonie and Kelly are around my age and clearly have these huge dreams for themselves. Makeup, runway, fashion photography. They're obsessed. And Baz, the boy holding me, twirling me, has dreamt of carrying on his father's trade his own way since he was little. I fix my gaze low, terrified that a million unleashed thoughts will betray themselves. I've had nothing but confusion choosing a future because I've never let myself envision one. How could I when any future I dared to dream of would be one without my mum? She wouldn't be there, and I simply couldn't let myself imagine those days. Me, as that girl, doing whatever thing I might do. It hurt too much. So I've always kept tomorrow out of focus.

But now it's becoming clear: I'm not broken or lacking in some gene that makes it easier to check boxes on enrollment forms. To plan for future days. I've been afraid of those days, and it's made *me* look unfocused.

When I lift my face again, it's like coming out of a thick London fog.

Baz is right there, face unreadable until he grazes two fingers under my chin and shoots a dark smile. "Let's get out of here?"

I feel myself swallow. "Sure. But isn't the point for us to be seen?" Pressed together, canoodling . . .

Baz hooks his arm into mine and makes a show of passing by the table, grabbing my clutch. We slip out without a word to his parents, or Kelly, or especially Armando. "One step up from being seen at an event is being seen leaving early."

"All right, then. Where are we going?"

"Doesn't matter," he declares, and we look like eloping newlyweds—him in a dashing suit and me in a blush lace dress that bounces as we flee into the night. The bowl of dark sky holds enough humidity for three cities. Keeps remnants of an earlier rain and the trill of insects that feast on bare skin.

Mine tingles with all the color, the urban orchestra of sounds beating against the truths I've just learned about myself. Loosened and let go, I suck in all the atmosphere I can through my sinuses. The Design District streets peal with girls' night laughter and clinking glassware from outdoor terraces. There's the red snake of taillights and pumped-up tunes bouncing out of convertibles.

We slow to a stroll in a shopping-and-gallery plaza. The rectangular lip of a large fountain beckons, a huge fly-eye sphere floating in the center. I sit and take in the strange and bulbous shape, and Baz says, "There's one thing *I* want to know. Not everything about our meet-cute was fake, right? It's clear you're a photographer, and you have a decent starter camera. But you didn't even mention it when you were posing at the studio."

"I guess it's more of a hobby," I deflect. For all the photos I've taken, I've shared only a few with friends and family. None sit in frames in my house. *Photographer*—have I ever seriously used that word to describe myself?

I catch the flick of his gesture from the corner of my eye. "I mean, the photos you brought to class weren't perfect. But Luna said you did really well with the editing tips."

"Hmm, did she?" I say, as smooth as glass, while a match strikes in the middle of my chest. No, my pictures aren't perfect. The world I shoot isn't perfect, either—far from it. Yet

I've held my camera over my small part of it, changing every shape and angle I could. That's what matters.

He bumps my elbow. "Hey, I teach workshops every month and see a lot of stuff. Yours stood out. You have real talent, and there's definitely room to level up your technique."

My own atmosphere heats to rival a dozen tropical nights. Baz probably thinks he's being encouraging, but he's coming for the one thing that earned me back some peace and control. Disease came hard for someone who was mine. Now I protect what I have left with my own crude and simple tools, just like the ones that built a coral castle. They're not fancy and refined. But they're my own.

I turn on the fountain rim. "Well, yeah, of course there's room for improvement, Mr. Sebastián Marín *Junior*!" The words come out sharply, as if I can't find a care about who's in earshot. "It's not like I'm an heir to a genius-level photographer who's been trained since nappies with some of the finest equipment. I've only had one class, so naturally, I wouldn't be perfect."

"Flora."

"What?"

"I said you were really talented. But you only heard the other parts."

I dissolve into a loud huff. While this is true, my temper ran off—again. Elsewhere. "Okay, yeah, I heard you. And thank you."

"Wow." He laughs. "I hit a nerve. But I think it's the best kind."

"How so?"

"You clearly care more about photography then someone who's just working at a, quote, 'hobby' level. Like you said."

I give a relenting nod, caught in the kind of game that Gor-

A British Girl's Guide to Hurricanes and Heartbreak

don and I once played where there's nowhere left to hide. "I do care," I admit. "A lot. Taking pictures helped me cope when my mum was nearing the end." I gaze up to find his dark eyes soft and welcoming. "But when she went into hospice, I buried *myself* in my camera in a way that helped me but really hurt my family. I wasn't honest, and I messed things up so much that it's been hard for me to trust myself again. I came here to heal and try to move forward, but my leaving made it even worse. My brother still isn't ready to talk to me."

"I'm sorry, Flora."

"Me too." I give a small shrug. "The people closest to me are the first to notice when I don't have my camera. But my photography has always been something entirely personal. Guarded, almost?"

"*That* I could tell." Baz rests his hand on my arm even though no one is looking. "Can you show me a few more photos? I'm super curious. No harm in me looking."

I pull my phone from my clutch because it's too late. I already bared part of my soul and gave Baz a taste of my hurricane, which he withstood as well as any Miami native. With a rough exhale, I click onto an older album.

My pulse tip-taps as Baz scrolls through the images, zooming in on a few and remaining infuriatingly silent. After too long, he hands the phone back. "You're really good at composition. Capturing an artistic mood, too. And that natural instinct is a gift. With that, you can be great. And I can help."

"You want to tutor me?" I roll my eyes. "I'll bet you say that to all the fake dates." This comes out funnier than I mean considering the amount of white-hot anxiety lurking behind it. Let him into the only safe place I have left?

— 157 —

He shakes his head. "Um, just the one Brit. I mean, it fits our decoy plan. While you're here helping me out and we're hanging around Miami hot spots, I can help *you* out with some new techniques and training. Have you ever wondered what it would be like to shoot with top-of-the-line cameras and lenses?"

Have I ever wondered?

Have I ever . . . dreamt? Of opportunities and a world as big and grand as this?

My hand instinctively flies up to my curls. Mum taught me how to manage what I was given so I could eventually go out on my own. Instead, I've not really gone anywhere because of grief. Because of guilt. Yet . . . have I unwittingly hurt my mother's memory, and the dreams *she* must've had for me, by staying stuck in one place? By circling the same spot, over and over?

I am still not sure what I want to be or study, but Baz is right. I *care* about photography—it's the one thing I do that edges out baking with Lila and hanging with my friends. And maybe figuring out who I'm supposed to be means opening up the one part I've closed off to everything but my pain: the camera I've held on to so tightly.

"Well? You taking my deal?" Baz presses. This time, instead of capturing it, he's the one who creates the lightning strike with a force hotter than pink.

"Deal," I say softly.

But my newly discovered truth booms as loud as thunder.

FOURTEEN

The next Monday, my Flora-Do List sends me to help out at La Paloma with some, quote, "shit Pilar never has time to get to." Turns out, I specialize in that sort of work. I *was* a bit apprehensive about showing my face around the bakery after my Studio Marín episode. Considering Pili and I hadn't directly discussed my involvement in the gossip overshare that outed her sister.

Yet I was ready on time, and only slightly nervous about riding into work with the bride-to-be. Straightaway I should've known that pragmatic Pilar would've reacted the way she did. Opening and shutting this lingering matter between us before we even reached the end of her street.

"Just making sure you wore your big-girl bloomers." This, she offered while looking me over a bit too closely as I entered her turquoise Mini Cooper.

Only a Reyes woman could get away with checking out my arse. "I always do," I said, clicking my seat belt. "Pink ones today. Extra posh just for you."

"Bueno, chica." Smiling, she backed out of the driveway.

"From what I've seen—and I see everything, tú sabes—the staff has moved on to juicier victims."

"That's basically what your mum said."

"Mmm. But should there be any trouble," Pili noted, "I have no doubt that you'll handle yourself. Just don't break my bakery."

Four hours ago I'd given Pili my assurance against causing any scenes that might disrupt business, but now, with my task items Flora-*Done* and one glance at my phone, I'm not sure I can keep my promise about *total* nondestruction. At least figuratively.

I'm strutting into the front showroom, newly changed into a breezy sundress and flip-flops, because that's what you do when your first photography lesson is at Miami Beach. After lunch, of course.

And when your instructor also happens to be a young Miami heartthrob who's trying to redirect his own dating narrative, he doesn't wait in the car park to pick you up. You tell him to park *himself* near the coffee station where whispers float as much as the scent of baked goods.

"Hey, you." Baz winks as I approach. We trade cheek kisses, and I hold up my sack of spoils for him to ogle. Two freshly griddled Cubano sandwiches—and oh, does he ogle.

"This is how I do school," I say, and give him a hold-up gesture when I catch longtime employee Marta waving me back to the bread rack. She's busy stocking bags of galletas cubanas—large white crackers often eaten with cheese and hard chorizo, or with guava jam.

When I'm close enough, Marta's right in my ear. "You didn't

say those sandwiches were for you and el hijo de Sebastián Marín."

"No, I don't believe I did," I whisper.

"Flora!" Right in my ear again. "Pero he's picking you up."

"Isn't it nice? Much better than the bus."

"Mis hijas follow him on Instagram. How did all this happen, chica?"

I shrug, backing away, ready to set her off in three, two, one . . . (Sorry, Pili.) "I'm wondering that myself. Adiós, Marta."

I make a quick escape and find Baz waiting outside the front door. "You're welcome," I announce. "And I told you so."

"¿En serio?" he asks, ushering me into the Jeep. The top's down today, splitting the sky wide open above the roll bar.

"The La Paloma gossip chain is on go time." He backs out, and I crane my neck and simultaneously cinch back my hair with a band. "I'm not sure exactly how far Marta's knowledge that Baz Marín just picked up a Brit with extremely fetching curls might travel. But it *will* travel."

His response is an amused high five before he turns up the volume on a bass-heavy beat. I stretch aching limbs and throw my gaze at the marbled sky. Soon, we pass over a bridge Lila used to run across. I remember it from my first visit to Miami three years back, but water this beautiful astonishes me every time. Teal and aqua and jeweled turquoise glitter on both sides—shades I'm not sure nature understands in England. With no roof, the muggy wind rushes by, and we're headed into a steely cloud mass.

"Are we okay?" I yell over the music, pointing at the gray

ahead. "It's not exactly easy to put the top up on one of these things. It rains every day."

Baz waves it off. "Yeah, but not this afternoon."

"What, are you a weather psychic? Do you know how many times I've gone out with no brolly into perfect blue only to be caught drenched fifteen minutes later?"

"Photographing this city means studying weather patterns."

"Ha. Well." I tug on my short ponytail. "This grows to very bad extremes in rain, so we'll have no one to blame but you if you're wrong. But I suppose I'll listen to your wisdom."

"Oh, you suppose?" he mocks. "Is this what teaching you is going to be like?"

I shrug. "Probably."

"Ay," he grumbles, and steers us down Collins Avenue, Miami Beach's pastel promenade of hotels and outdoor cafés. After a few blocks he pulls into a valet zone. Above us is a stylish white hotel simply called the Beach House.

Posh . . . posher . . . poshest. That's all that comes to mind as we enter the lobby filled with tropical furnishings and fruit-infused waters in glass dispensers. Baz catches me up quickly that this hotel is for members only, which his family is *not*. But the manager is close with Baz's father, who's shot many events here. As a courtesy, the Marín family and their guests may use the pool and club facilities.

"When you said outdoor working lunch, I pictured a park or something. Not *this*," I admit as Baz ushers me onto the sprawling pool deck. Just beyond, the ocean stirs in a dream-like panorama, and we find a table in a poolside garden, with plenty of shade from umbrellas and leafy trees.

"Just thought you might like it here. Plus, it's kind of the place to be."

I unpack our La Paloma lunch while Baz orders drinks from an attendant. A diverse crowd has gathered around us, dressed in slick pool gear and straw hats the size of flying saucers. "So, second-best chisme traveling outlet after La Paloma?" I suggest when he returns.

He opens the takeaway container with his freshly griddled Cubano sandwich, grinning on a deep inhale. "Try to convince me there's a better lunch. Anyway, totally. The Acostas are members here. We have plenty of mutual friends who hang at this club all summer. Friends who know more friends . . ." He trails off with a shrug.

I bite into my own sandwich. The roast pork and ham, with melted Swiss and pickles and tangy spread, bring me to bliss every time. "Has your mother been asking about us since the charity event?"

Baz swallows a mouthful. "Like, five seconds into breakfast yesterday, but I was ready. I'm playing it as you and I are dating and hanging out—not anything too serious. That keeps her endgame hopes alive, but it's enough in her mind to accept I'm, you know, taken."

The word has teeth, and my eyes zoom in on the image of him in his cream button-down shirt dotted with tiny sharks. The crisp navy shorts. Panning out, there's his light brown skin, and the mysterious tree tattoo winding over his forearm. And if there was yet another camera, someone hiding in the nearby bird-of-paradise bush with a long lens, they'd shoot a Brit in a sundress gazing at him. People might see the photo and think, *He's clearly taken.* My pulse thrums with this, the power of a captured image.

I blink myself back after missing Baz's last thought. "Sorry. What was that?"

"Was just saying that thank God you gave me some info about the Reyes family because Mami's more than a little jazzed over your connection to them." Baz rolls his eyes but tips his drink at me. We're eating La Paloma food, but he ordered us tart, refreshing virgin mojitos, plus a tropical fruit platter. "She wants to impress her friends when it's her turn to host dominoes and lunch in our yard. You and your secret recipes are her ace."

"What about your father?"

"Watches from the sidelines and makes sure everything with his partnership and deal's not, well—"

"Utterly disturbed to shit?"

Baz laughs. "Exactly."

It's our last word for long minutes, until it's clearly camera time. We keep the cold drinks coming but clear a space for Baz's large gear bag. Since finding out I've only worked with DSLR models, my first lesson will focus on mirrorless cameras, which utilize a different sort of technology. They're also so much lighter. Baz can wear a harness with two at once with no discomfort.

He presents Nikon and Fuji models, along with a few lenses, all of which I can borrow while I'm in Miami. "There are uses for both types," Baz says. "And I'll be helping you with that. Mirrorless takes some getting used to. But we have time."

While Baz takes a studio call from Luna, I reach for the Fuji. A patter of apprehension mixed with excitement skitters down my back. I acquaint myself with the feel, the roughened surface, the possibilities in this small black box. Am I making a huge mistake and kidding myself? Baz is worlds ahead in this realm I've only tested with my pinkie toe, at best.

"I know it's been a while," Baz says, back in my zone. "And a lot of this is new."

I clamp my bottom lip under my teeth and nod. "Can we just start?"

Baz in full teaching mode reminds me of Lila. When she taught me how to master French bread dough, she had my hands in flour and water within minutes. Baz is the same, encouraging me to learn by experiencing. And what doesn't click straight-away, we'll keep drilling in. Like baking, there's a sort of muscle memory that develops between a photographer and their camera. A sixth sense, where getting the right shot is as much about moving within the space by feel as it is by sight.

My photography muscle memory comes out sluggish. Mainly, there are two issues messing with my head. Firstly, it feels like my skills fell under one of those spell-induced sleeps. And mostly, for me photography has always been a party of one. I am not used to having someone watching me shoot; the fact that this particular someone is as renowned as Baz makes his presence even more nerve-racking. I'm showing him more of what I've forgotten than what's supposedly great about my framing technique.

"Sorry," I tell my instructor. "I'm, like, all thumbs and back-ward eyes." We've moved out from the pool deck onto the grassy strand flanking the beach to practice shooting land-scape features in full sun. I follow his cues (increase shutter speed, lower the ISO, open the aperture). Nearly identical models hang around our necks on webbed straps.

He stops our lazy stroll. "Don't hold back, Flora—shoot way more than you think you should. I can't help fix what isn't there." He gives a clownish wink. "Don't beat yourself up if it's not right the first time. That's my job."

Baz laughs at my overblown eye roll before he sobers. "There's some mental stuff going on between *you* and *this*, no?" he says, jiggling the Fuji around my neck.

"Most definitely yes. How do I break that so I can shoot freely like I used to?"

Baz averts his gaze toward the shore, following the lively blue current that never loses its rhythm. "Tell me about a photo you shot that you're really proud of. Go back to that."

When I think of feeling proud, I can't help but think of feeling powerful. Or the high of being in control, even if it was only for a short time.

"The wonky tree" bolts out of me so fast, I feel my cheeks heat. "Cripes. I mean, this. Here." I fish out my phone and search for the photo that's forever stamped onto my brain.

"I felt good shooting this scene," I say, showing him. "Proud, too."

As Baz studies my work, my mind travels nine months back to England, when I set up this shot. It's of a peculiar tree that grows outside a place called Elmwood House. Short and squat. The trunk is all twisted up, as if it changed its mind a dozen times about the way trees are supposed to grow. I always wanted to climb it, but does one do that? Climb the tree that grows in front of your mum's care home?

I photographed it instead. I cropped out the welcome

sign—the words *Home for . . .* , the smaller bits noting *Front Desk* and *Visiting Hours.* I blurred the building, so you know it's there, but it's not the focus of the shot. The tree became a great thing, and I grew it larger than everything else around it.

I explain some of this to Baz, why it's framed that way. A few bits about the woman who used to live inside the brick walls.

He rests his left hand on my arm so that another tree springs up between us. But I won't ask him about that one now. "You made the trauma into something smaller," he says softly.

I nod. "There was this huge rush in cropping out the hurting parts and minimizing them." But then doubt sneaks in. In a mind as twisted as that trunk, there's always room. "Is it bad? Did I not set it up right?"

"No, it's not that at all. The focus and the settings are spot-on. Bien hecho, Flora. You *should* be proud of this."

"But?"

"But I want you to really think about what you did. In portraiture and headshots, models go to hair and makeup first. We enhance what's there to make it look its best. We also do that with product and branding photography. But that's not all photography is."

"Isn't it about me getting to frame things how I see best?" I ask with a little sharpness. "To make an image come out the way I want it to be?"

"What about capturing what's really there, too? The truth of that?" He sweeps his hand across the beach. A horde of sunbathers and children with sand toys and all their sounds collide into a patchwork of life and color. "Do you think all of these people are perfectly happy and without pain?"

I shake my head. "That's impossible." The corner of my mouth quivers. "Unless an ice cream truck rolled in and started throwing out free treats."

He laughs and cranes his neck with whimsical hope. "You never know around here. What I mean is, would you sell your tree shot to whatever company owns Elmwood House, say, to use on their website?"

I shake my head, getting what he means. "It would be shit for sales. That one was just for me. I suppose it shows, then." When he nods, I add, "I told you most of my photos have been little more than personal."

"You did. And that's okay, too. Take my storm photo that you bought at the craft fair for way too cheap," he says, his lip curling over the last bit. "I was having a rough day. That's why I went out to shoot with Papi's friend even though it was super late and I barely got through class the next day. It was a huge stress reliever. But also, I wanted to make something into art that would appeal to viewers, too. That would make them feel something."

"It did," I tell him. "You did." The secret I keep over his photo throbs beneath my skin, but I don't let it out. I trap the feeling that maybe something—someone—led him there to grab that moment just for me. So bright and pink and strong when everything around me was sinking.

He smiles and turns me toward a cluster of palms, sending another kind of jolt against my bare shoulders. "You like shooting trees, yeah?"

"I do. They're one of my favorite parts about being outside."

"Cool, there's your next subject. And we'll set it up so that the viewer gets that they're looking at South Beach palms, but with something added. Nature makes the tree what it is, but you make it into art by capturing another layer."

A layer that's not about me as a hurting, striving girl making her camera into a weapon. But me as an artist trying to create beauty for another. A shot that could even go in a frame for a generous donor to bid on and take home. And didn't I hear at Canvas Miami that art can save people, in a way? It can touch one person at a time—heart-and-soul level—and spread.

On this famed beach with the midday sun heady-warm across our backs, Baz is trying to get me to see photography as more than just saving myself.

I lift the Fuji up from my chest again. I stamp out the familiar doubt, the sputtering gust of my breaths fighting the sensation of being watched and critiqued. *Easy, there*, I tell my insides. *We're doing something new today.* With the most brilliant equipment I've ever seen.

In a mirrorless camera, I get a digitized image of those trees instead of a bounced reflection. And there is magic inside the light between two of them.

"The sunrays," I tell Baz, pointing. "It's like they're dripping off those fronds." Sunlight shows itself the way it shouldn't (according to science), as if it's honey-thick and you could drag a finger right through the middle.

"Perfect." Baz sidles up with his own camera. "Let's see how much bokeh we can get with that light." I've heard of this term for the soft-focus aesthetic quality you can achieve with the right aperture or lens shape.

He guides my settings and technique, and I shoot freely.

Baz grabs my camera and checks the shots before I can. Grins.

And I grin, too, over my best photo from a time when I'm not trying to keep out hurt and disease from the frame. Instead, I let in all the light.

FIFTEEN

When it's the next morning here and afternoon in Winchester, I study the photos I took at Miami Beach. It's no secret that I'm not always the easiest person to teach. Baz still found a way in, calling up my sense of pride, my (apparently obvious) need for control. Harnessing those, he challenged me to do more based on what I'd accomplished before. To move forward and shoot another tree. Today, I stretch that same feeling across an ocean, pressing *Send* on one of yesterday's photos and a message I was told not to write.

The shot I picked highlights a swipe of buttery sunlight perfectly unfocused between two palm trees. A fingernail of coastline slips into the background.

Me: I wanted to reach out. This reminded me of you and her

Long minutes pass, and Orion doesn't answer. Though Dad and Lila warned that my brother needs time to process, I thought this photo might let some light back in between the two of us.

Me: Remember 3 years ago when Lila brought us to this beach?

And . . . nothing. The clock ticks in silence, all that warm light going dim.

Me: You were so ridiculously happy that day, it was annoying

I'm nearly panic-texting now. Can't he at least—

Three talking dots appear, and my heart runs rampant.

Orion: It's a good photo

I read over Orion's message, willing more to materialize. There's no greeting, no customary Pink nickname. *Flora, you really did mess up.*

Me: I've been thinking of you. Just wanted you to know

Him switching to FaceTime ranks at number twenty on my list of ten predicted Orion responses. The ringer becomes a siren, and I reach out with jittery fingers.

"Er, hiya," I say.

"Right," Orion says from his bedroom. "Look, Flora, was that all? I need to study."

He's never put me off for school. Or anything. "No, I mean, I'm sorry. And Dad did say you needed time to process. But when have I ever been one to follow a warning?" I add with hopeful eyes.

"Christ." He tosses a textbook aside and scoots back against his headboard. "Is that what we're calling this? Processing?"

The molten heat beneath his tone jolts something inside me. Familiar, like another kind of home. "Listen, please." I square my shoulders. "I don't have to tell you how hard that night at the piano was for me. I had to go, Orion. I kept making things worse. I was in a bloody spiral."

His gaze ices over. "You honestly think I didn't know that? Lila told me why you left. Dad, too. You think I would've fussed about you wanting a break to refocus? My own girlfriend needed the same thing three years ago!"

"It was Lila's trip that gave me the idea. And I thought you, being the way you are, well, you'd simply let me go—"

"Wait. Just *how am I*? In your view?" He barks out a laugh. "I'm massively curious."

I swallow forcefully. "You're one of the strongest people I know. And steadfast. A constant, too—like—well, like the way we always heat water to ninety-five degrees to make the best cuppa."

"Reliable, then?"

I exhale. "Yeah, that's it exactly."

"In fact, I'm so reliably strong that you could go off on any kind of whim and it wouldn't matter," he says, dashing a hand. "It wouldn't affect me. Because I'm just that stonelike, and it would pass right over me."

Had I thought that? My mind spins a dozen different ways until a grating truth emerges. I didn't think too much about Orion because he's always been our solid foundation. Just *there*. No matter how much I came and went. "I thought you'd roll with it, and it wouldn't change anything for you."

"Well, you were wrong. It changed everything. You're not the only one who lost a mother. Right as I'm getting through that, you set off a bomb, which I was ready to forgive and work through. The lying—everything. But then you abandon us in a way that felt personal. Like our family was never important or tight enough in the first place. That's what I've been fucking *processing*, as everyone says. What's become of the only family I have left?"

"I'm to blame for that," I press, my voice full of gravel and grit. "I created that space."

He shakes his head. "You could've come to me and said you needed to stay with Lila's family for a bit. Instead, we all find out on paper. How can I trust you with my feelings, as your brother, when I was only worth a note?"

"You couldn't, Orion." It comes out in a shudder. "I couldn't face you, and I'm still in the process of learning to trust myself again. So you're damn bloody right about that. And I'm sorry I didn't think my methods through more. That I just ran."

There's a short pause before he softens imperceptibly. "You did, then. And I'm sorry you thought that was the only way. Far from it."

I pinch my eyes shut. Typically, all it takes is a few sweets and *sorry*s to patch up the rifts between us. But this time . . . "It's not enough, is it? My apology?"

"It's not that simple—I mean, I want it to be. You have to know that." Orion wipes his eyes with his cuff. "But I fear you still don't see the whole of it."

No, it's not enough, then. I drop my head.

"Pink," he says. "It *is* a good shot. The tree. And Lila will love it."

I nod, though my photo, one that should be worth a thousand words in that old saying, didn't hold the right ones for my brother. I don't know which ones *are* right yet, any more than I know the perfect words to say to honor our mother.

But for the first time since I landed, I don't think I'm doomed to never know. And that, just like the way my recent photos look against anything I've taken before, is new.

Through the next week, I drag Orion's call behind me, knocked off-center by his reaction. But I decide not to get stuck on it. I'm looking and moving forward—finally. So I decide to add that feeling of *not yet, not enough* to the growing Flora-Fix-It pile I surrendered to Miami. Whilst playing the perfect photography student.

Besides the two cameras, Baz left me some homework this week while he's busy helping his father and assisting at the studio. Assignment: More full sun shots, managing different lenses and lighting levels. And reverse curating. I'm to include rust on metal fences, graffiti paint on walls. I'm not to crop out flaws in plants and cracks in sidewalks. Mentally, this works with my current rift with Orion. To reach him, I have to deal with the imperfect bits between us, too.

My phone buzzes as I'm trolling the neighborhood for interesting subjects.

Gordon: So, all I needed for proof of life from you was this Instagram link from Mum?

I click the link and nearly stumble face-first. A flurry of shots flip from the Canvas Miami account of me posing in blush lace, wrapped around Baz like an anaconda. And God, the caption:

Emcee Sebastián Marín Jr. of Studio Marín and Flora Maxwell of Maxwell's London stun at Canvas Miami's annual gala.

What mess is this? How did they get my name but totally flub my city? It's probably Armando's doing.

Me: I need to explain

Gordon: Not on my account. You look posh in the photos. Really pretty

Not on his account? His disinterest is *not* any better than his typical shade. Did he call me pretty, too? Oh, he totally did, and I realize I've been wandering in zigzags along the street. Ahead there's a house with a massive flower garden and an inviting stone bench. I head there and press Gordon's avatar. Texting won't do.

He picks up the call with "Oi, it's fine, Flora. No bother. You've obviously been having fun, and that's quite nice."

I flop down on the bench. "Bugger of life! No, not you, sorry. I just burned a layer of skin off the backs of my thighs. Anyway. Listen." I snap into myself and switch tactics. "It's not like you to not be curious."

"Well, I did look up that Sebastián—or Baz—bloke for shits, and he's quite the guy around town. And really talented. You two seemed friendly. Like I said, nice."

He looked up Baz . . . and *nice*? How is any of this nice? While I'm more than irritated by my sudden need to explain, analyzing *that* feels like trying to diagram one of the laws of thermodynamics. It's not happening. And it hits me that even though it's killing me to not reveal the truth to Gordon, I promised Baz I wouldn't tell anyone. Staying trustworthy to others seems like a crucial part of being able to trust myself again.

"It's more like I fell into this, er, plus-one situation," I say, because this part is entirely true. "And you know how photos can be." I think of a yellow macro flower with the insect bite cropped out. And a scene in front of a care home where the living, thriving tree is bigger than any disease. "It's easy to manipulate the viewer."

"*Now* who's the illusionist?"

"Takes one to know one."

He snuffs out a laugh, but it crumbles into an airy tone that sounds more pensive than usual. I wish I could see his face. I break off as a gray-haired woman creeps out from the house in flip-flops and a striped housedress. "Hold on, Gordy."

"Hello there, ma'am. So sorry," I say, hopping up as she approaches. "I didn't mean to trespass."

She motions me back down. "No, no, está bien. Siéntate ahora." She flips open her mailbox and grabs a stack of letters. Then waves.

"Muchas gracias. And you have a lovely garden. Muy hermosa," I call, and return to Gordon. "I'm here."

He's chuckling brightly this time. "Kudos on the Spanish—my mum would be proud. You could make a new hit reality show. Maxwell's Mumbles in Miami."

"Ha, bloody, ha. Aren't the gala pictures enough? How did your mum find those anyway?"

"Um, the Cuban chisme network? It seems Pilar searched that event and told Elisa, who sent it to my mum. And she sent it to me all excited about how lovely you looked. One click and a few swipes and there you were. My flatmate Matteo said I went to ash."

"Well, that's understandable."

"Is it?" he asks quietly in a way that makes me squirm along the bench. "I'm gonna ask you one question, and you can't think about your answer. You have to say the first word that pops up, okay?"

"Sure. But this better not be another golden owl chase game."

He sighs audibly. "Here's the scenario. Later today, you're scrolling Instagram. You see a thumbnail that looks eerily familiar but doesn't add up. So you click, and there I am in a dapper suit. And I'm wrapped around a stunning girl. Gut reaction—go."

My shoes scrape along the pavers, stomach sinking, and all that comes out is "You think Baz is stunning?"

"That's *not* what I meant. The first word—"

"But . . ."

"No buts. You're ruining it. The rules!"

"Okay . . ."

"That's your reaction? *Okay?*"

"No, I mean . . ." What do I mean? What am I even doing?

"Never mind," he grumbles. "It's too late."

"Wait, I do not lose games. I can do this!"

"You can't, though. Anything you say now, you'll have had too much time to think."

"Oh. Sorry?"

"Nah, you're good. It was a tough one. Look, I'm due back at the work site. Time to sweat another bucket over a parlor restoration."

I clear my throat. "Right. Say, I want to hear more about Key West."

"Soon," he says. "Matteo and I are coming into Miami for the weekend. Want to hang?"

"I do" shoots out like a bullet.

He makes a noise that's half sigh, half muse. "See, you *can* answer straightaway. Funny. We'll figure the rest out later. Bye, Squiggs."

"I . . . You . . ." But he's already gone. The little sneak.

After dark, Miami Beach transforms itself in the kind of illusion Gordon would love to master. At home, we call heading into this vibe going *out*-out, as opposed to simply going out for the night. Flashy cars are in constant parade. And clubgoers and diners turn up in silk, sequins, and shine, but they're not the only glowing ones. A neon haze spills over oceanfront buildings, the air misted through after an earlier rainfall. The palm trees I shot days ago are lit a searing yellow-white, fronds swaying against the cobalt sky.

It's Friday night, and I have one job: sell the ruse.

I'm at the Beach House again, with Baz—again. This time at a firepit table sat across from Kelly and Leonie. Tonight's hosts, the Marín and Acosta parents, are probably on their third drinks at one of the upper lounges while "los niños sit by the pool and catch up."

Insert me in my faded jeans and white platform sandals. A black lace off-the-shoulder top Pili picked up for me elevates my look enough to work. *Am I fashion?* I ask myself, more self-conscious than I've ever cared to be. The Afro-Cuban-fabulous Acosta sisters are straight out of a Reformation catalog with their floral minidresses in lilac and mint.

We're chatting about school, which seems bland given the lively setting. But I go with it as we share platters of Spanish tapas and stone-crab street tacos.

"Flora, what about you?" Kelly chimes.

"Well . . ." My tongue lags, too sluggish after listening to Kelly catch Baz up on her first year of community college while she builds her fashion photography portfolio.

"Are you thinking of a Florida university or one back home?" Kelly's throaty tone is reel and voice-over ready.

"You just graduated, right?" Leonie asks. "I'm gonna be a senior. Finally."

"Sort of," I start. "It works a bit differently in the UK. We don't really graduate the same way you do here. We finish classes in late spring, then sit for exams midway through summer. Then, assuming you pass the exams, you move on to uni. I'm still in the process of narrowing down my course of study." I send a silent plea to Baz. Do I admit I'll be heading back to England soon? I'm wondering if Kelly's ask was more future-plan fishing expedition than polite small talk.

But it doesn't matter. The sisters don't seem to be listening and are cheek by jowl over a private chat, their eyes beaming hotter over me than all the neon on this street. "Claro, she'd be perfect," Leonie mutters.

Kelly purses her mouth, appraising me like I'm in a Studio Marín replay. "The total look. And I have tons of ideas for her hair."

Wait. Whose look and hair? My hand instinctively crimps into my air-dried curls. "Did I miss something?"

"I won an after-hours photo permit at Vizcaya, worth hundreds of dollars," Kelly says, and I faintly recall Lila speaking of the historic estate on Biscayne Bay. "I want to photograph you."

My guava spritz goes down all wrong, and I sputter quite inelegantly. *"Why?"*

"The blogger I was going to shoot had to back out, and Leonie was gonna be my stand-in."

"But I'd much rather stick to styling," Leonie says.

"And Vizcaya is all about that old-world feel." Kelly gestures broadly. "You have a classic look and would fit right in."

This was *not* part of any Netflix dating-ploy agreement. I write it into my watering eyes, nudging Baz and his already-close thigh on the patio sofa. *Help me!*

Instead, he's a bobblehead. "Huh! She really would be perfect."

"Glad you think so, 'cause I want you to assist," Kelly says, all matter-of-fact, paying zero notice to my mortified glare. Her gaze is double-locked over Baz, so impenetrable that it stirs up my earlier suspicion about her true feelings for him.

Well, then. I swivel my body toward my date, brows as high as the moon.

"Come on," Baz says. "It's a great opportunity, and Vizcaya is incredible. I'm down."

Kelly scoots forward, twirling her long fingers in anticipation. "I'm partnering with a local gown designer for the shoot—so dreamy. Plus, one of my collab sponsors is going to provide designer accessories. I know it's a big ask, but what I have in mind for these shots will really amp my portfolio."

The entire space is one big puppy-dog expression. Even Baz. And yeah, I get that if he's assisting, it would probably look better if I were there as well. I thrust up my arms, relenting. "Fine. I'll do it."

Everyone's all gratitude and smiles as two servers appear. Photo-shoot talk switches to placing orders for truffle oil chips and fruity mocktails. Kelly and Leonie are back at the private chatter, probably about how to manage my hair.

I exhale and Baz notches into my side, *date-close*. His warm hand clamps over mine, in full view of everyone even through the firepit flames. "You look like it hurts to think."

I turn my cheek into his stubble. Soft meets sand as I talk through my teeth. "Because it does. In trying not to muck this up for you, I've suddenly gone from letting you show me some of your tricks with a camera to being on the other end of Kelly's. With you playing wing-guy. So that's how it's going, since you were wondering."

I feel his laugh more than hear it. "I promise it'll be fine and maybe even fun. As for our deal, you haven't flubbed anything. The girls have zero reason to be suspicious. Enjoy the night. Relax, sit back, and—"

I jerk away. "If you tell me to smile, you'll see why my family calls me a hurricane."

He holds up a placating hand. "Wow. Got it. That's no joke of a nickname, though. Have you ever been in a hurricane?"

I could tell him that I've been through the kind of loss that rips apart houses just the same. Or the kind of self-doubt that can't make up its mind whether it's going to stay at tropical-storm level or go category four. Or I could always brush it off with a demure *no, not yet.* That I've only lived the label.

But before I say anything at all, I lose all words as I stare—gobsmacked—over Baz's shoulder at the bar. The reason has auburn hair, which has gotten another trim, flashing as sleek and siren-hot as this Miami night.

SIXTEEN

Of all the joints strung along Miami Beach, Gordon Wallace is at this one. He's sidled up to a belly bar table, laughing heartily with another guy. He must've just arrived. The tilted smile and gesture of some sort of food item my way is a sure sign he's seen me, too.

I give a small wave and mouth *hold on* before snapping around on the firepit sofa, hoping Baz hasn't noticed before I can—

"What's up over there?"

Damn. Okay, then. "You know that Winchester friend I told you about who's studying in the Keys?" Baz nods and I point discreetly. "That's Gordon. I should say a quick hello and—"

"Invite him to hang with us," Baz says.

"Is that best? *Considering . . .*" I put the word into my brows. "Things?"

"Oye, Flora, you know those guys?" Kelly calls from across the firepit. "That's Matteo Lorenzo. He went to our high school, and his parents are members here."

Matteo . . . Matteo. The name swirls inside my brain until I recall that he's Gordon's program flatmate. *Pero wow,* I mouth. Sometimes Miami Cuban Spanglish says it best. Because Kelly knows Matteo and Baz. And I know Baz and Gordon. And Gordon knows Matteo and me.

"Well, isn't this cracking?" is all I can say.

"Seriously, go. We should meet your friend." Baz juts his elbow into our section. "Bring over Matteo and anyone else he's with."

I rise on wobbly legs even though none of my drinks were spiked. "I'll just go and do that."

The short walk lasts a century. Matteo's gone off somewhere else, but I'm certain the firepit group is eyeing my every step toward Gordon, who's bent around on his phone in a gray woven shirt and faded black jeans. I tap his shoulder. "Hiya."

Gordon flinches, pivoting into a grin. My eyes wax big as he goes in for a cheek kiss. I go in, too, and there's more than lips meeting air. He actually brushes my cheek with a little smack.

He answers my bemusement with a shrug. "When in Miami, right?"

"Right. Good on you for leaning into your Latino parts. Like you wanted."

"I'm trying." He motions toward Baz. "So *that's* why you said you couldn't hang until tomorrow."

"*You* said you weren't coming into Miami until tomorrow."

"I wasn't, but they ended up giving us the afternoon off. Matteo drove in with me, and we came straight here because he said I should 'get my nightlife on' or something equally cringey. His boyfriend was supposed to meet us but got called into work."

A bridal hen-do group breezes by in party-store veils and

tiaras. Gordon whisks us away, and we end up in an alcove shielded by a wide column and bushy potted plants.

"Good one," I say. "Making us disappear. I hate being watched."

"Sometimes circus school comes in handy," he deadpans. "So, your plus-one date seems to have multiplied. You two looked cozy—not that I was spying." He gives a shrug. "Not that I wasn't. But clearly I've gone lax because I didn't see this coming."

Our eyes meet; all the words he said at Coral Castle spin on replay. About getting back to friendship. That he'd stepped over some fuzzy line but won't make that mistake again. (Because of him or me, though?) God. And inside this hidden space, the urge to spill everything about Baz shoves my insides into a game of Twister.

But I hold my tongue.

Gordon getting hold of my gala photos proves the Cuban chisme network is stronger than I thought. Beyond the matter of my promise to Baz, one runaway word could spoil this ruse.

"I didn't see it coming, either," I tell him. "We're sort of, um, hanging out."

I crane my neck around the beam and spot fresh platters of tapas. Baz and the girls are all in, so I take the time to admit what I can. Namely, Baz shooting Pilar's wedding and his offer to help with photography lessons. I end there, on borrowed cameras, absorbing Gordon's wide-eyed stare.

"I know, the opportunity sort of fell into my path."

"I am glad you've got such a capable teacher, Squiggs, if that's what we're calling it." He barks a low laugh. "Apparently, all a guy needed was a Fuji to hook *your* fancy. That James bloke from the pub should've figured that out. As well as some un-notable others."

Wow—he really went there. "These things happen, and I'm only here for a few weeks," I say, bristling inside and out. "Anyway, Baz and his friends want to meet you."

His jaw hardens like stone for a second before it cracks, sending his mouth askew. "Why not? Might be fun."

Twenty or so minutes later I'm not sure *fun* is the word for the state of my situation, smooshed between Baz and Gordon on our side of the firepit. But there's this: I'm no longer the novelty in our Friday night hangout. Gordon might as well be onstage. Kelly and Leonie, and even Baz, are happily munching appetizers, listening to my friend talk about England and architecture. Matteo's here, too, tucked into the chair next to his former schoolmate sisters.

"Wait," Leonie says to Gordon. "You actually live at your family's inn?"

I butt in with "It's loads better than he described it. Look up the Owl and Crow."

Kelly pulls out her phone for a search but scrunches her nose in confusion.

Gordon springs up and crouches at her side. "No, that's a shop in Wales. It's just here." He types and taps, then hands over the phone with a firecracker smile.

Kelly returns it, and him catching every pink-lip, pearly-white bit isn't wrong so much as . . . different. Of course I've seen girls around Gordon. I had a front-row seat during the whole Lizzie episode. But I don't recall much about those interactions. This one's already imprinting itself onto my memory, as green as jealousy. Sure, I know what that is, and what it feels like. But why is it creeping in now? I can't make the ends add up, and I certainly didn't ask for it.

Subject change, please.

"My brother and I grew up tramping all over the grounds," I announce cheerily as Gordy returns. "While minding his mum's demands to keep our squealing to a civilized level and swiping treats from the cook."

"Oh my God, it's like something out of *Pride and Prejudice*," Kelly says. "I'd love to stay here. And this is your *house*?"

Gordon knocks back a garlic prawn in record time. "It is. And we'd love to have you and your family sometime. Just say the word."

"Oh, you *must*," I add heartily, realizing that I've been stabbing at the ice in my drink with a stirrer.

"Fun fact," Gordon says. "Jane Austen's buried at Winchester Cathedral. And yeah, the third floor of the inn is our family flat. I always thought it cool that people from all over the world were just downstairs from me. Sometimes guests would give me little trinkets or tell stories." He turns to me. "If you ever run into Mrs. Worth at Tesco, never tell her, but I think the inn taught me more than any schoolroom."

Matteo scoots forward. "And at the internship orientation, we had to tell the group the first thing that made us want to study architecture. El hombre Wallace over here said his right away. The Owl and Crow."

Gordon tips his hand in concession.

"Why, Gordy?" Immediately, I want to take it back. Shouldn't I know this—the spark that led to Architect Gordon? One of the ways he's the most Gordon of all?

"It's not what you think," he says, not seeming to mind my cluelessness. "That the Crow is this grand, important structure that made me want to design my own. It's more the opposite, but it feels entitled saying the real reason."

"Go on, bro," Baz says. "It's all good."

Gordon shrugs. "Part of me wanted a real house that was just for my family. I wanted to know what that would be like. I've never lived in a place where I didn't pass a stranger every time I came in from school." He shakes his head. "One time I nearly tripped over this couple snogging away on the staircase as if no one else were around. Like, all sprawled out on the landing, and here I am with my Batman schoolbag and after-noon snack."

We all snort laughter at this. "Sorry I missed that one," I say. "But I never cared. Your home was always an adventure."

"I know, and I wouldn't trade my life. It's more that having a different sort of home made me really keen on the way oth-ers lived." Gordon takes a swig of the Coke Matteo "enhanced" from a hidden flask. "I began to research and draw different types of houses. And now all I want is to design them and earn enough to build one of my own."

Matteo hooks his thumb. "Same. And your architecture story is way better than mine—the LEGO set I got at six that made my parents want to take out stock in the company."

"Oh, this one didn't tell you he still buys LEGO sets at the London flagship? His eyes bug out of their sockets before we even get inside." I scrunch my nose and ruffle the top of Gor-don's hair before I realize it; hopefully the group sees it as a platonic-friend thing.

"Hey, now," Baz stresses. "LEGO puts out an architecture

collection pro series. The real deal." The way he trills his fingers along my shoulder is not at all platonic. He's added a wink and a little brush of his frame against mine. Because that's what we're here for.

Gordon stares for a quarter second too long before arcing his hand in agreement. "Right? See?"

The guys flanking my sides share this tremendous dude-bro expression, and *no*, it's not at all awkward being stuck in the middle of that. I hastily reach for another tempura roll just for something to do with my hands.

Midchew, when I'm certain a bit of sauce has dripped onto my chin, Señor Acosta materializes at our firepit table. "I see you've found some friends—even better. I'll settle your tab so you can all get up to the lounge. There's a live salsa combo, and if you can stand being in the same room as us viejitos, you don't have to be twenty-one to dance." He turns to his daughters. "Sebastián and Iva think they can out-move your mami and me. Which is total porquería, and I need witnesses."

Señor Acosta pivots, catching me tucked under Baz's arm. His eye twitches over a miniscule nod. "So, muchachos. Who's in?"

Us. We're in, after Baz and Kelly find out the duo from Winchester has had some salsa lessons with a Miami Cuban. The four non-Brits figure that's enough for Gordy and me to have some fun on the floor without looking like complete dolts.

That remains to be seen.

We caravan up to the lounge. A twinkle light–studded dance floor and a lively band fill the wide space, but the view out-shines this show. The terrace spills outward, blending indoor and outdoor seamlessly. I stride to the railing; the waves roll dark and heavy just below.

While Baz is with Leonie and Kelly surveying their parents' dueling dance moves, Gordon creeps up next to me. "Not bad for a couple of Hampshire rug rats," he says.

"No, look at us. *God.*" The breeze comes in cooler up here, and I want to take a long pull of it, fresh and briny. "Sometimes I wonder how Lila left all this. For our bloody fog and gray."

Gordy bumps my side while Baz and Matteo cheer at something on the floor behind us. "She fell in love with your half-brain twit of a brother."

I laugh, but it comes out weak under the rift between Orion and me.

"And she fancied herself a curly blond sister," Gordon adds, though it's hard to believe I had anything to do with Lila moving life and country.

"It was the fish and chips."

"Likely. Besides, her real sister is only a flight away. She can always come home again." Gordon gives a pensive smile. "Lila was only supposed to be in England for a few weeks, too. Look where that got her."

My secret nudges hard from the inside out, wanting even a bit of that Atlantic Ocean freedom. It takes everything to keep it hidden. "I'm not Lila."

Gordon moves to answer, but our group closes in around us and the music changes.

"Our turn." Baz faces my friend. "This is your song, Gordon—'Llorarás.' It's by Oscar D'León. He's Venezuelan like tu mamá."

Gordon eyes the dance floor, frowning. "I'm not sure Mum

left me enough in the genes to do Venezuela proud out there."

Kelly hooks her arm into his. "Let's find out."

"All right." He winks, and it's like a bulb clicks on inside his head. "Lead the way, Cubana."

Kelly whisks him off behind Leonie and Matteo, and I can't look away. Cubana? And the little wink and giggly laugh? Is this supposed to be Gordon a) purposely trying to flirt, b) simply being cheeky, jovial Gordon, or c) all of the above, and what the hell is life?

I jolt back to Baz with a hard blink as he pivots, hooking my arm. He missed the entire Gordon-Kelly exchange.

"Don't look now," he says covertly. "But my mami is all over this scene in 'let's analyze the dynamic' mode."

I need to slow whatever it is I've been rolling in my brain and focus on my job. And Baz's see-everything mother. And *Baz*. I give Señora Marín something good, beaming as I draw him closer.

Baz dots his lips to my forehead. The brush, the tiny flame is all for show, but that doesn't mean it doesn't sear.

"I might make you look pitiful out there," I say. "The name of the song does translate to 'you will cry,' right?"

He leads me onward anyway. "Why do you always diss yourself like that?"

"Muscle memory, same as the camera." I glare at my white platforms. "And these make for shit dancing shoes."

Baz waves me off as the band moves into the chorus. At least I know the basic step well enough. When to go right, and when to swing left. What to do with my hips, my arms. In salsa, it's touch and release, twirl and extend sideways—arms out—then snap back until we're chest to chest.

"Flora es una mentirosa," Baz says on a laugh, just above the music. "You're doing amazing. Shitty shoes and all."

He might be a little bit right, even though he's clearly holding back. The lock and swirl of his hip, the play of muscle and rhythm are rooted deep beneath his skin, hinting that there's more where that came from. Salsa is a quick, go-everywhere-at-once kind of dance, so it's hard to watch others on the floor. I only get flashes:

• The Maríns battling the Acostas in the opposite corner, besting everyone with their moves.
• After a quick half-turn, I catch Matteo and Leonie, laughing as they keep up like near pros.

We go on and on, winding around like heated clock parts. And on the next stretch, my limbs burning with exertion, I spy Gordon and Kelly, her dark, lithe body against his solid form. She wore the right little dress and perfect strappy heels. And he's so tremendous, so natural out there, I'm ashamed to feel surprised. It's as if his Venezuelan-Cuban parts have simply made a home for him this time. A good and rightful one. No one on this floor would deny his heritage. I wait for him to catch my eye, but he's lost to this dance. His smile's so sharp, it rips a gash down the center of me.

The band drives on. I try to lose myself, too, sinking feet-first into the kind of music that can mend as much as break you. It pulls me close with all its minor bends. With layer-cake harmonies and expert piano trills. Baz seems to notice I've gone all in. He lobs a grin full of challenge and dare, then heightens our moves and all the things we do.

"Need some air?" he asks, slowing our steps after we've danced and danced like this. We're locked together as our feet still keep enough of the beat.

I nod and follow him off the floor. We all but run onto the smaller, northward-facing terrace, with half the people as the main balcony but just as much ocean. "Good on you. Thought I might combust."

"Because you were doing it right."

"Was I, though?" I grip the rail, still panting.

"Sí, bella." Baz drags both hands through his hair, pushing the dampness into the cropped, sun-touched waves. It's not fair that he looks this good after dancing that hard. "Although your friend Gordon wins debut artist of the year. He's cool. You pick good friends."

I open my mouth to say something irreverent and self-deprecating. It's what I do. But not this time. For all the mistakes I've made, picking stellar friends is one thing I've gotten right. In the sentimentality of that, I blurt out, "Well, I do in Miami, too. I mean, I only make friends with genius photography teachers with cracking salsa moves. The rest of this town can piss right off."

Baz plunks his hands next to mine, beaming. "I only make friends with Brits who can play a convincing fake girlfriend and handle my photography bullying."

"No idea where you'd find such a fool," I say as he edges closer. The air is ripe with clean sweat and tree flowers. Beyond the wall, the band plays a new song, but the salty current thrums its own rhythm, arrogantly, in a way that makes me envy it. I'm still hot and heaving off the floor, with my face inches away from the pale blue linen of Baz's shirt.

I close my eyes, simply wanting a pause, but my mind is made of stronger stuff—fast and furious, like the city I chose for my escape. A hundred thoughts whirl. New dares to dream, and my brother's hurt, and Gordon walking away at the inn. The Gordon I saw tonight. There's the soft-sharp memory of my mother, the pink blossoms she named me after and the lightning she left when it was time to leave *me*. My family's words float over it all, and I'm just trying, trying, trying . . .

Baz draws me into his chest. "You okay?" His tenor plays in my ear. "Is this?"

I nod against his shoulder, and I don't want to cry like the song said we would. But my eyes fill anyway because he's so kind. His body eclipses so much of my *too much*, even in the dark of night. "No one's here to see us," I point out. "Kelly. Your parents." The little cocoon we make on a balmy terrace.

His lips crease into a line as he thumbs my cheek. "Not everything has to be fake."

"I didn't mean you were being, like—"

"Shhh. I know." He curves his fingers so the knuckles poke out, grazing the underside of my jaw. And inside my own little storm, against the blue-black Atlantic, I raise my head, so our mouths are close, and just so.

"You did say no back-alley snogging, Flora," he whispers.

"If you think this is any kind of back alley, you've not been to England." We share another chuckle until there is a point when he slants a grin and moves in, leaving only the final bits for me to take if I choose. And I do choose, brushing my mouth against his mouth. He slides deeper, past the warm, jagged seam of our lips. We move like this for a few hushed seconds. But when I pull back, the scene is changed. Like a theater set that's been stripped away to rafters and bolts.

My eyes hinge open, and I don't know where to put what just happened. "Hi."

"Hey there," he says while I'm still in the outer bounds of his arms. "Pick a number. One, that was amazing. Two, it was the weirdest thing ever. Three, you have no fucking clue."

"All of them?" A sort of giddy panic comes, the kind that makes you ramble. "You're a damn good kisser, and that was so nice. Like, really, really nice. But I feel a little knocked out of sorts."

"It's okay, just breathe. And no way in hell am I going to tell you to smile."

I do anyway, but it wobbles.

His lips purse tight before relaxing. "How about this? Next week I'll take you to Little Havana to shoot. And eat Cuban food, of course, because I'm not a monster. And I won't kiss you like that again unless you ask me to."

"Thank you, I mean . . . I will." I hold out my hands. "Wait— oh bloody hell."

"I get it, Flora."

I exhale in relief, long and steady, because it sounds like *I see you.*

SEVENTEEN

The next morning, I'm perched on the edge of my bed, my thoughts volleying back and forth in a dizzying sort of way. The kiss with Baz was fun and hot. (Incredibly hot.) And isn't it nice to be kissed by someone who's not a raging twat? (Yes. Yes, it is.)

But I've got another, troubled side. I drag it to the bedroom dresser, fiddling with a few items—the brass owl, the lace doily. I don't expect these recuerdos to give me some grand epiphany, but there's something calming about this space. I lower my head, shutting my eyes into the small morning sounds. Birds are feasting in the garden. The air conditioner cycles on. The house is full of people today; cabinet doors shut, water runs, footsteps pad. And my insides are still full of last night.

Typically, when I've been kissed, I know whether I want to go in for more or not. And it's not that I don't want more of those incredibly hot kisses. I simply don't want to be rash and flighty—not only about Baz, but about *me* this time. My trip here used up all the rashness I could spare with my family. And then too much that I couldn't.

Baz did say that the way we'll carry on is up to me, and he and I will be good either way. The fact that I still get to keep growing my photography skills while flitting around Miami on my end of a bargain tells me that maybe I don't have to have everything sorted all the time to keep moving forward. I can just sort out today.

Steadied and more at ease (Was it the recuerdos after all?), I lift up, casting one last look at the storm photo. My phone chimes with an e-mail, not a text.

> Dear Flora,
> Just found out your camera needs a replacement part and will take a few more days. Papi insisted on covering the repair cost for you, so don't stress.
>
> Next, sorry it took so long for your headshots from Papi's class. I wanted to edit these myself, and, you're welcome, I got up way too early to finish them. 😊
>
> You take a mean headshot, Winchester. Not bad for a fake model (kidding).
>
> And since I have you, here's your photography assignment before we make it to Little Havana for some lifestyle work. Take pictures of people this time. I left a list of portraiture tips below.
> Can't wait for our next dance,
> Baz

As my gratitude soars over the Maríns' generous camera help, my fingers race to click on the attachments. I'll study

Baz's portraiture guidelines later; I'm way too curious about the student shots he sent over. The first four of me on the chaise lounge are plenty nice, and of course the editing is top-notch.

It's when I reach the final photo that I get a tinge of surprise, even when I should've seen it coming. It's the one where my face is a landscape of a dozen emotions, my head gazing away. The pose Baz used in his editing class that literally developed into a big wedding gift and a bigger ruse. The rest that comes after feels as open-ended and far away as England.

England. Rarely do I think of home without thinking of Lila. I save the images as my friend's name materializes in my head. *Check in. Do something.*

I click onto her Instagram first. A minute later I'm so glad I did before ringing her. Today's not a normal day. I read through Lila's post, studying the beautiful tribute with old pictures before sending my message.

Me: Good afternoon/morning, love. I saw your Insta. Thinking of you

Lila's quick to text back.

Lila: Thank you. Besitos 😘😘

I feel them as good as real.

Me: Sending hugs

Then I set off into the hallway toward another Cuban woman.

Pilar's in the kitchen filling up a reusable water bottle. "It's Abuela Lydia's birthday," I say softly.

She caps the bottle and turns. "It is. Ryan and I are going to Woodlawn Park to visit her before I head to La Paloma." She casts a pensive smile. "Every year, I bring Lila on FaceTime and set my phone by Abuela's grave so they can have a few minutes."

My heart aches—a hairline crack for their loss that fissures into mine. But I find I'm peacefully grounded, too. There's a lot of love in this room.

Pilar's face sobers. "Your mami. How can you not think of her? I'm sorry."

"It's okay. But you can thank your abuela for me. She helped bring my favorite family into the world and all. Nothing major, just that."

Pili pulls me into a strong hug. "Gordon's out back eating cake for breakfast. You know you want some."

I find the enormous wedge of Cuban butter cake with Grand Marnier–infused syrup. Abuela's signature recipe, the only choice for a birthday this home still celebrates. First I brew a pot of the English breakfast tea Pilar ordered—from my own business website, mind—as I'd forgotten to bring any.

Minutes later I edge through the patio door with a tray piled with two cups of tea and two hearty slices of cake.

Gordon's perched on the brick steps leading to an overgrown lawn. "Not bad for a couple of Hampshire rug rats," I take my turn saying. "Cake for brekkie and a garden full of cool lizards."

He cranes his neck as far as it goes. "Morning." It comes out gravelly, and he scoots to make room for me and my offerings. "You brought more?"

"*More* is your secret code word." I sit, offering him a fresh slice and taking him in. He's unshaven, and his hair's a little dizzy from sleep. I hand over his tea. "Figured you didn't take the time to fix your own cuppa. And yeah, this is the kind of house where it's almost wrong not to eat two pieces of cake."

"Too right," he says. "You're a star."

"No, that's you, dance-floor hero. Who knew?" I say this now because it's the first time I've seen Gordon since returning from the terrace last night. We all danced some more, but Gordy left early to take Matteo home and was already out cold by the time Baz brought me back.

"Believe me, I was as surprised as you," Gordon quips. "As much as I was over some other South Florida realizations." He tips his hand. "Apparently, when you tell *some* people you're half Latino around here, they assume you're lying because diversity is evidently some trend. Like I'm using it as a pub trick."

"Which is disgusting," I offer. "Who said that?"

"A couple subcontractors my team ran into last week at a Key West nightspot. I dunno, maybe it was the alcohol talking, because the majority of people have been really cool and want to know more. And I do, too. I mean, I want to learn more Spanish," Gordon adds. "Mum tried early on, but it never clicked. Lila's taught *you* quite well."

"Still working on my accent," I say. "But it took me three years of total immersion between pastries and biscuits. Brutal, but it's Lila, so do we expect anything less?"

"We do not. Maybe I can have Matteo and the guys do that for me. Or Baz if we find ourselves on another hangout." Gordon traps the words between us for a beat before stabbing into his cake.

I kissed Baz last night. As soon as the thought forms, I bat it away like another flying creature. "Oh, he'd be down. Massive

Gordy fan, he is. Surprised he hasn't asked for your number."

"Fuck off, Flora," Gordon says in a deep russet tone that can't shade the light in his eyes.

I crane my head back, laughing, but it comes out a bit strangled. "You two getting on is the last thing I expected. Not that it's bad. Maybe weird?"

But I kissed him. I kissed Baz Marín. I pinch my own arm, hard, and what is wrong with my brain?

"Sure it's weird, Squiggs." He swallows the last of his slice while I'm only halfway through mine. "But life is weird, yeah?"

"Yeah." I want to lean my head on his shoulder. There's a spot I claimed there, long ago. A well-used notch, like a threadbare chair you'd never sell. But I don't make the move. I study him instead. "Can I take your picture?"

"Huh? Now?"

"Baz wants to work with me on portraiture. You know, humans instead of landscapes. I thought about going over to La Paloma to shoot some of the bakers. But . . ." I lock on to his face. "Why do all that when you're here and human?"

"Are we sure?" He tests the tea, giving a sign that it's cooled. His throat works over a few hearty gulps. "Funny, you've never shot me seriously before. Just iPhone pictures, or random one-offs."

"You've never drawn a house for me."

"Shitty excuse for friends, we are. Why do we even bother?"

I find myself staring at my hands. It's all I can do. And I am not easily offended. I'm the usual offender.

"Flora." This time it's his floppy red head on my shoulder for real. "Since when do you totally miss my cheap-shot jokes?"

I exhale, big and messy, angry at myself for my extreme

reaction, and unsettled by the fact that the truth I'm hiding doesn't feel solid in the way that true things should. "If you ask me if I've got PMS, I'm going to stab you with my dull fork."

"There's my mate." He grabs that fork and digs up a wad of icing, then feeds it into my mouth until I swallow enough sugar to turn sweeter. "Your favorite part, that. But the cake is beyond, too. Fitting for Abuela Lydia's birthday."

I give a little jolt. "You saw?"

He nods. "I thought I'd go and visit. Thank her for all she did for my mum growing up. I never said it when she was alive."

"You were young."

"Yeah." A soft smile. "Want to come to the cemetery with me? After, we can scrounge some lunch."

My next breath jitters, and I'm already picturing all the ways his offer could go wrong considering my history with graveyards. With the wakes that come after them. I make phantom lines with my flip-flop along the pavers. "That's a shit pickup line. I hope you didn't use that one on Lizzie for any dates."

He sends a *look*; I can't sort out the ratio of pissed off to amused. "Don't worry. I won't threaten any future girlfriends with such a good time."

"Only me?" I ask, so quietly I could deny it ever happened.

A lizard darts by. Gordon tracks its little feet until it disappears behind a shrub. "Only the best for you."

So this is the view from the friend zone. *You put yourself there,* I remind myself. And then, sometime between an England inn and a Miami coral castle, he thought it right, too. He thought it best.

But the word *best* is misleading. Because it's possible to have a better day than the best day you've ever had. And it's possible to make a better friend or have a better love than the one you feel is best today.

I risk a glance, find him staring back and waiting. And the only answer I get is the word, *time*, straight out of Baz's Pablo Neruda poem. That maybe time really does matter most between us and everything else in this life.

"You never answered my hot date proposal. So, graves and goulash?"

"Or graves and gazpacho," I say, playing along.

"Or graves and gyros."

I shake my head. "*Gyro* does not work, and you know it."

"Graves and Gordon, then?"

I nod once. "Sorted."

EIGHTEEN

After Gordon cleans up and I study Baz's photo tips, we pile into the rented Toyota. With the sat nav in charge of getting us to Woodlawn Park, there's time to catch up, and I insist on learning about Key West.

At a traffic light, Gordon cues up his phone so I can scroll through photos while he narrates. He's been busy capturing neighborhoods with a bygone flavor, and their flowery gabled cottages and pastel homes trimmed with gingerbread wood-work. He details the typical conch-style architecture—marked by wraparound verandas and shuttered windows—made popular in the nineteenth century by Bahamian immigrants.

Gordon gestures with his non-steering hand as he tells stories of Cuban cigar barons and their escape to Key West during the Ten Years' War. Shipping and cigar money paid for grand Queen Anne structures marked with turrets and pointed rooflines.

"Plenty for you to draw," I note, and return his phone.

"Yeah, and learn, style-wise. And fix, most of all. We just started on a Victorian passed down to a descendant of a shipping baron. There's not enough left in her estate to pay for upgrades and retrofitting. I'll send more shots of the place next week—it's amazing. But parts have gone shabby and might not make it through the next hurricane, so that's why she's a prime recipient of grant funds."

"And your time."

"And loads of our time," Gordon agrees as the sat nav tells him to turn into the cemetery drive. At once we fall quiet. Stories pause, and it's just the engine revving around curve after curve until we reach the closest car park to Abuela Lydia's final resting place.

Gordon grabs the pink bouquet we brought. I bring Baz's camera bag for safekeeping and follow my friend onto the nearest walkway. At the mouth of a brick path, I slow and take it all in. The area is marked with the most beautiful flowering trees and shrubs. An enormous Gothic mausoleum right out of England stands in the distance. But my earlier fears prove true, and my feet aren't ready to move.

Gordon hangs back, eyeing me with concern.

"Today's the first time I've been to a cemetery since Mum's memorial," I admit. "I agreed to come—wanted to—but . . ." I shake my head. "Hell." I'm weak and exposed, teetering on the edge of a cold, dark place where grief meets guilt.

"I didn't know." Gordon shifts in his gray Vans. "I can't promise to keep out all the bad stuff like with the window mosquitoes, but you don't have to go alone." He holds out a hand.

It hits me that this is another way that I can move forward for real. I clasp our fingers, and we go. Together.

My heart rate stills as we wind through brick paths, past

old trees with rough, peeling skin. I lean on Gordon, taking the steadiness of him and adding it to my own. This is how I stop feeling so weak. Each step feels like another win, and by the time we locate the right granite marker, I'm ready to be here and read the carved inscription:

Lydia Elisa Rodriguez. Una Madre y Abuela Tan Querida.
So beloved.

Two bunches of flowers already fill the adjacent vase. "Pilar and Elisa came," I tell Gordon.

He nods and slots in our pink daisy offering. "Well." He clears his throat. "Happy birthday, Abuela. I hope you can see how amazing your business is. It's quite famous, and you should be proud. Oh, and thanks for giving my mum another home all those years ago."

After a solemn nod, he sits cross-legged in the tree-branch shade. And I sit, too. "Um, hello. Unlike Gordy, I never got to meet you. But I feel like I know you as well as my own nan. And I hope you know how much your family loves you." I pause as Gordon scoots closer on the downy grass, plunking an arm around me that will never be fake. "Happy birthday. Your cake recipe is delicious, by the way."

"Oh Christ, yes," Gordon says. "And thanks for letting me inside your bakery kitchen when I visited. And feeding me pastries and chasing after my arse when I went back for more. Then always letting me have more and not telling Mum. I think you even straight-up lied to her face a few times about how much I'd eaten."

I laugh at this, at the pure Gordon-ness of it.

His phone pings with its typical series of barks. "No, Gordy. That digital dog isn't at all out of place here."

"Yeah, yeah," he says, fishing his mobile from the pocket of his shorts. "I need to ring Matteo. I'm his ride back tomorrow."

I wave him off. "Go on, then."

He jumps up and pace-walks on a nearby path whilst chatting. Animated and wandering.

I turn back to face the grave marker, alone for the first time in hours. "There's one more thing," I say to Abuela Lydia. "I haven't been to my mum's cemetery since her burial." As soon as I free the words, a notion drops into the empty space. That maybe all the places we put departed loved ones are inexplicably connected somehow. Like a network of grass and bone and memory. I was afraid to visit Mum at home, largely because of the guilt that would've come along. But I don't want to be that girl anymore. That daughter. So whether it's true or not, I decide to treat this place like Mum's more *here* than any other place nearby. Just like I reached far across oceans for my bedroom mementos, I plunge into that grassy web and hope it's deep enough.

"Can I say some things . . . Mum?" The way she looked when I was seven or eight comes to life. Vibrant and carefree. A heart-shaped face and delicate blond waves. "I know it's been too long, and I'm so sorry. But here's the thing—I can't get over the feeling that you've seen and understood everything I've been through lately. Just like you always knew when I hid sweets in my room." I look up smiling, tears breaking through. "I also think you sent me to that lightning photo, so I'd feel seen and loved. I believe that." I nod three times into the balmy air. "And I hope you feel just as loved where you are. Of course, I hope there's a beautiful piano for you to play, too. And I . . ."

And I . . .

And I *can't* go on anymore. "Clair de Lune" floods between my ears, my hand clenching into a tight ball as emotion rises fast. The kind of feeling that makes me want to break something so the whole world will stop and acknowledge the sound. The kind where I am louder than that tune and its darkest coda. Where I rise to prove that graves like this don't win even though they remain standing. They don't take everything.

I move away from the plot when even the shape of the granite stone becomes too much. Gordon's nearby, continuing his chat with Matteo. Eyes fixed, I don't even realize what I'm doing until I'm holding Baz's camera. The rush of pride and control, the power to change and reframe, storms in like a familiar remedy.

(I didn't stay close. I shot the world instead.)

And now I simply want to photograph my oldest friend.

Fueled and inspired, I stand, wiping my face dry and forcing an audible exhale. Gordon's under a shady tree with foliage that droops low over his shoulder. If plants could eavesdrop, this one would be the ringleader. Gordy doesn't budge when I approach. He's texting, face set in concentration, bottom lip pulled out. *Click.*

He still hasn't noticed. *Click, click, click.*

I check my work, adjust the settings. I can get more light into that clean-shaven face. Enough to match the brightness inside him.

Baz sent a reflector, along with tips to use it—more precise and advanced than anything I knew before. I unfold the metallic-framed circle and stride closer.

He notices me now. "Oi, what are you up to?"

"I like this view and that tree and your adorable, ruddy face as it is, right now. So I'm going to take your picture." He barely has time to pocket his phone before I shove the reflector in his hands.

"Why am I holding a pancake spaceship?"

"Since I've no assistant and don't want to set up the stand just yet, you're going to bounce the light into your face with that spaceship." I position the reflector.

I back up, taking test shots along the way. And I find I quite like the lighter feel of the mirrorless camera.

"Er, when I said you could take my picture, I meant somewhere scenic after we left the graveyard."

"This is scenic. You won't see gravestones in the angles I'm using." And I like the idea of reframing the somber space. To make forever art in this place of forever rest. "You haven't stopped for snacks, either, and mucked up your look." A navy linen tee and crisp gray shorts I found in the overnight bag he brought from the Keys.

He laughs, and I shoot again.

I move deeper into my work, tuning his placement of the reflector and directing him. Peaceful and pensive Gordon, cocky Gordon—I bring them all out.

"You're enjoying this way too much," he says on a break. "Bossing me around."

"Don't get too jealous."

After a few minutes I set up the reflector stand so I can get his entire body. This makes him tense up and lock his joints too much, so I try one of Baz's trusty relaxation techniques, which is different from the personal, self-centered way I've approached photography in the past. These shots are about highlighting what's already true and real about Gordon—no framing tricks necessary.

Yet no matter how genuine my subject is, Baz talked to me about how it can seem manufactured to pose someone. He maintains we can add authenticity into what is, by nature, an inauthentic moment by leading the subject into a place of comfort and safety. And I know Gordon's. A few dirty jokes later he loosens up again, easy and natural. I string my finest swear words all in a row until he's howling and limber with mirth.

And God, his smile. Sly and sweet and cheeky and gleaming. Sometimes dark around the edges. I capture it like I want the world to want a slice.

Over the next half hour I move him like a game piece, more king than pawn. I sit him on an oversized boulder and lean his arse against a wooden footbridge, his swagger on show with crossed arms and his mouth pulled into a hint of mischief.

Viewing this one, I decide to make it my last. Besides, Gordon has started to whine about lunch and that I'm starving my portrait model.

"*Starving*, are you?" I wind around to the car's passenger seat and click in, holding my overheated face directly in front of the blasting air-conditioner vent. "Mr. Two Pieces of Cake."

Satisfied the car's cooled enough, Gordon shuts his door and starts off. "That's only slightly more than an appetizer. Plus, I've something in mind, and it might sell out. And that would make me very, very sad."

Leave it to Gordon to cry over lunch. "Fine." We ease out onto the main road. "You going to tell me what's on the menu?"

"Not a chance. Only that it's something I tried my first day in Key West. Matteo made all of us go there straightaway."

"Interesting."

Gordon doesn't answer, but it's not more than a few minutes later that he pulls into the car park for the Publix supermarket.

"We're cooking our own lunch?"

He swings into a space. "I like that you still have no idea what you're about to eat. Come on." He drags me into Publix, sending me to the far end of the shop for cold drinks and warning me not to find him and ruin the surprise. I'm to meet him out front, and I don't argue because it's best to go along with these matters with this friend.

While I wait with my bag of water bottles and fizzy drinks, Gordon finally emerges with a sack. "Sorry. Was a long queue, but I have the prize." He waggles his brows.

"Looks like a sandwich," I say, noting the outline of the items inside the plastic.

"The Cubano and medianoche are not the only famous sandwiches in this town. Behold the Pub Sub." He holds up the bag like the cub from *The Lion King*.

"Excuse me, the—oh. You mean *Pub* for *Publix*."

An exaggerated wink as we slide into the car.

It's not that far to the next spot where Gordon parks his rental. Alice Wainwright Park is a small, fairly hidden space set on a long stretch of Biscayne Bay. There's no beach here, only a shin-high sea wall separating the grass from the deep cobalt panorama of gently lapping water. The kind you could stare at until you're hypnotized.

"The Publix clerk said it's a good spot for a picnic. Did I do okay?" Gordon asks sheepishly.

"Come on, you know you did."

He finds a spot under plenty of trees with bushy leaves that make a shady canopy, knocking degrees off the thermometer. We sit, and I open our drinks while he arranges whatever I'm about to eat.

"Trust me on this." He unwraps a sub sandwich filled with fried bits. "Welcome to heaven on earth. The chicken tender Pub Sub."

I lean in, giving it a whiff. "Like cut-up chicken strips from the supermarket freezer?" Also tomato, shredded lettuce, and mayo, it seems.

"Just try it, Squiggs."

I go in for a bite and quickly realize that Gordon scored and I'm eating my second favorite Miami sandwich. "Holy shit, that's amazing."

He laughs, taking a break from food-shoving to down a good portion of water. "I guess I did do all right."

I am too much into this sandwich to reply. But my blissful expression and repetitive nods seem to clue Gordy in well enough.

"Good, good." He dashes a flimsy napkin across his chin. "Say, Woodlawn Park was okay for you, then? I got caught up chatting to Matteo, and then you started taking my picture before I could ask."

"I had to work through some things," I say, toying with my sandwich wrapping. "But I'm glad you went with me. Leave it to you to make a girl laugh her first time back in a cemetery."

"Um, you're welcome?" His face bunches up in mock confusion.

"No, it's good. I mean, that's *you*."

"Learned that early, didn't I? Making people laugh at the oddest of times."

I bump his side. "Made it your trademark."

"Yeah, I guess it's as carved into my identity as the place that built it."

"What place?"

"The inn," he notes. "Same as my architecture obsession."

I scrunch my face. In all our years, he's never brought up anything even orbiting this topic. "What does the Crow have to do with you being a bloody laugh factory?"

He faces the gently churning bay just ahead, sobering so much, I'd call it sour. "And a prankster. And don't forget goofy jokester, illusionist, and court jester, as you've said. Shall I go on?"

"Um, no, but you should explain. What did you mean you learned that early?"

"Humor? Being funny?" He gives a crooked smile. "More it was the power of humor. How laughter rarely changed *anything* about anything hard, but it could change the way some of those things went down. For my family it was guest reviews. Remember the Owl and Crow was passed down from Dad's family?" When I nod, he adds, "He's always taken his legacy, and the responsibility, seriously, which translates to acting all uptight about everything being perfect for guests."

I concede, knowing Spencer Wallace—Gordon's red-hair benefactor—well enough.

"Well, not all guests leave positive reviews, no matter how hard we try to cater to them. While negative reviews are a part of owning a business, Dad was never okay with that. He took

the critical bits hard. One day Mum was totally over his mop-
ing and griping and dramatic stomping off into the garden."

"Ooh, this should be good." Catalina "Cate" Mendoza Wallace is none to be trifled with.

"Mum decided no one was going to out-drama her," he says.
"So she started acting out the reviews when they'd come in
like they were telenovela scenes. With extra swooning and
gasping and hand motions."

"That's brilliant."

Gordon beams. "Even prune-faced Dad couldn't help but
crack up. And chill a bit. Right away, I started getting in on
the act."

I snort a laugh. "I can't believe I've never witnessed telenovela Gordon."

He wiggles his fingers like he's conjuring sparkles. "I am
quite good—and was, even as a boy. So good that Dad doesn't
even have that mopey reaction to negativity anymore. It's like
he can already picture Mum and me and our hijinks. So that's
what I meant. It didn't change the reviews. It changed the
mood in our home, and I never forgot that."

A small dawn breaks inside me. "So this is what made
funny Gordon. The pranks and jokes, all that?"

"Flora."

I look up.

"When your mum was diagnosed and everyone found out,
I was the only person you'd let sit with you at lunch. And we
ate alone in the library near that cool fish tank, because the
librarian allowed it as long as we didn't spill."

"Yeah," I muse, my memory catching up. "Interesting, the

things people let you do when they realize your mum is eventually going to forget you."

"I know. But kids don't usually think through the why of things. They just go with what's really immediate. You did that. But now you can look back and see everything."

"Too right," I say as moments come into the light. "My classmates made cards. Some brought flowers. There was one day I was out, and I came back to find my desk decorated. And of course, that was so sweet and lovely."

"But it was also shit, right?"

I avert my gaze.

"What, like you can't admit that to *me*?"

My face falls, and I collapse with it into a heap of a shrug.

"Because you felt your pain a little too on display," he continues, "and it began to feel like pity."

Pity. The first raindrop of so many of the storms inside me. "It did," I admit. "And I was too confused about what was happening to separate my grief from friends simply being nice and my teacher trying to help. Like, I didn't want them to be extra kind. I wanted things to be how they were before."

"So why do you think I hid that rubber snake in your cubby? Like, sneaked into your class and risked a demerit?"

"Whatever your reason, I hope it was to get me to chase after you. Because I sure remember doing that."

"And you threw that snake straight at my head without a word because you knew I was the culprit." He rubs the spot. "Sodding hell, Flora. You and your aim. If that hadn't been rubber."

If it had been a little brass owl at the end of another chase. "I . . ."

"And that made way for all the next parts. First I stole that book of Dad's with the off-color jokes and taught you swear words that neither of us had heard yet. And that's saying a lot with my mum in residence."

Chills trail up and down my arms. "You mean you planned that stuff out?"

"Sure, I did, and it worked. You laughed, like, really hard, and often couldn't stop. We started walking home together more. Then I kept drumming up ways to be goofy and silly. My class-clowning entertained you. So there you are."

"I thought you were just being you. I didn't know you'd made me your newest experiment."

"What?" His eyes snap wide. "That's not how it was—"

"How it sounds now is that I was just another telenovela project. Like, being funny worked with your dad, so why not see if you could turn a sad girl's frown upside down?" Emotions pelt me from all directions, so muddied it feels as if I can't trust them again. "Did you even want to be my friend for real?"

"Fucking hell, Flora," he snarls. "How can you say that?"

I snap up, finding his face pulled tense and tight and his neck flamed and burning red. "I mean, I know you're my friend now."

"Do you?" It comes out darker than an England winter sky.

"Yes. *Yes*, but I never knew any of this about you—us—and it's *all* coming back." The piano, and diagnosis, and little-girl loss. The lingering guilt that it took three months to even talk to my mother at any grave site.

I gaze long at the expanse of Miami across the bay, then narrow my lens over the smaller bits around me. Rocks and scattered leaves and petals. A city in macro. "It *was* hard being at Woodlawn. Very. Before we started your photo shoot, I had an extremely heavy moment. So I'm sorry everything got turned around into *this*."

"No need." There's no life to the words, and he's gazing somewhere aimless and distant. I can't even follow.

"What?"

He pivots his neck just enough. "No need to be sorry. Of course it was hard. I get it."

"Right," I whisper.

Two, five, then maybe fifteen seconds pass before Gordon juts up. "Look, it sounds as if you need a minute alone or whatever. We should probably go."

It takes me five more beats to gather our rubbish. "Yeah, we should."

NINETEEN

"What happened between you and the camera since last week?" Baz asks. We're in Little Havana for my next lesson on lifestyle shots. "You're shooting like it's the only thing keeping you from exploding."

I slide out a wry laugh. "It might be. It's been a tough few days." The one uptick: Nan's Canon DSLR is back in my hands. While Baz still wants me to have access to the studio's equipment, today, I'm learning how to master my own.

Baz tightens the leather harness around his neck. "So you're putting all that back into the lens?"

"Something like that," I say, but don't elaborate. For one, he's a new addition to the box of random parts I still have to figure out. Especially after kissing him. Right now, Baz is my instructor, but he's also a friend who's loads of fun to be around, with enough chill to let me figure out whatever's going on between us. The way *that's* going? My figuring-out settings need more help than the ones on my camera.

And then there's Gordon. We haven't even messaged since he dropped me off after Pub Subs and tense words. Now he's four hours away after staying at Matteo's for the rest of the weekend.

So, yeah, the camera follows my spiraling thoughts. It's with me as my feet trail down Calle Ocho—the main avenue cutting through Little Havana, alive with Cuban culture and history.

As Baz schools me on the mechanics of the perfect lifestyle shot, I can't get enough of this setting. The rainbow hues of mosaic tile walls and Technicolor murals soak into my lens. For a beat, I catch Baz looking *me* over more than my technique; he slaps on a lopsided grin. He's as assured and at home in his Cuban-ness as this street. I wait to capture him unaware in his white tee and blue shorts, breezy against the background of shop fronts.

"Sneaky," Baz says when he catches on and peers into my screen. "But this is exactly right. Look at the way you framed me on the block, so it's about more than my face. It's the context that matters."

"I mean, your face is nice, too," I note. "Marginally."

It's fun when he sputters. "Oh, marginally? I'm still learning your range of compliments. Where does that one fall?"

"Right with me realizing that for every shot I take of you, I'm noticing twice as many people checking you out as they pass by."

"Shut up, Flora." He grabs my hand. Our eyes lock. My smile catches up to his, but he simply gives my palm two squeezes. "If you have time to notice la gente, it's time to move up in difficulty level."

I don't know what this means until he's urged me down the avenue.

"You can't shoot Calle Ocho without going to Máximo Gómez Park." Baz points to a courtyard enclosed by walls of white plaster and black ironwork. The nickname Domino Park marks the entrance gate, and inside, pavilions with terra-cotta tile canopies offer shade. "This is where the viejitos come to play. Legendary."

Lila's spoken fondly about Cuban domino culture. Here it comes alive in a riot of guffaws and yelling, and in the constant clacking of tiles. We pass through the gate to find every built-in square table occupied with game players of all ages, but mostly retired folk.

"Let's watch for a sec," Baz says. I'm pressed against him as we sink into the controlled chaos of heated matches. I zoom my artist's eye on the way players strike their winning tiles onto the table with a flourish. Heckling sneers and evil-eye glares are common accessories.

"This seems really intense," I say into Baz's ear. "I don't want to intrude."

"Hold on." He strides into the noisy middle and appears to recognize a few of the players. Game play stops, and wide arms draw him close. I comprehend bits as he seeks permission for me to shoot, and in seconds boisterous calls summon me forward.

"¡Oye, Florecita! Ven."

"Sí, qué bueno."

I step up. "Muchas gracias. And please carry on with your games."

They waste no time. *Clack, clack, clack.*

This hub is a candy shop of lively images, and the unwritten uniform is the short-sleeved guayabera shirt or bright polo.

Hats are requisite, too, in panama styles with rims stained with cigar smoke, or faded ball caps. I set up and shoot a few scenes, and after a few minutes Baz checks my work.

"These are good, but we can level them up," he says.

My features sharpen. "I did all you said with the settings and the framing. It's not enough?"

"You took solid photos. But we're going for extraordinary. Isn't that why you asked me to tutor you?"

I take the Canon. "*You* offered to tutor *me*."

"Okay, pero you haven't run away yet. I usually get your read receipts on my texts in seconds."

Busted, I compose myself. "Well, that certainly speaks well of you, esteemed teacher."

"Ay, qué tremendo paquete," he says, exasperated. "Do you want to learn how to turn this shoot into something extra, or are we done?"

I glance briefly at the camera. "I don't want to be done." This is true in deepening layers, the feeling ballooning inside me. *I don't want to be done.* If I hadn't decided before, I do now. I'm not supposed to take pictures just as a grieving person looking for a remedy, but as something more. As . . . a photographer. The rest is blurry, but this one thing materializes in clear focus. "Show me. Please."

A poster-sized smile. He moves forward and seems to be doing more watching than shooting for a time. But then there's a burst of *click, click, click.*

Baz returns to my side and shows me about five photos of one of the players. And *oh.*

"Yours are, I dunno, more alive and present. How?"

"Lifestyle work is about more than the subject itself. It's

capturing their energy. So I waited and tracked Ramón and shot right when his movements had the most forward momentum."

This actually makes sense, and it's something I never learned in this way before. I give it another go. And another.

An hour later we eat takeaway Cubanos from one of Baz's favorite Little Havana joints. Our shady bench sits inside a history book along Cuban Memorial Boulevard. The long plaza is strung into a web of trees and monuments honoring Cuban revolutionaries and soldiers who fought in key military campaigns, including the Cuban Independence Wars of the 1800s and the Bay of Pigs invasion.

By the time our sandwiches are gone, I gain an understanding that lies beyond facts about anti-communist crusaders or the year 1961. I understand Lila better. Sitting here inside the pulse of her heritage, listening to Baz speak of Cuba with such resonant love and longing, I truly realize how hard it must've been for Lila to leave this place. And more, how much she's had to carry with her to keep it close.

I'm glad Baz wants to sit awhile longer. The breeze twirls in, soft and fragrant with flowers and tropical green. It could be straight off the island itself.

Motion grabs my vision, and I giggle at a trio of wild roosters. Calle Ocho is filled with loads of colorful rooster statues, but it's fun watching live ones poke along the path. "Adding that to my list of things you'd never see in Winchester."

"Oh yeah, they rule around here. For us the rooster is a symbol of power and strength." I scrunch my nose at this. "I know, you'd think a lion or bear. But this has stuck for generations."

Power and strength—I've always held both so high inside my head. Those words in this place make me feel it's right to ask the question I've kept hidden. Today, it's wide open like another history book. Baz's forearm tree tattoo butts against my side, faceup toward the sun. He gives a startle when I grab his left wrist for a better view.

"Tell me what this means?" I ask, tracing the lines of the gnarled tree with exposed roots. Thumbing the tattered Cuban flag tossed at the base of the trunk.

Baz nods thoughtfully. "It's a ceiba tree, or kapok. It's considered a holy tree in Cuba." He glances up, pointing. "We're sitting under one."

I'd missed it; a huge piece of the mystery was shading us all along.

"My abuelo—my father's papi—was a photographer in Manzanillo. He worked at a studio while my abuela taught school." Baz turns, eyeing me straight on. "After Castro assumed power, families who had the means filed papers to leave the country. In 1968 my abuelos completed their paperwork. But while Castro didn't stop the application process, he made life a living hell for those who were waiting. They lost their jobs. And many were sent to labor camps. My papi was too young, but Abuelo had to go away to one of these camps to work."

"God, that's horrid," I say.

"Major understatement." He bites it out. "Conditions were deplorable, and there was rampant abuse and illness. My abuelo died in a field accident, never making it home. Abuela had to come here alone with her only son."

"I'm so sorry. You never got to know your abuelo."

"No. As you can imagine, this history—my history—has always fueled my papi. To honor his father, to carry on his trade and not only be good at it, but great."

"Like the difference between a good and an extraordinary photo."

He cracks a smile, nodding as he lifts his forearm again. "On my eighteenth birthday, I got this ceiba tree tattoo. I asked for the Cuban flag to be tattered because of the way my family was torn."

I touch his inked skin with more intention. "Your abuelo's memory and legacy mark your dominant hand, the one you use to work."

He nods once. "My work is my duty, but it's also something I do out of love, you know? I don't need to graduate college to work in photography, but I will, because Abuelo never had the chance. And that's also why I'm studying photojournalism. It has little to do with my papi's empire, but this way I'll add another angle to our work and another piece to the Marín legacy. And hopefully win some prominent awards. Selena is doing that, too, by painting."

His heartfelt words land hard and weighty. "What if you're like me and you've done the opposite?" I dare to ask. "What if you haven't added any sort of honor to your family's legacy?"

He shakes his head. "Flora—"

"You don't know, Baz, what I've done. All I've squandered." I point to a bright and beautiful mural across the street. "When I was fifteen, I defaced my city. I used to tag walls because it was some twisted way for me to feel seen, to leave a mark when I felt I was being erased from my mother's memory. But it was wrong, and I hurt people and businesses. My father still doesn't know, but he saw the damage and was rightfully upset. So disappointed. All along, it was me."

Baz stays quiet, urging me forward.

"Orion and Dad have handed me one opportunity after another, and I've done so much skipping out. Like showing up late and blowing off vendor meetings. Weeks ago I flubbed a chance at a mentorship and embarrassed my dad and our shop. I intentionally stayed away on the day my mum died and lied about that, and when I finally told the truth, it shattered my family." Pink lightning flashes through my mind, and the one who captured it tucks an arm around my shoulder. "And it wasn't until I got here that I realized I've spent years living in circles." I look up, meeting Baz head-on. "You know, like when you're about to land at the airport and there's no gate. So the pilot keeps the plane in a holding pattern. Around and around. That's been me, circling my mum's life, waiting for, you know . . . that day."

My throat burns, thickening with words I've barely voiced before. They rise up from all the places I've kept them.

"All that circling, trying to just keep her—keep *us*—made me afraid to dream of a future that didn't include her. So I never did—not like you and Kelly and Gordon have. I didn't even know how. But since being here, I've had the space to break free from that holding pattern. Now I'm trying to land in the perfect place."

When I lift my eyes, Baz jostles my gear bag. "Wherever that is, something tells me a camera is there."

In this plaza dedicated to Cuban history, all I can do is sink into my own. "Yeah, and at home I never wanted to let go of my camera. Now it's become something bigger. Photography is the first thing that I've been excited about in a long time, but . . . so much doubt is still there. I'm not the best at trusting myself."

"Well, trust this." Baz holds up a finger. "You're good at it—and photography is way too important to me to throw that out lightly. With more training, you could have an amazing career. We can talk about different specializations? How to get there?"

Just the sound of this plan throws sparks from the center of my chest. "Clearly, I'm never shooting weddings."

Baz snorts out a laugh. "Por Dios. Too soon." He drops into a half smile. "Listen, I'm in a photography degree program, and I told you why. But Papi never went to college. He took trade classes and studied with experts. Nothing Studio Marín has or *is* came at the end of a degree."

This truth nearly knocks me off the bench. I close my hands, staring at locked fingers. "But I'm *supposed* to go to uni. My brother applied on my behalf to an organization that provides scholarships for children of terminally ill parents. They chose me. It's a lot of money I can apply to any university program next year."

"Wow. So even photography, right?"

I shrug. "That word has never come up in my home. I've been steered toward courses like marketing or public relations. Fields that would help in our business expansion. But I dunno, simply having that paper would bring some honor and pride to my family. That I followed through with something. Still, I'm not sure that type of study is best for me."

Baz looks up at the kapok tree for a beat. "So you've found

your dream. But maybe choosing another way to have it besides college means disappointing your family and throwing away a huge opportunity."

"Again, Baz. *Again.*"

"Yeah." There's a short pause. "You know how I said you were using reframing in kind of a limiting way?" When I nod, he adds, "There's a healthy way to reframe stuff, so we can see past it and move on."

"I do get that."

"Good. Because who said dreams never hurt, Flora? Just like most good things worth having come from a little pain." He holds out his left arm, baring the gnarled tree. "Or a lot. This hurt like hell," he says through a wry laugh. "But I wanted it for my family members who never made it to Miami. I did this for them. It lasts because of the pain it took."

It lasts—the opposite of flighty. The other side of wasted and squandered, and blown away by the wind. Or a storm.

TWENTY

Baz's challenge follows me home and lingers into the afternoon. Ideas stream down with the water as I shower away the sweat of Calle Ocho. Afterward, as I work styling product into my curls (the way Mum taught me), my mind whirls until it stops on a single mark.

Who said dreams never hurt?

It's not like I've never heard this before. But I was so wrapped up in trying to *find* a dream for myself that I hadn't considered the painful part. The part etched into Baz's arm and into his father's empire. And into my own family's work and legacy.

In the clearing steam, I remind myself that I'm no stranger to hurting things. I've gone through pain, and caused pain, to get what I need and find control. Haven't I defeated tougher trials than securing my future? Haven't I risen, proud and tall, over a hundred of life's greatest pains? *A hurricane girl knows this well,* I think, giving a final shake to my hair.

In the tiny hallway bath, I trade my dressing gown for soft blue lounge shorts and a matching tank. When I pad out to the living room, Elisa's at her mum's old piano with a duster. The sight halts my bare feet on the carpet.

She turns, not startled so much as lit up. "There you are! You've been so busy all over this city, I have barely seen you, cariño."

I don't know what to say except "I could've done that dusting, and more. You haven't left me a to-do list in three days."

She waves it off. "You've had enough going on with Baz and all those new cameras and lenses in your room. Now come sit. Catch up with Mami Elisa so I can at least *say* I'm keeping track of you the way your papi would want." She plunks down on the piano bench and pats the empty space.

My bottom lip drops, heart twisting. A piano bench is the last place I'd choose to rest my legs.

But when Elisa moves, I realize she's holding something—a silver-framed photo. Even from here I recognize the context from the colors. The flamingo-pink Instagram-worthy wall of the café where Pilar treated all her bridesmaids to lunch. And me. I was there, too, eating seared ahi and blue-cheese pull-apart bread. Coconut crème brûlée.

So I go for the photo. I approach for that, if only to see. Elisa guides me onto the bench as she makes room at the top of the piano for the new shot. Everyone in this family lives in frames here. Years' worth of love and memories. I never noticed before, but a doily runs along the piano top, a match to the one in my room and the design painted on Pili's wedding favors.

And in this new frame on top of an old recuerdo, there are women. British and Cuban women. Mothers, daughters, and sisters. Elisa's in the middle, cinched between Pili and me, and I'm holding Lila's image to the camera, beamed in from FaceTime.

"Abuela Lydia was at the party. I felt her," Elisa says, and when I lift up, her eyes are glassy and rimmed with red. So are mine. Because for the first time, I see her as someone kindred, even though we're more than thirty years apart. She has lost a mother, too.

I nod (it's all I can manage), and Elisa says, "I thought it was time for a new photo." She dashes her hand out. "And there's plenty of room for more."

This gets me good, and my tears stream freely. Because there is still so much living to do. It's what she would want—my mum. She would. She *does*.

"Sometimes I come to this bench when I'm alone in the house," Elisa says. "I like to remember mi mamá here, because she would work through her beginning lesson books, and it was one of the only times she would simply sit. She was always in motion. I didn't care that she didn't play well."

"Mine was masterful," I whisper. "I grew up next to her on the bench."

"Sí, chica."

"But I don't sit at pianos anymore. It's too hard." I run from them instead. And when Elisa's eyes plead, *Tell me everything—dime todo*, I do. I tell the woman who placed me by her side in her family picture—a mother at a piano who has also lost a mother—all my hardest things. I place her into my life.

It all floods out: The May afternoon wake and the running away. The donation gift and the speech I still must write. The guilt and regret tainting all those days.

"I'm trying to do better with her memory," I say near the

end. "And I think I have been. But the piano is still so hard."

Elisa's close, her frame strong against mine, arm hooked around my back. Her perfume is aired out since morning but still there. "What was that song you said was your favorite?"

"'Clair de Lune,'" I supply. "By Debussy. It means 'moonlight,' but whenever Mum played it, I always thought it sounded like the rain when it first hits the window. Not a big stormy rain, but a light spring shower." I shake my head. "It's so beautiful, but now it only reminds me of her disease. And of so many mistakes I made." Running, lying, evading, escaping.

Elisa thumbs a stray curl from my face. "Sometimes we need a new memory to add to an old one." She gestures to the line of picture frames. "It does not mean the old one doesn't matter anymore or that it becomes less. It means the new one matters . . . too. También. And over time, they both change, nena. They change with us and inside us."

On this bench, it hits me that Elisa Reyes is the best reframer I've ever known. And maybe . . . "You wouldn't know how to play 'Clair de Lune,' would you?" I ask with a little cheek, lighter than I've felt in hours or months.

Elisa throws her head back in a firework laugh. "You know I don't." She goes soft. "But we can find it on the Spotify. And we can listen together?"

We can. I think we truly can.

I pull out my phone, cuing the music app, but the sound that fills the Reyes home just then isn't from any piano. It's Pilar.

"¡Ay carajo!" she bellows. The garage side door slams shut, and Pili swears six ways in Spanish all the way to the living room.

Elisa spins on the bench, and I follow. "Mija, what is it?"

Pili approaches, and oh my Lord. Her face. That's very much what it is.

"I had a makeup trial run at Macy's, and look at me!" She lets out a feral growl. "I'm a reality star who got into a catfight with a rainbow and a clown car, and this, *this* is what's left."

My jaw has hit the floor because she's right. Pilar Reyes is every bad YouTube makeup tutorial I've ever seen brushed onto one person. Halloween-worthy fake lashes and glittery eye shadow. Thick cat-eye and cut-crease eyeliner—for a bride? Atrocious contour and, wait . . .

"Did esa fulana put a fake mole by your lip?" Elisa notes, seeing it, too. She reaches out—

Pilar jolts backward. "No! It might explode if you touch it!"

I've already cued up my photo app. I can't resist.

"What is this shit? You're going to show Lila, aren't you?" One arm wings over her hip. "Because su hermana is a Bratz doll?"

A giggle bubbles up at the corner of my mouth. "I most certainly am."

"Ay, qué cosa más grande." Elisa shakes her head. "This disaster will wash off, you will put on some Pond's, and we will find you a new makeup person."

"Already done. The freelance artist who did Tiffany for her wedding. She took one look at my selfie and penciled me in." Pili flinches like she's only seeing her mother and me for the first time. "What's going on here?" She picks up the new photo from her bridesmaid lunch. Finally cracks a smile.

Elisa tips her head onto mine. "We are just having a little time together, remembering our mothers." A pink rose blooms across her face. "Óiganme, I brought home some chocolate cake with raspberry-and-cream filling. I was going to serve it after dinner, but . . . eh. Let's have it now?"

The three of us decide that sounds brilliant. Elisa fetches three plates heaping with berries and cream and pillowy, soft cake. And we do something both our mothers would've probably frowned upon. Pili drags over a side chair, and we eat right there at the piano. We descend into gossip and silly stories. There's me, smearing whipped cream on Pili's cheek because why not at this point?

We never do play a recording of "Clair de Lune." It's not that I forget. In fact, it hums along in the back of my mind on this wooden piano bench. Rising above the faint raindrop melody, there's cake and laughter and time. Like a new song.

Later Pili washes the bad face away and goes out for drinks with a friend. Elisa sticks close to me in a non-hovering way that only deepens when Alan comes home, primed to fix the wobbly pantry door that's been irritating his wife for days. Once the toolbox is out, though, he checks every loose cabinet and anything else that might be even remotely off in the steamy, fragrant space. Said wife and I team up to prepare the dinner we've only slightly ruined by eating dessert first.

"Ay." The single word from Alan comes as he adjusts the volume on the kitchen TV. I hadn't been paying attention to the telenovela episode the couple's had streaming while we cook up picadillo, arroz blanco, and tostones. But now I'm rapt as a National Hurricane Center emergency warning rolls across the screen.

Hurricane Jessica expected to make landfall early next

week. Jessica originated as a tropical wave off the west coast of Africa. . . .

A newscaster adds more information, that the storm is due to hit Florida sometime next Monday—a week from today.

Elisa steps up. "Your Vizcaya shoot should be fine on Saturday."

Vizcaya—right. I hadn't forgotten so much as let it drift during my afternoon with the Reyes women. My gaze narrows over the TV. "It won't be all rainy and windy?"

"Likely no, but the tides will change. You'll see," Alan says. "One day it's clear; the next we're in a cyclone. Many ignore the warnings and are fooled by the calm weather." The telenovela program returns midscene. "We always prepare, and we'll keep a close watch on the surge. Don't worry."

I find some calm—enough—trying to believe him as he drags the toolbox into the garage. As I return to my frying pan, my phone buzzes.

"Siempre el tiki," Elisa quips, rolling her eyes with amusement. She hands over my mobile and takes my place at the stove. "When I was your age, boys had to call on the wall phone, and I had to stretch the cord all the way from la cocina into my room."

"Why do you assume it's a boy?" I retort, and open the lock screen, scanning. My wide eye snap makes her dissolve into a knowing chortle because not one but two boys have logged texts into my message screen.

Gordon—*Gordon*—had called earlier, which I missed. He'd then texted, which I also missed.

Gordon: Kelly contacted me through Matteo about Saturday. Bloody storm should hold. Thoughts?

Perplexed, I switch to Baz's text screen and hope for some explanation.

Baz: Hey, Kelly said she asked Gordon to pose with you Sat at Vizcaya. Has a new idea

Um, wow. So much wow. I switch back to Gordon.

Me: Just saw

Gordon: Which part? The hurricane or the photo shoot?

Me: Both?

Gordon: Matteo said it should be clear, and I'm to be dressed up. I've heard I'm best in some sort of costume. But it's up to you if you want me there. I need to tell Kelly now, so she has enough time to sort out my kit

Something is not right, and by something, I mean us. But Gordon did reach out. And while I have loads to say to him, I don't have a way into those words right now. Maybe we both could do with a little costuming.

Me: Tell her yes. Let's do it

TWENTY-ONE

"I'm already beat, and we haven't shot a thing," Kelly says over a huff.

It's just before dusk on photo-shoot Saturday, and while Hurricane Jessica is still due in on Monday, she's cooperating today. My outfit is another matter.

The Acosta sisters work to stuff my manicured self into their father's SUV. The struggle is due to the fact that I'm not wearing a gown; I'm wearing a theater production. A multi-layered confection in frosty blue organza with a train as long as Pilar's.

Underneath, my insides are swirling in a mild anticipatory fizz. Gordy and I still haven't texted anything more than basics, and nothing during our jam-packed makeover sessions with Leonie. Originally, I thought a little stage scenery would help pad our reunion. But I didn't think long enough over the fact that there would be witnesses. Key witnesses, which sends my stomach into a nosedive.

Kelly leans in the cab to click my seat belt. "Sorry your look is so major. I need more drama and, you know, extra in my portfolio."

My door shuts. Extra, meet Flora.

"What about Gordon?" I ask after Kelly pulls the SUV away. Gordon's been holed up at Baz's after driving in from the Keys this morning. "No hints from that one."

"Your bro's owning his look," Leonie says. "Now Baz wants a suit like that for himself."

"Totally. He already contacted my sponsor," Kelly muses. "Watch him blow his next paycheck." I catch the flutter of her lashes in the rearview mirror. The bit corner of her lip. She averts her gaze when our eyes meet, and I don't know what's real in this ruse anymore. Random scenes from the beach club pop up in all directions. The flirting and fakery, the terrace—I cough out a muffled noise of frustration and beg my mind to quit.

"So, yeah, I wasn't wrong picking Gordon," Kelly adds. "He let me put him in whatever I wanted, and I think his look came out perfect. I made him change after the final check because the guys had time left for video games."

Baz and Gordon, the budding bromance, part two. Setting: Miami, land of stranger things.

My personal awkwardness aside, I'm convinced Miami is also home to some of the most beautiful corners of the world. Kelly turns onto the Vizcaya grounds, and I'm instantly transported into an early-twentieth-century ode to Italian Renaissance architecture set in a verdant forest.

"God, the pictures lie" drops out of my mouth.

"That's why we're here," Leonie says.

A wide roundabout is as far as we can travel by SUV. The villa entrance looms behind a symmetrical maze of hedgerows and marble pillars. As a guard approaches, Kelly checks her phone. "The guys already parked, and they're coming over now. We'll keep you in the AC as long as we can." She rolls down the window and flashes a digital permit.

The uniformed attendant points ahead. "You can unload here, and you have two hours past closing."

The sisters dart around to the back to pull out several gear bags, and I get a double glimpse of nineteen-year-old male in the distance. Gordon and Baz. Baz and Gordon. A duo of unlikely blokes, chuckling as they stroll around a pillar topped with a lion's head. I don't know where to look first; my heart is a thunderous machine when they realize I'm here. When they slow and slightly drift apart, squinting into the tinted window glass.

In a whoosh of heat, Kelly opens my door. She and Leonie gather up the trailing dress fabric and help me from the cab. They loop my train around my arm, imploring me to keep the delicate hem off the ground. My feet, clad in lent Valentino heels, find solid pavement. I'm staring at the pointy toes, afraid to look up and spill too much. Or spill the wrong emotion to the wrong guy in front of the wrong audience.

Kelly tosses Leonie the keys to park the SUV. "¿Qué bolá?" she says, signaling Baz. "If you try to kiss or even touch my model, it's your funeral. My photos will be perfect, ¿entiendes?"

This throws a brick into my nervous little bubble, and I lift my head.

"Don't worry, I'll admire her from a safe distance," Baz says.

I cast him a quick smile and shoot out a flappy wave. He's dressed like the girls in simple black.

And yes, Gordy is right there, marking the perimeter of my vision. Time moves at half speed as I get my first good look at him. And holy wonder, what a picture he makes already. In front of this historic villa, Gordon Wallace wears Italian tailoring like another skin. Pewter-colored trousers barely graze below his anklebone, dusting over black elongated loafers. His jacket flares and curves in every right place. Fitted but not tight. And the white shirt and slightly deeper-charcoal tie are both clean and modern.

"I won't touch her, either," Gordon quips with just enough gray to make me wonder if he's wearing a costume on the inside, too. I meet his eyes, searching for the us we know in this foreign place.

"Oh yes, you will," Kelly says, sending my pulse skittering. "*That's* why we're here."

Baz flashes me a cheeky, amused look I can't decipher and runs over to assist with Kelly's gear. They divide up the bags, likely discussing photography matters I should probably observe. If I weren't total mush.

Complicated, complicated, complicated is the new song in my head as Gordon strides my way. (How I kissed Baz, and he left me with an open invitation. How last weekend Gordon pulled a new string inside me, unraveling old wounds. And I pulled back.)

"Hiya. Didn't think you'd turn up quite like *this*," Gordon says, immediately blanching, but too late to stop my face from twisting up quizzically. He juts out his hands. "No, fuck—that came out all wrong."

I'd cross my arms, but this *train*. "Really?" I deadpan, my gaze sharpening. "Because I was going to say the same about you."

He snaps into a mock glare, stepping up close to raise the wager. "Not bad for a couple of—"

"Yeah, yeah. Hampshire rug rats." I shrug. "You'll do."

He's unmoving, but his eyes are twin candle flames. "You as well, Flora."

Flora, not Squiggs.

"Damn, you two! I haven't even given you my photo story yet," Kelly barks into our moment. We break apart, and I find Baz, loaded down with gear, pivoting out of a long stare. He strides up to Kelly, and they motion for us to follow down a sculpture-dotted walkway.

"What's a photo story?" Gordon asks. "And do you need help with . . . that?"

"Oh, you mean my comet tail?"

"I was thinking of calling it your procession of adoring fans, the fabric edition." He silences his phone and stows it. "I'm quite sure Kelly won't fancy any barking-dog notifications disrupting her shoot."

I laugh at both points, and he follows without a hint of awkwardness—for once in forever. It feels like a Miami oasis. "A photo story is like a mood script for the shoot," I tell him.

On the walk to the first location, we learn ours. We're to play a star-crossed couple that's slipped away from a ball inside the villa. The garden feels as old as this tale, leafy and dewy with birdsong and moss-covered stone and coral-reef matter.

"Stand here and hold the bars like this, please," Kelly directs as she positions me at the threshold of a massive gate with floral ironwork. Leonie unfurls the train behind me. "Pretend you're sneaking out to meet someone."

Baz has the reflector ready as I flash my strapless, pale blue bodice to the camera, its delicate folds pleating from bust to hip before the skirt expands. *Click, click, click.* I hear it a dozen times. Along with cue after cue.

Soon she places Gordon on the other side of the gate. As directed, I reach toward him longingly. *Click.* For the next series, I lay one hand on his shoulder as he turns his cheek into my touch.

"Okay there, Squiggs?" he whispers between shots.

"Yeah. This is just . . . different."

Kelly waves her arm. "Gordon, grab Flora like you've been waiting all night for her to find you. I want to see lust. Pull her through the gate. Oye, Leonie, her clip."

"Oh, she wants *lust*, does she?" He winks at me and plants one hand around my waist, drawing me in. "Hi there."

"Hi," I manage, feeling the train being swooped around our front as Leonie fixes the sparkly barrette above my ear. Gordon was right earlier; I've never turned up in front of him in such finery. And my hair's never been asked to do this. To cluster into a tight bouquet at the side of my head in a modern flamenco style. And *I've* never been asked to stare so long at Gordon, in a way that would be downright rude outside a photo session. Held in pose after pose, I discover more than handfuls of easily missed details. I realize how much everything *works*—the way a thousand things construct the unique shape of him. A burst of self-consciousness comes with the next shot stream. Gordon's been staring back just as deeply. What shape do I make, and has any of it changed?

I get no answers. Kelly's "Okay, perfect, break!" wedges us apart, and Baz moves us into a lush part of the garden with weathered staircases and reflecting pools. Here we're looser, with more space to make the poses feel grand and cinematic, straight out of a story. That's fitting, because one keeps reeling inside of me—but it's my own story, not a stage version with a costume dress. Not a fake-date ploy or a scene where I've cropped out all the bad and difficult parts. A real picture that fits into a future. And maybe a dream.

My wish remains, pealing softly as we set off for the next stunning vista. The crew springs ahead to set up, and Gordon and I are told to come slowly so we don't get too tired or hot. Leonie gives me flip-flops for the walk, and Gordon gathers up my train this time.

"I came here with my family years ago," he says. "But it's even more incredible now that I've learned about the architectural history of the region."

"It's like a tropical fairyland," I say in wonder. "I want to come back."

When he doesn't respond, I turn. Find him staring into the damp thicket. "I said it wrong, last Sunday," he whispers. "My explanation came out badly."

I shiver and swallow hard; I guess we're doing this. "It wasn't all you. Sometimes I *hear* things badly."

"Hmm" vibrates between his lips. "I usually have chips to help with that. Pub Subs didn't cut it."

I hold a secret smile as we follow the others and their dark shadow of photography black. "Guess not."

Gordon's pulling me along by the train, not too fast, but it's strange being attached to him in this way. "I wish I'd said that I noticed the way you reacted to classmates and teachers," he starts. "And I wanted to be something more usual for you. Sometimes we treat grieving people with too much care. We're afraid to make them feel . . ."

"Human. Like they're more than their grief."

"Yeah. So I wasn't pranking you and being a jokester and pretending to be your friend just to be funny. I did it *because* I thought I was your friend."

"You were. And I'm sorry." I look up at him, chin crumpling. "You were the one person who didn't treat me like glass. You seemed to know when I needed to be a kid. To muck around even when I was being rotten and obstinate. You've never stopped, all these years."

"Seeing through *your* muck?"

"Seeing me," I say, and the truth of it runs me over and all the way through. *Seeing the real me.* It's from the center of this feeling that I make a choice and a change, so much greater than the shift from jeans to ball gowns. "I've had to keep a secret. I'm not dating Baz the way I let on. It's an agreement to help him with a business and family matter. There's loads more behind it."

Rarely do I outtrick Gordon. Our steps have slowed, and his face flips through a pile of expressions. Shock, amusement, awe, and a tinge of something bent and blue that I can't name. But then he guffaws, tossing his head back. "Wow." Two beats pass, then "Bloody hell, you had me fooled."

"I learned from the best," I say through a gritty laugh. "Keeping it hidden was about staying true to my promise to Baz. I mean, this is something I would've told you—before— without thinking. But I felt like I couldn't. Now things are

different, though. Maybe *I'm* different, and I'm not okay with this one promise making me feel entirely untrue to myself. Not anymore."

"Hey, we're ready up here!" Kelly calls, and apprehension rolls down my back.

I come to a halt. "Wait. Please don't let on that you know. Baz is shooting Pilar's wedding, and he's been so cool with helping me with photography. That part's true."

Gordon raises a palm. "I swear on your cat aversion, and my LEGO Death Star model, and all my house drawings—"

"Apúrense, beautiful people!" Kelly calls again.

I exhale and snap my focus back to the shoot. Baz and Leonie are setting up a tripod just ahead. And I realize I've been ambling along the north face of the villa without truly seeing much of anything. Gordon loops the train back over my arm, and the remnants of my hasty reveal scatter into complete awe at what's in front of us.

"This has always been my favorite part of the estate," Gordon says. We're at the wide expanse of Biscayne Bay, what is essentially Vizcaya's backyard. A massive shipwreck-like structure juts across the water, opposite a dilapidated dock.

"What is that thing?"

"A limestone barge that served as a breakwater for the villa and the boats that docked here," Gordon explains. We stroll forward onto a landing tiled with a massive sun motif while Kelly and Baz take test shots along the water. They scour the best angles as the sun drops westward behind the mansion.

"Oh look!" Dozens of mermaid statues are carved in crumbling stone along the barge, as if they're studying their reflections in the water.

"Yes, they're much loved in these parts. There's talk of restoring them," Gordon says. "But some feel they're best left alone to wear." He pauses to look over my shoulder. "Either way you'll be photographed in front of them tonight."

"And so will you."

And so will we.

"For this scene, I want a classic dance feel," Kelly declares as Baz arranges Gordon and me on the sun-motif plaza. Which is not at all awkward. "Pretend you're alone but hearing the music from the ball inside the villa."

Baz switches to taking test shots while Leonie rushes over with her tools, fixing my red lippy and fastening up my train, working a bit of product into the wilt of Gordon's hair. "Shiny," the teen makeup artist says, surveying her work.

After she backs away, Gordon grabs my hand, elevating us in a formal waltz pose. "We've never danced, you know?"

This can't be true. "But we've been to a hundred—"

"Not clubbing," he says. "We've never slow-danced."

Again, his memory shows up better than mine. "Well. Did you envision our first dance dressed in clothes we can't afford, acting for the camera?"

"No," he says on a stilted laugh. "But if you think about it, that's rather on-brand for me." He shakes his head. "For us."

On-brand? I don't get the chance to question him before Kelly calls for us to move. At first my mind is spinning more than my feet. My head scrambled under this elegant hairdo.

"Come on, Squiggs," Gordon says, bringing me in. "We can do this." A faraway longing clings to the words. But he sets off with purpose to the sound of the sea. I drop my eyelids and let him lead. Feel Leonie unfurling my skirt and ducking out of the shot. And with the air swirling into the fabric, over my bare legs, I'm dancing with my oldest friend.

"Your dress is flying," Gordon says into my ear. For some shots, he pulls me against his chest in a way that eclipses all the times we've hugged.

Other cues have him stretching me long at the end of his arm. I envy the freedom we make and want to steal some from this borrowed gown. But beneath every sway and turn, I keep wondering what he meant by acting being our brand. And why did it not sound like part of a comedy show script, like usual? Why didn't it feel that way?

"Amazing. That dress did its thing," Kelly says, squealing over the shots with Baz. "Wait until you see this magic."

We halt. The secret music of the sea and forest cuts away.

"Last stop is right next door. The teahouse," Baz says, packing up.

Panting from the brisk moves, Gordon and I walk toward the adjacent gazebo. We step from an ornate footbridge into a tiny domed palace. It's lavishly windowed with a glass ceiling, so the light plays along the mosaic floor, and the sides flare open to the wind and the water lapping below. The current moves with only slight restlessness; it's hard to believe a major storm is two days away.

"Hello, most beautiful place I've ever been," I whisper.

"I know. And you're dressed to match," Gordon says.

Leonie comes up, breaking into our gawking. "This is the end, so we're going to mess up your looks a bit. That okay?"

"Er, I guess. Sure," I say after silently conferring with Gordon.

Leonie grins. "Awesome. Gordon, you're gonna love me right now. Lose that tie."

It begins like this, the undoing of our outfits along with our story. And in five minutes Gordon is down to shirtsleeves, polished cotton rolled to his elbows. And then it's my turn. With a few yanks my hair tumbles.

I catch Baz's stare as I shake out the waves. His shy smile seems knowing in the strangest way. A little too on display, I feel myself flushing as red as my lips.

Kelly steps up. She's switched cameras, and I'd ask something professional about that if I weren't down to brain dust. "You two have sold everything so far. But this is gonna go beyond lust. I want it *all*, so pretend we're not here."

Beyond lust, Gordon mouths. We share a private giggle before we step into place.

This scene starts with me, hair rioting in the middle of the gazebo, arms extended, my train rustling up and wild. Then Gordon moves in and shakes the hem like he's launching a lover into the wind, our eyes locked.

"Gah! Amazing," Kelly calls, crouching low on the tile flooring. "Now move up against the wall, Gordon, and you follow, Flora. Just sell it."

Tucked between the tall, open alcoves, Gordon leans against the paneled wall. "Here," he says, winding my arms around his neck. Open palms press against the bare skin of my back.

With each click, we lean in until we're close enough to count each other's eyelashes, and our mouths hang slack in an almost kiss, giving the camera an unfulfilled ache. He's all minty breath and clean sweat, and I've never touched him quite like this. Never felt his hands on places that have only been grabbed and gripped against dingy alley walls. Not this way, like something beautiful.

I try to forget we're being watched as I get comfortable with the swell of his biceps and pecs. Learn the strong cording of his neck. My skin ignites as he fists pieces of my gown against my thigh, then bends me toward the ground in a dramatic dip.

The last shots have Gordon leaning against an ornate railing, bracing me between his legs and facing the camera smugly. The sea teases behind us, and his arms clamp around my waist, my hand rising to cup his cheek. I close myself up until my senses are down to two—the ones about feeling and fitting somewhere. Fitting right here, dizzy and daydreamed until new parts of me unwind. Tingling, dreaming parts. The kind that whisper, *What if he asked again, right now? Those sweet and shy things at the inn? Would you push him out another door, or would you pull and take and . . . ?*

And would I dare?

The question twists a hundred ways as minutes, or more, tick by. I don't become fully aware again until the zip of canvas bags and muffled words fill the teahouse.

"That, amigos, is a wrap. And I mean, *wow*."

I find I'm still cocooned in a delicious fog, emerging slowly into the sound of the others debriefing and the rushing thrum of my pulse.

"You killed it, Kell," Baz says. "But I'm still right about that garden gate shot."

"In your dreams, Marín," she retorts, and tosses him a reflector like a giant Frisbee.

By some miracle or curse, Gordon and I are left alone in the teahouse. Leonie and Baz run to get the cars. Kelly's the last to leave, toting out gear and telling us we have fifteen minutes to chill and enjoy the scenery without working.

Gordon leaves the suit jacket off. Air floats into the gazebo, fresh and wonderful, and twilight rises in an inky shroud over the bay. "I guess we sold it. The story," he says. "Kelly bought our acting."

He was only acting. Was I only acting, or . . . ? I decide to test another kind of water. "Besides dancing, we did a lot of things we've never done."

A smirk. "You mean me feeling you up?" And curving his mouth into the swell of my neck. And sweeping his lips across my ear, *and* . . .

I turn. We meet. Smile.

"It was good fun," he goes on. "It's the coolest stage we've ever had, this place. And I bet we'll fool anyone with those shots. As much as you fooled me with your, er, agreement."

Something inside me freezes. "So it was *all* fake? A game between mates?" Even after he knew my truth?

Gordon snuffs out a breath, peering just over my shoulder. "It's what we do best."

"That's what you meant before about us having a brand." A thousand more questions blur my vision.

"Flora." He cups a hand on my shoulder; it's the coldest touch I've felt in hours. "You know that bit at Coral Castle, weeks ago? The Repentance Corner?" he starts, and waits for my nod. "I told you that I'd found a way for us to be friends again after what happened at the inn. I realized I needed to get over it. Seeing you with Baz helped that along."

"And now?" I ask, broadsided by the tinge of hope slotted into my words.

He shrugs, his forehead pinched. "Now I feel it was probably for the best, even if it was really hard. And, look, earlier you said I've always been able to see you."

"You have," I tell him. "You do."

"Good. But I realize I want the same. I deserve the same. I want to be seen, too. All of me."

"And I don't? See you?"

His mouth curves but only halfway. "It's not so simple. I've realized I'm one specific Gordon to you. And I may be the absolute best at being that guy. But through everything, all our time here, you mostly want to be around good ol' entertaining, funny me. Prankster me." He tugs the cuff of his dress shirt. "Costumed me. That's always what you notice first, and what you seem to need most. Of course, that's partly my doing. I'm the one who's been throwing rats in your window, and golden owls, and . . . God knows I have a million more examples."

"But?" I ask as my personal storm arises, well before the one forecasted on the news. This one is sad and silent, plucking at the seams underneath my skin in a way I can't explain.

"But," he says, "sometimes even a million doesn't add up to enough."

Not enough, not enough, not enough rings through my head. The limestone mermaids hear it, too, and sing a taunting rhyme as they crumble into the sea. And in front of this window, in front of my oldest friend and every Gordon he's ever been, I rip all the way through.

TWENTY-TWO

Different. It's bloody *different* this time. I admit this to myself the next day, well after I thought I'd be done feeling odd and squiffy. Typically, when I'm caught in some sort of rage, my episodes don't last long. My temper usually blows through my little world, then slows to a calm where I pick myself up and carry on.

But this time it's different.

I raise my chin defiantly, glaring at no one but myself. At the end of yesterday's shoot, I didn't yell at Gordy or cry. I didn't pick up my skirts and strut away, bringing all that drama of the shoot to life.

But I could have, because how dare he? I don't see Gordon? Now that's a load of rubbish. And I should have told him so, but I was just too . . . *It* was just too . . .

A tear leaks through, and I despise it. Knuckle it away. How easy and cathartic it would be to jerk open my window, yelling to all of West Dade, "Hiya, I'm Flora Maxwell, and I'm knocked for six, and I don't know what this is!"

This mantra repeats inside my head as real knocking

sounds through my door. I recoil and try to get myself together. "Yeah. Come in." Even my voice is scratched.

It's Alan. He waves himself through, saying, "Channy from next door is going to help me board up your window because we have not had the ones from the back bedrooms replaced yet. I didn't want you to be frightened by the noise."

I find a smile. "Thank you. I've never been through anything like this before."

"But we have, many times."

True. And the whole family's been working like bees for Jessica's landfall tomorrow.

"You called your papi, claro? And Lila has been through dozens of these. She will keep your family calm."

I nod. "I told them I was with hurricane experts."

Alan backs away, shaking his head over a chuckle. "I wouldn't tease the sky with that kind of talk, Florecita. We can prepare, but ultimately, Jessica has the power, not us."

Alone again, I perch on the edge of my bed, gripping on to the word *power* as Vizcaya comes around again, our final moments like blown-up photos in my mind. First the one in the gazebo when Baz texted to say our cars were ready at the roundabout. And a silent garden walk back that felt like a trample into a thorny thicket that time around, and Gordon on the phone leaving a message for Cate.

No, the hurricane isn't here yet, Mum, and I promise I'll be safe.

Then the awkward goodbye with too many eyes watching, with our brief hug and his "You really did look so lovely, Flora," before he decided to head back to Key West to avoid any motorway gridlock the next morning.

And above it all, the roaring headache I didn't have to fake to exile myself again in my room. The one that was still there at dawn along with all the blistering feelings that hadn't passed on.

This time it's different.

There's knocking again, but it comes like an echo of itself, faint and chalky. I slip back down, down, and away to wherever I was—

"Óyeme, Florecita, I know you're in there."

One eye wiggles open, and I barely detect that some words were said.

"Hey! Seriously?" *Knock, knock, knock.* "Even *you* are not so much of a flighty pajarito as to run off to wherever with Jessica coming!"

Snap! Two things ring clear: it's Pilar, and I must've dozed off. "Erhggmm yes hi wait" comes out wrapped in cotton. I rub my face, swinging around, and—it's bloody half past five in the evening?

Post-nap legs fumble to the door. "Whatzit?" I eke out to Pili's annoying springy form dressed in joggers and a tank top.

"Bueno, sleepyhead," she says. "I'm glad you're enjoying the calm before the storm. Pun intended."

Calm? Is that what this is?

She ignores my blank face and hands over a large unmarked shopping bag. "I'm going to Ryan's now. But Marta found this in my office at La Paloma this morning."

I know the sender before I even read the hangtag. Uniform block letters belong to someone trained in blueprints and precision. He must've stopped by the bakery for food for the drive back.

For Flora

"Gordon—probably a storm care package," I muse, noting the weighty heft to the sack. Did he set me up with a dozen Pub Subs? "Hey, how relieved are we that Jessica didn't wait a couple weeks and ruin your wedding weekend?"

"Oh, that was not happening, amiga. I would've shot up to the sky and kicked her out myself," she says, and I believe her. "We'll lose power, but I'll be back as soon as the roads are clear. You'll be safe with the best parents in Miami." She kisses my cheek and braces my shoulders. "Okay?"

"Okay enough," I say as she leaves. A quick flip of the wall switch fills my dim room with light, curiosity and dread twining inside my belly. I plunk myself and my mysterious gift on the bed, and I'm stuck staring at the bag.

Seriously? It's from your oldest friend, and you're not a coward.

Just open it!

I finally go in, yanking out a large square housed in Bubble Wrap. Realization erupts, and I'm trembling by the time I reach for scissors and neatly slice through the wrapping.

Gordon drew me a house.

My head fills with unshed tears—not just because of the fact that, after all these years, I finally have a Gordon Wallace original, but because he remembered. Gordon remembered every word I said three years ago at a celebration dinner at Bridge Street Tavern. Lila was there, and all our friends. We were talking about Gordon's first part-time job at an architecture firm, and I said that Winchester could do with some original homes beyond our classic styles. I told everyone my fantastical specs for such a house. It occurs to me now that it's one thing I actually did dream about. And Gordon remembered every detail.

Air freezes inside my lungs as I witness what Gordon never forgot. *Flora's House* is scripted at the top corner. And on the large parchment square, he's drawn the most whimsical, adorable structure I've ever seen. Flora's House is a fever dream of color and perfect oddity.

The three-story Victorian is tinted in a gradient of purple shades, straight from my imagination. Black gingerbread moldings trim the house in minute detail, flourishes curling everywhere. And he added to my design, too, with a walkway done in pink jester diamonds, leading up to a magenta door. The porch bursts with wisteria vines. And on that porch, there's something that makes my heart beat so hard against my ribs, I can't breathe around it. My magic cat sits on a doormat. She's black with a perfect surprised white circle around her mouth, waiting for her owner to come home. *For me to come home.*

I give a messy sob when I spy another secret. From the top gabled window peeks the little tan dog I wanted to adopt from Win-Fest. Flora's House gets all the pets. I can't stop looking—Easter-egg clues are everywhere. A gray mouse pokes out from rosebushes. A brown owl and black crow perch together on a blooming cherry blossom tree at the side lot, like friends.

At once, I am more seen in this drawing than I could ever be in any photograph. I'm more remembered than any three-year-old memory that still lives. And I'm celebrated—every pink-jester, purple-shaded part of me.

Shaking, I reach for my phone and start texting.

Me: Gordon, I just got my house. And I love it too much

After long minutes, there's no ding of anything incoming, no three dots pending.

I switch to calling, waiting for eons until the connection goes to voicemail. Where is he? Why isn't he answering? "Gordon!" I spurt after the beep. "Read your bloody text. Oh, and thank you. Christ, thank you so very much, and ring back, okay? Please just ring me back."

I toss my phone, trading it for the Flora's House drawing, where Gordon has put so many details of me. But no matter how hard I stare at this sweet and wonderful gift, the image stays flat and one-dimensional. Nothing lives behind the windows. No family or friends, no mother at her piano. The pink door leads to nowhere, and certainly not to any good future. I finally got my coveted picture from my oldest friend. But as for anything else, I'm—

A whimper drops from my mouth. *You're too late* might as well be tagged across the structure in graffiti red.

In trying to protect Gordon's heart from me, I pushed it away . . . from me. And just when a change sparks there, when it's different and we're dancing and I'm daring to *feel*, he said I was right to press stop. To keep us how we've always been. We're only jokes and pranks and games. Of all the house styles depicted in his room, we're the one carnival fun house. He thinks I don't see all of him well enough to be more to him. To be enough for him. Just when I find trust in myself, and my truth, he loses it. I'm too bloody late for Gordon Wallace.

His drawing is full of memory and friendship but makes a piss-poor hugger. A shoddy object to hold.

No one is here for real. Alone is the way I tackle most everything, but I am no longer enough for myself and my good company. The fear and abyss of that send me grabbing and reaching for anyone I can find. Lila's asleep in England. Pili's gone.

There's only one person left. I reach for my phone again and click on Baz's text stream.

Me: Hi from almost Jessica. You good?

The small talk is as fake and glossy as our dating scheme, but it's something. Immediately, three dots pop up. Even the promise of connection sends a ripple of calm, head to toe.

Baz: Hey you. Yeah, Papi and I prepped the yard and a hundred other things. Bring it, Jessica. How about you and Casa Reyes? Doing okay?

Me: Sure. Yeah

I type this automatically, so used to those throwaway words. Another message comes through, the bitter aftertaste of my lie still coating my tongue.

Baz: Nice. I'm working on some editing. Anyway, be safe and we'll talk after everything clears

Gordon's Vizcaya parting words flash through my head again, swirling over everything, and my fingers move ahead of my brain.

Me: Baz, wait, please

Baz: Still here

I will him to stay on my screen, to simply keep me company.

Me: What's your favorite photo you've ever shot?

Baz: Why does that sound like asking what my favorite color is? Or if I prefer chocolate or vanilla?

God, he's right. Before I apologize like any good Brit, the phone vibrates again.

Baz: Fine, it's a fair question (also, chocolate, duh)

Baz: Would have to be the photo of you on the stool at the studio

Me: You are a bold-faced liar

But I laugh, and my pulse is skittering. And that's more than something. More talking dots appear.

Baz: Okay seriously, there's one of my sister on the beach, her head in her hands. And everything lined up perfectly—the light, the sky, her pose, her dress. It's on my Instagram

Me: Sounds like it comes with a story. I could use one

Ringing makes me flinch until I get that Baz isn't texting back. He's calling back.

"Baz?"

"Hey." He waits a beat. "So you said you're okay."

"I did."

"Why am I thinking that's not true?"

"Are you sure you're not trying out a minor in psychology or text interpretation?" I ask pointedly.

An exasperated sigh cuts through like static. "Flora."

"Baz."

"You're not okay, are you?"

My heart takes a shuddering breath, makes a shift, and where there's usually fight and storm, there is only a weariness that's so much deeper than any poor excuse. "Not exactly."

TWENTY-THREE

Not exactly.

That's all it took. Two honest words to Baz across the telephone line. It's the reason I'm standing in the guest room of the Maríns' Coral Gables home with an overnight duffel.

From somewhere below, the garage door whirs closed, and Baz's gray Dunks clomp onto the floor tile. "The *Clueless* Jeep is tucked in tight!" he calls. Then, closer, after he's trotted up the wrought-iron staircase, I hear, "Hey, you practicing your turned-into-stone pose?"

I pivot as Baz crosses the threshold. "More like something from my *Total Disbelief* series," I tell him. The Mediterranean-style house is slightly less than massive, and I'm counting on getting lost multiple times. "You're *sure* I'm no bother?"

He sidles up. All his parts are so close—the unshaven jaw, the rain-dotted navy sweatshirt he threw on before coming to get me. "Listen. You were on the line when I asked Mami and Papi."

"Yes, but—"

"Flora." He arcs his hand wide. "We have more than enough

room, and Mami is always happier with someone to dote on. I'm the worst at letting her, and my sister is in sunny Florence."

"Right. Okay." I've tried to get better at accepting nice things, but old habits love to pop through during stressful times. Like now, and a few minutes ago when the early dusk sky was angry and menacing out the Jeep window. "Thank you. I know I keep saying it, but it's already so horrible out there, and you made the drive anyway."

"Nah. I should've checked in. I mean, it's your first hurricane." Peat-brown eyes draw me in. "I was trying to catch up and help around here. And the Vizcaya shoot was, you know, busy. And long."

And so many things he doesn't even know about yet. Emotions. Shifts. The everywhere feel of Gordon against my skin, then the finger-snap loss of him. Through all of it, I'd sensed the heaviness of Baz's gaze as more than Kelly's sharp-eyed assistant. As if he were—I don't know—trying to solve a Flora-shaped puzzle? Perhaps his keen sense of disturbance came from the same spot that made him know I was not, in fact, okay today.

When my tongue stays put, he steps closer. "I thought the Reyeses would've put up more of a fight at me whisking you away, no?" His brow line jerks upward on an invisible fishhook. "At una mujercita staying in close quarters with this rakish dude she's been hanging with."

"Rakish, are you?"

"It's been alluded to in social media comments. And yes, I read them."

"Interesting." I tip my hand. "We're calling *this* home close quarters?"

He rolls his eyes. "You know what I meant."

I do. This bedroom is twice as large as my usual one and set with sleek pale wood furniture and a crisp white comforter. "Everything's perfect. But don't think I didn't have to answer twenty questions before you got there."

"Only twenty? You got off easy on the scale of Cuban Mami Questioning."

"Oi, I know," I say over a dry chuckle. "It was mostly about me having a separate room and you not sneaking into mine after we lose power. And then Alan brought up the fact that your home is probably equipped with better generators and those fancy impact windows and all that. He looked at Elisa and was like, 'Bueno, querida, it's Casa Marín. Why not?'"

He laughs at my manufactured lilt. "True, all of it."

"But it got worse," I add, my hands flailing. "They figured out that with both Pili and me gone, they'd truly be *alone*. In the dark. All night long. And thank God you showed up right then because eww!"

"That's horrifying." He looks left, then right, and waits for a solid three count. Shrugs. "About the other *thing*. I'll leave any sneaking down the hall to you."

I let out a single nervous laugh, belly dropping. The sting of Gordon's rejection wars with the nearness of Baz, two steps away with midnight invitations and sparkling eyes. But is he only joking? My mouth wiggles into a smile any clown could've drawn on. "Er, right, then."

A metallic crash cuts through the room and makes zero percent of anything better.

"What's going on?"

"Probably a patio umbrella or something a neighbor forgot

to stow away," he says, and strides to the window.

I follow. The rain has gathered force, streaming in a trembling sheet. He picked me up just in time, and my heart thumps at how close it was. "England is, like, the birthplace of weather, but Winchester hasn't seen anything like this. The closest was Hurricane Ophelia when I was younger, but that mostly hit Ireland and Scotland. We only got minor showers."

Baz says nothing, but his face pulls sideways.

"What?"

"That's not really Jessica. Not yet. Like in a wedding, if Jessica is the bride"—he pauses to point at the drenched and blustery world outside—"this is like the flower girl and las damas de honor and all the things that come down the aisle before her."

God, this is just the prelude? "Well, that's just lovely."

"¡Niños!" Iva Marín calls from the ground floor.

I follow Baz's nod toward the door but trot back briefly to fish a paper from my duffel.

"¡Vengan acá!"

This time it's Baz's father. As we shuffle down to the kitchen, it's more than a little weird to see Sebastián Marín, the photographer fawned over by a fleet of assistants, bent over the great marble island with a wineglass, phone, and two backup radios. In jeans and a simple blue shirt, he's less the experimental fashion icon I'm used to, as well.

Seeing us, he springs up. "Flora, welcome, and I hope you feel safe and comfortable here."

I barely get out so much as a "Yes, thank you" before Baz's mother darts out from a walk-in pantry with a large basket. She rests it on the island and busses both my cheeks, her fragrance lingering. Not the legendary Royal Violets scent many Cuban mothers and grandmothers still cherish. Hers is spicy warm with a hint of bergamot.

She reaches for several large water bottles and slides two over to me. "These are for your room," she says while Baz cracks open cherry Cokes and holds one out. Twenty minutes here and I'm already assured of being well hydrated.

Sebastián adjusts the volume of a small television as Jessica spins over the Atlantic, floating in and close. "Oye, Flora, there is plenty of comida. Please come down anytime you need something."

Plenty is an understatement. I scan the ample spread on the counter. Besides wrapped sandwiches, fruit overflows from baskets, and hard cheeses and cured Italian meats are neatly arranged on trays. There are energy bars and peanut butter and stuff that won't go off even if the generator fails. Alan and Elisa made similar plans, but this is another level.

"Thank you, truly. And for taking care of my broken camera, as well."

His parents smile warmly, and Baz wastes no time stuffing Parmesan slices and pita crackers into his mouth, crumpling sheepishly when I catch his eye. It's so Gordon-like that I instantly turn red and traitorous as I reach for my phone. *Inbox: o. Messages: o.*

Where are you? Why aren't you responding?

Stowing the device, I realize I've creased the paper I brought for Iva into a right mess. "I got that recipe you wanted." I try to smooth it out the best I can.

Iva takes the slip, her face brightening as she reads. "Ay, the mango mousse domes. With all the secret ingredients?"

"Yeah, it's all there, I promise." The bakery gets so many asks, Pili was hesitant to reveal it at first. But after seeing how much Baz has been helping me, she had a change of heart.

Iva's deep into the instructions. "There's a passion-fruit infusion in the sponge cake?" She looks up, musing.

I nod. "Abuela Lydia—the founder—came up with that. The La Paloma bakers still take the extra step today. Pili only asked that you don't pass it around or put it online."

Iva plants one hand over her heart. "Oh, I would never."

"No; she'll make it for her book club and pretend it was barely any work," Sebastián says, and peers at the page over his wife's shoulder.

As we snack, the Maríns track the updates cycling through on the TV screen, sipping their wine and appearing nearly unfazed. And I'm not far behind. I'm with a friend and his kind family. I'm safe and dry in a storm fortress with backup resources and three kinds of fizzy drinks on the counter. Sure, this is all new to me, but I didn't reach out to Baz earlier because I was scared of Jessica. I'm more tangled because of Flora—my enduring grief, the tension over my future, the rift with Dad and Orion, my soreness after Gordon's parting words, and the raw emotion over seeing his drawing. My heart is a cyclone, and my Miami bedroom felt too small and solitary to contain it. And while this hurricane will come and go, my life and the fight to set it straight will rage on.

Behind me the rain has changed, slanting in sharp angles against the glass patio doors. Between me and the water, I win this one. I'm the most slanted force of all.

A TV warning signal blares through the open kitchen, shrill and sharp. The announcer's baritone voice calls over the watery conundrum outside, snatching all our attention.

"Ay, mira," Señora Marín says.

I take in fragments.

Jessica upgraded to a category two hurricane. Landfall in six to eight hours. Projected wind speeds up to one hundred miles per hour.

Baz comes up beside me. "Wind speed determines the category of the storm, and if it changes. So here we go."

I swallow hard. The screen switches back to an announcer desk and an orange-bordered update. *Key West.* Jessica has shifted course, and the strongest part of the storm is heading right for it. Right for Key West.

"Gordon!" I shout entirely too loudly. Everyone turns from the TV to the displaced Brit behind them. I'm red and heated as I whip around toward Baz. "Gordon's staying in the Keys."

Iva says, "Isn't that your friend that you were shooting with yesterday? And from the beach club?"

I nod rapidly.

Baz holds out his hands. "Chances are he's fine. And it could all change again."

"That meteorologist is saying his area will be the hardest hit, right?" Every breath is a gulp, and sweat laces the back of my neck. All that calmness and security I'd felt minutes ago is a memory.

Baz checks the screen again. Nods solemnly. "Looks like Key West will be getting the dirty side. The worst rainbands and flood risk. But listen, stay calm, okay?" He braces my shoulders. "Just relax—"

"Don't tell me to stay calm!" I screech. From the outskirts of my vision, his parents are slack-jawed and wide-eyed, as if they've let an unhinged dolt into their home and happy hurricane watch party. It's me; I'm the dolt. "I'm sorry. I'm terribly sorry, but Gordon's never been in a storm like this of any category. And he's not in a big place like yours with all this protection. It's a flat with three other blokes, and who knows what kind of shape that building is in. And—"

"Flora," Baz says, right at my eyeline.

"He hasn't called or answered my messages."

"Maybe he's been helping others around the key. With Matteo."

"They said Cayo Hueso has already lost power," Sebastián says. "He might have everything shut off to conserve. Especially if they do not have proper generators."

Some of the fight leaks out of me, but not enough. I check the screen. Zero in on the angry gray menace that has more than a town lassoed in its rough outer bands. Jessica is coming straight for my friend. For my . . .

Iva rushes over. "Niña, why don't you go into the family room? Sit for a while and get away from the news. We will update you." She turns to her son. "Go with her. There's a puzzle we started, or you can show her the photos that Kelly sent."

This kicks me into sense and motion. "What photos? You mean from yesterday?"

"Yeah," Baz says. "Before I left to pick you up, she sent over a few from each series. She's editing and wanted my opinion on some stuff."

I draw a few breaths and beg my heart rate to slow. "Can I see?"

Fifteen minutes later I'm slack-jawed over Kelly and Leonie's Vizcaya vision, and the digital reflection of me in a gown that grew wings in the breeze. "I was there, and I still can't believe this is me." Or me like *this*, with Gordon. It only took one day, so little time, for everything to turn about. That same Gordon is gone and silent, and that breeze turned into a windstorm.

"Oh, it's you. Firsthand witness here," Baz says, curled up close to share the screen. "Check out the drama show happening in your eyes, and the way you're using your arms. So much better than when I tried to get you to pose at Papi's class."

"You mean before someone set me straight."

"Thing is, though, I didn't teach Gordon, and bro's eating up the lens," Baz says into the laptop screen.

"He's always been good on a stage." That's what Vizcaya was. The truth of it cycles through my head as I click onto another scene. There, my body snakes against Gordon on a grand terrace, his bent mouth and the cocky flare of his cheeks playing for keeps. One more swipe and we're twirling at the lip of Biscayne Bay with a mermaid audience. Then messy and pressed together in the window bay. Almost kissing, touches blazing.

"Just acting," I say, knowing it's true.

"Sure, Flora."

I clench my jaw. The one Baz held at Miami Beach, not stopping. Not faking.

Baz clicks back to the mermaid barge shot. "You didn't dance like this with me."

"At the club? That was salsa. I was trying to keep up and not trip in shitty shoes."

He leans back, hands clasped. "So when you landed on me on that balcony, you tripped for real?"

My heartbeat leaps ahead. "Baz."

"No, really," he presses. "I want to know. Did you kiss me by mistake, too?"

I heave out a sigh and want to crawl beneath the carpet.

"Humor me. You ever think of kissing me again?"

Oh God, oh bloody hell. "You're so amazing and all those Instagram groupies aren't wrong about your looks and did I mention talented and—"

"Just be honest."

"I thought about it a lot," I manage, mortified. "But I stopped there. It's so not you, though." Disappointment falls low and dark across his face and—"I knew it! I told you!" I'm pointing now. "I *told* you at the studio with Luna that every fake-dating scheme eventually turns shit! Remember?"

He nods once. "You're absolutely right. People end up getting hurt."

"Christ, Baz, I didn't mean to lead you on, really." With so many unknown and odd sensations, my remorse is painfully clear. As well as feeling like complete rubbish. "I'm so very sorry."

In a flash a tree branch cracks sharp in the wind, and Baz's face breaks into total amusement.

"Why the hell are you laughing?"

He doesn't stop. "I really had you going there. Easier than I thought."

I spring off the sofa, hand on hip. "Easier?" Dawn comes hours too early in my brain. "You mean you were just pulling my leg? Faking?"

"Completely. Call it an experiment. And turns out I was right."

I gasp, wishing I had something to pelt at him. "So that whole bit about you being all affronted over our . . ."

"You mean our one kiss that was just a cool, fun moment?"

I actually growl even though we're in total agreement. "Why not just say it was a one-and-done and we're better off as friends? Before now?"

His shoulders pop up, and everything slows a notch. "I wasn't sure before, and I was trying to gauge your true feelings." My eyes nudge him to go on. "I wanted to know if what I saw at Vizcaya was real. Because watching you was like intruding on something super private. And I was okay with it, which is a huge red flag. I want someone to look at me that way, you know? Someone I'm looking at, too."

"Oh. Well. I do hope you find that."

"Trust me. It's cool, and I'm not in any rush. But with you, now I know for sure, based on what I just saw in my kitchen. That wasn't just concern over a friend, Flora. Your heart shattered in front of all of us. Clearly, I'm not the one you want to kiss."

The fight leaks out of me. And as Jessica rolls in, my personal storm is weakened down to a puff barely enough to break a dandelion.

Baz takes my hand, drawing me back to the sofa. "You didn't lead me on, okay? I'm not the one who got hurt this summer. In our Netflix fake-dating show or anywhere else."

Not knowing whether to nod or shake my head, I stare at my socks.

"Something happened with Gordon, right?"

"Isn't this a little too weird?"

"Not if you need a friend," he says with all sincerity. "And

I don't mean someone you call a friend while secretly pining over them. Just a friend."

Air leaks out in relief, even as the hurt doubles every second along with fear and regret. "Back home, I pushed him away. I had to because I wasn't in the right mind to sort out anything, and I thought I would hurt *him*. But here, everything in my heart began to change . . . and it doesn't even matter because he realized I was right to shut him down. He thinks we aren't good for each other."

"Bullshit," Baz says.

"He told me himself, Baz. Then he left a gift that gutted me. And now I can't reach him. Key West is gonna get hit so hard, and I need him to be okay." I need *him*. "But I'm too late. I lost my chance."

"Not according to what I saw."

My eyes glaze over. "Gordon was following Kelly's cues. He was acting."

"I didn't mean the finished photos." He pulls out his phone. "Remember the test shots I took for Kelly? When I got home and looked them over, well, see for yourself."

A dozen candid snaps are on his photo app. And there's Gordon, gaze fixed over my profile as Leonie touches up my makeup. Another shows him bent against a tree, and it's his sad-Gordon face. I know that face. I let out a helpless whimper over him soft-eyed when he thought no one was looking.

I whip up toward Baz. "Okay, fine. So he's feeling *things* here, but he told me himself it's not enough. It's like he's trying to *un*-feel. He's trying to let me go because he thinks I only see him in a certain way, as a funny prankster clown. He thinks I don't need or value him deeply enough."

"Did you tell *him* any of this?"

"Not . . . exactly. I didn't think he'd believe me. My thoughts were only beginning to clear, and maybe I didn't believe me, either. So I got angry inside and let him walk away." Because that's what I do. I get angry instead of honest. Once again, I didn't trust myself.

Baz gestures absently. "And you didn't shoot your shot, which is not the Flora I know. Look at all you did to get in front of Papi. Look at how you worked and schemed to get me to shoot Pilar's wedding, and the way you've pushed through all this new stuff with photography."

He rises after another glance at his phone.

"Wait, where are you going?" I ask.

Baz sets his laptop on the coffee table. "Papi needs help getting something down from the garage."

"You're leaving?" I spurt. "Now? After you make me admit all these blasted . . . ?" I trail off in a huff.

"Feelings?"

I grimace at him.

"Yeah. That's exactly what I'm doing. Go have a shower or something. And take up your lantern and water to your room before we lose power." He backs away. "Hey."

"What?"

"From one photographer to another, you need to buck up and shoot your shot."

TWENTY-FOUR

Now that I'm alone, Baz's words and too many stirred-up emotions are piling above my head, higher and heavier. I've got to move before I'm buried alive. I grab my water bottle and lantern and trudge through the miles of cream marble leading to the staircase. Massive family portraits track my every step. Along with faces, these walls hold shots of island beaches and coarse jungles, the streets and structures of Cuba crumbling like the Vizcaya mermaids.

Outside, parts of Miami are being destroyed, too. And as for my insides? Well. *Shoot your shot,* Baz said. How do I even dare?

In my room, I drop my supplies and flop onto the white comforter. Lila's sleeping and I need to conserve power, but I pull up our thread and text, I'm still okay, please tell everyone, and tell me if you hear from Gordon

Of all my friends, Lila would be the best storm companion. A molten volcano in all this wind and water. And if Lila were here, annoying me with her advice, I'd finally admit something so raw and vulnerable, I can only push it out in whisper form.

"I lost Gordon."

I say it again as the first tear breaks, then another. I finally let them fall. Let them multiply when I see that losing all the unexplored possibilities of him feels the same as losing another part of me.

Trapped beneath a storm, I find there's nowhere to go but backward. My memory dives deep, beating from the inside out and tested like the rafters of this house. My mind ticks through the years, and Gordy and I fall into a living photo album, just like the one I devised for my mother. Our weekend hijinks and getaways and inside jokes are there in full color. We're a filtered lens of picnics and hangouts and motorbike rides to secret places. Cold pizza and pastries and running all around the Owl and Crow, costumed and putting on shows. But at eighteen, wearing a blue dress and dancing in his arms, it didn't feel like a show. We touched, and it didn't feel like friendship.

It felt like everything.

My stomach plummets. I've told him next to nothing. I have to tell him.

Before my next thought lands, I'm reaching for my phone. My heart's teetering on a wire through every ring, dipping when I hear his greeting. "Oi, it's Gordon. Say your thing."

"Gordy, it's me again." Such obvious, weak rubbish, but I keep going. "Please, if you can call or text, I need to know you're safe. And Christ, that's not all."

I draw in a trembling breath.

"You were wrong yesterday. And I was a coward and didn't say anything, but I'm saying it now. I see you. All of you. And if some other girl claims she sees you more than I do, well, I'm going to have issues with that. 'Cause it's just not true. There's not one part of you that isn't the most special and important to me. Please ring me back!"

I press the red button and grab at one of the water bottles, sucking down liquid until I'm near choking. And—no. That wasn't it. My attempt was basic, and I can do better.

I dial again and wait impatiently through the ringing and aching sound of his voice, tears falling through the beep. "I am *not* done, okay? Yeah, you're a funny bloke, Gordon Wallace. And your pranks are tremendous. But you're not half as funny as you are wonderful. And kind and ridiculously talented. And you smell really nice, and Lord, you *feel* really nice when I hug you. You've grown up—I mean, we both have—but you're just . . . You're beautiful." I pause, shaking and heaving. Missing him so much, I can barely breathe around it. "And you're wrong again. Funny Gordon isn't the one I need the most. I need every Gordon the most. Because you're *everything*."

I end the call, bent and battered along with this house. The space between the walls changes, as if the atmosphere is different. The rooms go dark and silent. Power cuts away. Something's down, the grid, a station. And I'm down, too. Down to last chances, I cling to just one more. Out of time, I scrape for seconds. And there's only one way.

A rush pounds through my ears as I tap his avatar for a final push. Overwhelmed, Coral Castle drops heavy in my mind. The man who built it, the unrequited love, a dream that hurt with sweat and heartache. And all for a girl who never saw it.

For so many passing years of *us*, Gordon's been building a castle of his own. His isn't made with pyramid secrets and magnets and endless tons of limestone. But trust and loyalty and fun and humor and . . .

He thinks I never saw it.

Tingles dart from the base of my spine because *this* was the shade and shadow behind his eyes before we left Vizcaya—I'm sure. But he's wrong. I don't just see him for who he is; I see every tiny and tremendous bit he's ever done for me.

"Oi, it's Gordon. Say your thing." The beep is blaring and monstrous.

But the thing I must say, I've never said to a boy. I didn't even recognize it for what it was until it became too late. But now it's here, and . . .

"I love you." It's scared and shaky. I clear my throat. "I love you, Gordon. So much," I repeat as strong as I can, with every ounce of trying and wishing and dreaming I have left. It comes out a little bit pink.

Some hours later it's the sound that wakes me, but I can't be truly awake. Impossible. Only nightmares and movies put their people in the center of dark tunnels with trains charging toward them.

Consciousness creeps in. It's the middle of the night, and I fell asleep next to my phone with a screen as dark as Miami. Tearstained, my heart wrung out to nothing. Gordon didn't ring back. He didn't text.

I jolt upward and realize the sound isn't a train, but a noise I know well, straight from England and my shop on the corner of Jewry and High Street. It's as if every teakettle across the world is blaring hot and ready at once.

The wind? It has to be. Though I never knew wind could act like this. I clutch a pillow, deadened and alone. As I'm gaining consciousness, the sound doubles. Outside, the world is moaning, the kind that makes you want to sympathy-weep along with it. Overnight, Miami's grown legs and lungs. Jessica is here.

She's ten times louder than she was when Baz and I sat on the couch with pictures. I thought I had some reference for the idea of storm and gust, but this is a terror. Losing a mother, I thought I knew grief. But Jessica wails like she's suffering a million double deaths.

And God, what's happening near Gordon? What the bloody hell is happening here? I creep to the window. I haven't looked outside in hours. But when I lift the shutters, I see beyond my face in the dimmed reflection.

She's a hurricane, that one. For years I've been ignited by that nickname. But I never experienced a real hurricane. I never heard the bone-melting, teakettle whine of wind. Never saw the reality of this identity I've kept so close.

I barely make out specters of the tumbled outside. Massive trees bend like twigs. Debris and loose matter are swirling, flying, shooting. Under the noise, it's shattered glass and uprooted metal. Jessica is a monster. Her evil eye, her claws and talons scraping, drawing blood across the city. A monster. Not even Baz's finest camera lens could reframe her into anything less.

I get a rush of disgust mixed with sheer appreciation. *You're a right bitch, Jessica. You win.* People take cover from you. They respect and fear you. They prepare for your coming and stock for days. They board their windows and secure their loved ones. They see you approach and flee your path.

No one tells you to stay close. To not go far. No one denies or pities you. No one could ever forget you. But for years, haven't I more than emulated you? Haven't I strived to be the Flora version of this Jessica?

This monster?

Here the feeling morphs again—and instead of rushing back to bed, I must get closer. I have to own what I've been, once and for all. I fumble for my lantern. With a fresh wash of pale light cast over the rug, I'm trembling as I throw on a dressing gown and trainers. In the long upstairs hallway, I'm alone. The Maríns sleep soundly, and Baz is shut into the room next to mine. I clutch the lantern and creep down one landing, and farther down as another crash hits somewhere close.

The front door looms, strong like steel. It traps Jessica on the other side, and I know I shouldn't. I'm certain I mustn't. But I can't stop the urge to confront this monster head-on. I rest the lantern, my hand cupped over the doorknob, the other at the dead bolt. I squeeze my eyes and I'm pulled, called, and summoned. *She's you and you're her and you only need to see. To see, to see.*

It takes everything I've got to wrench the door open. Then one, two, and a few more steps and *no, please no.* Because this is utter tyranny. Another kind of madness. Instantly, I'm soaked and nearly pummeled at the edge of the flagstone walkway. An entire treetop whizzes by, and this is too much, too much. This wind isn't wind. Wind is the lively drift that kicks back your hair on boats and flies kites and puffs out sails along tropical coasts.

This power spells death for living things. My cries are silent out here, useless as my fingers grip and slip along the porch rail. I can't hold on. My feet lose traction, and my hair and cheeks are blown outward. Hollow and—

There's a human-inhuman noise and a pain. A good and working sort of pain, like a muscle pulled with a yank. I shut my eyes, sinking, sliding. Sobbing and numb.

"What the fucking hell?" The voice is both muffled and frantic.

"Baz?" I'm shoved inside now, a heap on the entry tile, chest ballooning and deflating as something shuts. The door. It's quieter by a half but still blaring. I'm warmer by a third but still drenched.

In the light of two lanterns, he throws a blanket over me and another over himself, crouching low. "Why would you even think of going out there?" His voice is shivered and scratched. "I just pulled you out of hundred-mile-an-hour winds! You could've gotten—I heard you going downstairs, and something felt off. God, Flora."

"Sorry. I'm sorry." It's all I can get out. "I . . ."

"Hey, hey." Baz pulls me close on the floor, wet and all. "You're okay. Just let it out."

I nod into his chest, my insides bubbling over in the arms of a friend. After a fuzzed amount of time, I lift my head. "I know it's careless. But I had to see for myself."

"See what? Yourself being carried away?" he says, his hand kneading my back, warm and strong.

As our skin dries, I tell Baz about my nickname and what it became, inside and out. "Since Mum got sick, I vowed nothing would get the best of me. I'd destruct anything before it could get close enough to hurt, or I'd purposely make things look different with my camera. I kept this wild, romantic idea of a hurricane in my head. And whenever anything hard has come into my life, any storm, I've tried to be a bigger storm."

He nods toward the furious tantrum behind the door. "But now you're in a real hurricane."

"Yes, and it's bloody awful. Video footage lies. That's *nothing* close to what it feels like for real," I say. "I don't want to be like that anymore. It hurts people. It hurts everything."

He drags the edge of the blanket around me. Pulls tight. "You've been through some real-life category fives."

"I've tried so hard to beat them."

"That's not how Miami deals with storms, though. Could you be stronger than what you walked into just now?"

"No." Impossible. Jessica won, not me.

"We get some kind of hurricane almost every year. But you saw for yourself—we prepare and stick together."

"That's the total opposite of what I've done, especially back home." Realization opens wider. "I've made sure I battled everything alone." I shut out Lila and Dad and Orion, and Jules and Gordon.

He gently curves a hand around my shoulder. "No matter what we do—in Miami and, hell, in life, too, right?—there's always going to be another storm."

My eyes spring open, chest swelling. *There's always going to be another storm.* I shift until our gazes lock.

Baz nods. "Yeah, like another accident, or disease, or shitty day. And some of those, we *can* beat. But others, we just have to ride out, stocking up and sticking close to our people."

"I haven't been good at doing that," I admit. "And I twisted the way things looked instead of facing them. It's why I couldn't be honest about how I handled my mum's death. And why I still haven't said a word about photography or anything having to do with uni yet."

Baz takes my hand, squeezing. "And why you couldn't get honest about Gordon."

The name brushes against the battered parts of me. A tear falls fat and round again. "I left him a voicemail and finally said what's in my heart, but what if it's not enough?"

"You want the wingman view? From your extremely loyal Miami friend who's really good with a camera y tan guapo tambíen?"

I let out a stifled sob, a light in all this dark. "You forgot humble."

"Hmm," he says on the breath of a laugh. He thumbs the rise of my cheekbones, and I motion for him to go on. "You shot your shot. And unlike you and me and Netflix shows, it was all for real. And real means something."

For real. These are the new words I try to exchange for the other pairs that fight to get in. (*Too late, too lost,* and *not enough.*) It's my biggest reframe yet.

TWENTY-FIVE

When Jessica packs up and leaves later that Monday, the sky turns violet. It's science, Señor Marín explains to my gobsmacked face. An abundance of atmospheric vapors, mixed with the setting sun and the low cloud ceiling, create these plummy tones. Baz and I venture outside, in eerie tranquility this time. Jessica tossed an Instagram filter over Miami.

Coral Gables stumbles, awake but abused. The greater city slogs through floods and outages, while felled trees and downed power lines make it unsafe for us to drive. Instead, we stretch our legs and arm our cameras. And later, when I scan my work, one shot calls from the screen, as loudly as a pink-lightning photo. This one is another color, and that's fitting. I've changed color, too. It's time to let Orion know.

The feeling rises too strong to save for later, or to wait until I've found those better words. I see now that I never really needed them. I needed an open heart instead. From there, my message to him is simple.

Me: You're my only brother and the best one in the world. I'm truly sorry, with all my heart

With the text, I send my best photo of an impossibly violet sky, the only one in the world.

No time lapses before his reply.

Orion: Thank you, Pink. I love you. Stay safe and I'm coming there soon

My eyes pool as I type.

Me: And then we're all going home

As the next morning comes up dappled blue again, I'm more settled over Orion, even after those few, small words. But my heart stays purple. It's the color of both royalty and sympathy. American soldiers wear a Purple Heart medal when they suffer damage. Mine beats for the one person I still can't reach.

I keep missing Gordon. Worse, everyone else seems to be finding him. Yesterday while I cleaned up and ate, I found a message from Lila.

Lila: Gordon's okay. He got through once to Cate on e-mail. His building flooded, and the cell tower is down in KW. I love you

This morning I missed a text from an unknown number while I was having a shower:

Hiya, it's Gordon. My provider won't work and I'm on Matteo's line real quick. No internet here and we're on mobile hot spot setup. Internship mates have been helping at the historic house site—major damage, owner didn't evacuate and now in hospital

God, the poor woman and her home. And more, I missed Gordy by five minutes and now he's gone. Baz came running from his room at my frustrated scream. Then kept me busy with an annoyingly useful lesson on camera lenses.

The hours bleed together. My heart spills another kind of red and angst.

I'm officially sick of Scrabble and even Baz's "advanced level" photo-editing instruction. We've also spent hours weighing the pros, cons, and requirements of different photography fields. Looking over others' work, and mine, I have my chosen field narrowed down but not completely set. An idea about how to execute my plan has begun to develop. It's so new, I'm still keeping it to myself for a while longer. Getting there will hurt, and there will be a cost. Like so many things worth having.

But two days after landfall, Miami beams with restored power. I get moving and packing as fast as I can, and by mid-morning the roads are clear enough for Baz to drive me back to the Reyes home.

After enduring bear hugs and bursts of utmost appreciation from Elisa and Alan (over butter cake and cafecito, the way they do), Baz stops by my room before heading back to Coral Gables.

"Well, I guess this is it," he says, nodding toward my borrowed gear bags. It's time for him to take back his beautiful equipment, and for me to carry on with my own.

I throw my arms around his neck. "Christ, thank you. So much. You helped with loads more than photography."

"All good, and everything's going to work out." He pulls back. "Let's officially call it quits on fake dating, but we can stay friends for real, yeah?"

"Of course. I never had to fake that."

"Don't forget my offer for FaceTime lessons," he says. "When you get home after the wedding, send me some new photos. Ones you're proud of?"

Proud. The word settles in a throbbing ache after Baz leaves with a final cheek kiss. I have so much to rebuild. But right now I can't even think past another kind of art, and the boy who created it.

Cross-legged on my bed, I reach for Flora's House. My custom image is like one of those pixelated illusion prints that appears three-dimensional once your mind lets go. I go in, too, willing myself past the sketched front door to reach any part of Gordon I can. *Gordy, please, call or text, or anything.* I sink deeper into my thoughts, way past the point where I can hide my tears and knuckle them away.

"Hey, now, chica. ¿Qué pasó?"

So deep, I missed Pilar coming in.

She rushes over, catching up and piecing clues together the way the best of friends do. I'm sniffling over the drawing as her gaze ping-pongs. My puffy, wet face, the sketch, my face again. Then "Ay, mi amor." Her chin crumples. "You're in love with Gordon."

I can't even deny the truth, and that's *new* for me. So after expelling an inflated sigh-sob, I let Pili into the saga—the things I said, and the words Gordon said, and the terrible space and silence between us.

With me under one arm, Pilar dials a number on speaker. "So, news alert, Flora's in love with Gordon," she starts, even before Lila makes it through her greeting.

"What? Oh my God!" Lila says through a squeal. "Wait until Orion hears!"

"Seriously, Pili? I'm literally right here." I blink in disbelief. "And they're flying here in four days. You couldn't wait until then?" I untuck myself from her hold, my hands flailing. "What happened to the stuff we say between us staying that way?"

"Please. You ratted *them* out to the chisme network a few weeks ago." Pilar's mouth softens. "Besides, we love you. *And we love Gordon, so let us have this one nice thing?*"

Oh sodding hell, I'm thinking as Lila giggles and claps from the other side of the world. "Gah!" she says. "Carajo—I knew it. Three years ago I had this pegged, but you were like, 'Gordon? Nah.'"

"Excuse me, but I was fifteen," I retort. "People realize stuff later."

"Bueno, of course she's in love with him," Elisa says, inciting a virtual whirlwind. "Finally she says it!"

Pili and I whip around to the door. The Reyes parents are there, grinning and bounding into my bedroom.

I try to insert a word or two, but it's no use with Lila on speaker, and everyone ogling the Flora's House drawing, and screenshots flying across oceans. They go on and on, louder and louder. *Do his padres know? How long? Did Gordon say anything? Baz is wonderful, but you can tell he's just a friend.*

"You're quite welcome for the entertainment." Despite my raised voice, I go unnoticed. But as I lean back against the pillows, I'm hit with overwhelming warmth. This is care and family, and the kind of shoring up that Baz mentioned. I'll never crop these people from my life. They're mine, and I don't have to hurt alone.

"Okay, now that all this has been established, there's just one problem," I blare, waving my arms. The room halts on a pinpoint. "I'm here, and Gordon's, I dunno, somewhere in Key West, and something's going on with the phone service and we keep missing each other. And . . ." I trail off over a need as strong as my dream. "I want to go after him this time."

Pilar gives a blubbery sob.

Alan and Elisa share a weighted look and a series of gestures. It all looks so secret and insider. "Pili, can Flora take your car?" Alan finally asks.

"Sure," Pilar says.

I lose my next breath. "You mean . . . ?"

Elisa nods. "Claro, we'll drive Pili to La Paloma to prepare for tomorrow's reopening, and if, *if* the highway is clear enough, you can go in her car."

"But only if I pair your phone with the Bluetooth in the Mini," Alan says. "And you don't text while driving."

"And do not turn the music up too loud, and stay on the right side of the road." From Elisa.

"Mami, por favor," Pili says, shaking her head.

"All I am saying is that you can get distracted when you're so emotional." Elisa jolts up. Cuts to the doorway. "I will pack some lunch."

For the next few minutes as chaotic conversation streams through the West Miami house—about Bluetooth, sandwiches, Pilar's Mini Cooper—I fight a smile because they're letting me go. They trust me.

The Overseas Highway spears through ocean water so crisp and sparkling blue, it stings my teeth like the first pull of champagne. Coral and limestone reefs rise from the surface like stony turtle shells. And while the roads and bridges themselves are clear, the small keys I pass over still carry enough Jessica debris and felled palms to cause delays and backups. Many businesses are still closed.

But luckily not the dockside café and market called Burdines on Marathon Key, roughly three hours into my drive from Miami. A sign a few minutes back promised the best chips in all of the Keys. My favorite snack, and hopefully a clean loo? Sorted.

I pull into the car park beside a charming, weathered wood structure. After I cut the engine into silence, my phone chimes to life with not one but two voicemails and a missed text. *What?* Gordon's name on my list sends a flutter down my back. The Bluetooth must've failed, and the Do Not Disturb mode on my phone was still engaged. I let out a furious growl. I was driving for hours, anxious and jittery and singing to Lorde and classic Joni Mitchell, and half the world was calling me. Gordon was texting me.

I expand his message.

Gordon: I just got mobile service back. I've left Key West for good. I'm in Key Largo and getting close. We need to talk so stay put

"Stay put? In Miami? No!" The message came in more than an hour ago. I didn't alert him before leaving because I didn't think he'd get it, and I've missed him yet again. We've gone the opposite way, and we more than need to talk.

Frantic and trembling, I try to get through, each ring like a death toll.

"Oi, it's Gordon. Say your thing."

Damn all phones and voicemail boxes on the planet. "Gordon, pick up. Where are you? I'm not *in* Miami. I came to find *you!*"

My cheeks flame as I cut the call and click the first voicemail.

"Amiga, ugh, it's Pili. Gordon called my cell right as we were leaving for La Paloma. I told him you left for the Keys.

Anyway, if you get this, don't go any farther. I'm so sorry. I hope you two find each other. Besitos."

"Noooo" streams out as I beat my fists against the wheel.

An unknown number comes next.

"Bueno, Florecita, it's Alan, and Gordon just called. Sorry, nena, but I do not think I set up your phone correctly with the Bluetooth. I think the settings on your phone were off, too."

Oh, he thinks? I clamp my eyes shut. Do I stay? Turn back? Pooling sweat and my rising body temperature win over decision-making, though. I exit the Mini before it becomes a steam sauna. It's time to regroup.

I creep around strewn palm fronds and dwindling puddles to the marina side of Burdines. The dock is clear of boats, but the water laps a gentle lullaby around weathered tie-on pylons. No tables sit on the upper deck patio—not yet. Under the seafoam-green awning, damaged bits are everywhere, but a sign lists items from the post-hurricane edited menu. *Fries. Deli Sandwiches. Salads.*

Not mentioned, but just as important, a sparkling clean loo is inside the balmy market that smells of fish and lemon surface cleaner.

"An order of chips—er, fries—please. To go," I tell a sunburned clerk wearing the name *Bill* on his name tag. But "to go" where? That's the problem I leave on this counter along with a few dollars.

"You're driving all the way down?" Bill asks. "Key West still isn't up and running quite yet."

"Honestly, I don't know. But I'm sure your fries will help."

"Oh, they'll do," Bill says. "But give us a minute to cut up a fresh batch? Some guy just took a double order for the road, same as you."

"Did you say double order?" My mind pings, and tingles creep down my arms. "When?"

Bill lifts the brim of a green ball cap. Scratches. "Maybe five minutes ago."

No. It couldn't be. But I still ask, "Was he a Brit by chance? Redheaded?"

Bill fiddles with the order tablet, nodding. "As a cardinal. You one of those psychics from South Beach? My wife frequents some joint off . . ." He continues, but I'm gasping, pivoting, trying to catch my heart as it flies up and out of my chest. And bolting.

"Hey, miss, your fries!"

I'm already through the door and dodging an ice machine and tackle bins until I reach the waterfront patio. I look left, then right, pulling out my phone.

Me: Are you at Burdines on Marathon?

I skip around fuel pumps and a thatched cover for bikes, skidding to a stop when I hear a text message alert behind me. But not just any alert. It's the annoying dog-barking one that hardly anyone uses but . . .

I spin like a dervish. Gordon's simply there, so real and present he clouds everything else on this little key. He's got his phone in one hand and a white takeaway bag in the other. His mouth parts, eyes wide and as stuck as his feet. Instantly, we're back in the Reyeses' kitchen when he landed in Miami. Paces apart. Where do we start?

In movies and the same Netflix catalog that gives us baking

shows and fake-dating disaster plots, the star couple runs into each other's arms. Bonus points for slow-motion effects and moody indie ballads.

And I thought I'd run, too, when we reunited, overjoyed and relieved and empty for all things but him. But I can't move any more than he can. My bones ache with apprehension—I can't read a single word behind his gaze.

"Why are we just standing here?" I finally ask, barely recognizing the wheezed sound that comes out.

"No sodding clue." His voice scrapes with exhaustion. "In that horrible storm, I thought a hundred times over about how this would go."

I nod, feeling my chin crumple. "You drew me a purple house."

"You came to find me."

My hands shake. "Yes, and dammit, Gordon Wallace, you still haven't told me if I'm too late. Or *anything*. After I sent you the equivalent of three drunk word-vomit voicemails and totally ripped myself open."

A flicker of a smile. "You weren't sloshed, though. Your drunk-message voice is giggly, and your *T*s skip all over the place."

I sputter into a laugh and take a wary step, but he holds out his palm, and my world crashes down.

"No, *no*—wait, then. Trust me." He scrolls through his phone. Taps the screen.

My ringer goes off.

"Don't answer," he says. "Let it go to voicemail. And unlike someone I know, I'm gonna try to get it all into one."

My nerves are one more Wallace trick away from utterly

igniting. "What's all this? Another game? I don't have any-thing to pelt at you this time."

He preens and speaks into his mobile at the tone. "Hiya. So it turns out I'm absolute rubbish at moving on from you no matter how hard I try to convince you otherwise. I tried to accept it and play it cool, but it gutted me seeing you with Baz, no matter how casual you two seemed. And even after learning the truth, I closed up for a bit. But I realized that I need to take a chance and believe that what I've wanted for so long is actually happening, as much as you needed to take one and say it. So no, you're not too late. Squiggs—Flora. You've *always* been everything and—"

"*Beep!*" I yell, and toss my phone on the nearby grass and simply go.

He throws his own phone with a riotous grin. The takeaway bag slips from his fingers, and he grabs for every bit of me.

"Mailbox full," I say into that perfect collarbone-to-neck space I've already claimed.

We hold on safe and warm and tight, just being, until he brushes my curls and spans my cheek with one hand. He wears gray shadows and bloodshot eyes, and I note a few new bruises and scrapes. He's been through so much, his skin as storm-battered as I was on the inside.

"You cut me off before the best part," he says.

"Snogging for the first time is the *second*-best part?" I ask in the dizzying rush of me and him.

He smiles and drops his gaze and—poof—Gordon eyeing my mouth like this is my new favorite of all his tricks. He thumbs the underside of my chin, and I could disintegrate. "May I?"

I nod rapidly. "I didn't drive all this way for chips."

A millimeter closer. "Think we'll argue over who's the better kisser?"

"Do you even know me, Gordy?" I ask, and before I can think about firsts or who moved where and when, we fall into each other. I float up to my toes. He nips lightly and sinks deeply, and I lose another battle. Not me, it's him. He's the best at this, and I never want to stop. At once the answer to my own question is yes, yes, and always yes. He knows me. He sees me.

All of me.

Even that part. My chest clamps in a vise grip, and worry sneaks into the smallest crack between us. He must sense the shift. The swell of my bottom lip is the last part he lets go of when he edges back. "Was that okay?"

"More than okay." I rub the soft, damp skin at the back of his neck.

He flashes a smile. Nods. "Then what is it?"

"Something I have to say before we go on any more, because you might think you know what you're getting into, but—"

"Flora." He pecks my forehead. "Just tell me."

I take a clearing-out breath. "I strike hard, Gordon. My temper—you've seen it. We just went through a hurricane, but I'm one, too. I'm a hurricane."

"That's all, then?" One side of his mouth turns upward. "A hurricane? I know what to do with those."

Air whooshes from my lungs. "All these years being my friend, you probably do. But I don't want to be that way anymore. I'm going to get help straightaway. But working on my temper and how I cope will take time. I might slip, and it would kill me to hurt you."

He sends me a piercing look, squeezing my hand. "See, there's a way to shore up a house, starting with the design. The layout and materials and foundation elements. You never build the house to stop the hurricane. That's impossible. You build it strong enough to let it come anyway and to keep standing."

"You're strong enough to withstand me?"

He shakes his head. "To love you."

The words feel forever old and solid, but tiptoed and shaky all the same. "Oh Christ, you do?"

He kisses me hard. "*I love you.* You'd already know that if you hadn't cut off my message. But it's not about being strong enough. Just together enough, okay? If you need to work on some stuff, then brilliant. But if you slip or fall behind, I'll still be here."

My heart swells with everything a real hurricane showed me, that there's always going to be another storm. But never another Gordon, and I need to hold on. I launch myself into him again.

In three or thirty minutes, Gordon points to the takeaway bag. "Want to eat cold, greasy chips over on that little beach before we head back to Miami?"

"I do." And there is something new and wonderful about the short walk we take after grabbing my abandoned order from the Burdines counter, linking arms and stealing kisses. Marathon Key was ravaged hard, like all the rest. But we find a spot, untouched and clear. A patch of soft white sand, the shade from two palms Jessica spared for us.

Turns out, cold chips with Gordon and plenty of snogging on the side is the best meal I've ever had.

"Leave it to you to create my favorite picnic ever on a hurricane-ravaged beach," I muse.

The joy on his face is contagious. "I know what you like." He lobs a sly gaze and adds, "About that—my internship was cut short, and I'll be at Matteo's until the day before the wedding, when my parents arrive. What will we do with all this free time?"

"We can play cheesy tourists until Lila and Orion get here," I say. "Swim in the ocean and practice our Spanish in Little Havana. Maybe a pontoon boat ride."

"That's all, then? Sunbathing at South Beach and dodging mosquitoes in the Everglades?"

"No, that's *not* all," I say, and seal it across his lips. "But we'll have to get creative. There's no way Elisa won't put up a roadblock in front of my door now that she knows we're a thing."

His mouth curves, slow and lazy. "Is Alan's stepladder still at the side of the house?"

I nod.

"Good, 'cause I know of a window."

TWENTY-SIX

For the next three days, I perfect a form of photography that wasn't on Baz's syllabus: the selfie. I subject Gordon to an album-ful. There's us eating Cubanos on Calle Ocho and stretched out on the beach after a swim. Gordon presses his cheek to mine in front of Design District murals, with Miami returning to life in the background.

Shooting me and him and us, I don't have to crop the world to reclaim some control over it. I capture the world I have instead—the one that will see days like these, in tropical sunlight. And darker weeks in hurricane gray. There will always be another storm.

But I can get better at drawing close to my loved ones. When fighting back is best, I'll let them in to fight with me. And for the things I *must* do alone, they'll be waiting at home with all the doors and windows open. Today, that home is in my heart, and the boy who knows them best is right beside me.

Together we watch the arrivals board at Miami International. Lila and Orion's flight already landed, but customs can be a slog. My phone rings, but instead of Lila, Baz pops onto my screen over FaceTime. He underscores his greeting with a slow clap when Gordon jumps into the frame, boyfriend-close.

"I know what this means," Baz starts, grinning. "And I'm your number one fan. But hey, real quick, I have a big ask about the wedding."

"What's that?"

"Do you think the Reyeses could secure a last-minute reception spot for my assistant?"

"Sure, I'll let Pilar know. Who's assisting you?" Then it hits me. "If it's Armando, then we're gonna—"

"Kelly. It's Kelly."

Gordon and I share a knowing look, but before we can ask any nosy questions, Baz says, "We've been hanging out the last couple days. You know, editing the shoot photos and stuff."

I let out a little gasp, and Gordon's right there with a fist pump.

"No, you clowns," Baz says. "It's not like that."

Gordy snorts a laugh. "It's not like that *yet*."

"En *serio*." Baz rolls his eyes. "I'm hanging up now."

He does, and Gordon kisses my cheek, and in that rush of joy and contentment, I look up absently. My England crew emerges at the end of a long hall.

They don't see us yet. But anxiety arrows through because here, along with Lila and my brother, is the second surprise visitor of my Miami summer. I reach for Gordon's hand. "Did you know he was coming?"

Sensing my nervousness, he pulls me in tight. "Not a clue. But it says something when Lila and Orion keep secrets from both of us now."

Dad has come to Miami.

I would've sworn on all the magic cats in existence that I wouldn't cry. I rarely do during moments like this, but their eager approach hits all my tender spots today. After all I've been through in Miami, sinking into my brother's redeeming hug and absorbing Lila's *let me look at you* plea before she squeezes me flat makes me a threat to waterproof mascara.

"Aww, Pink," Orion says, and kisses my forehead.

Lila's turned into a ball of sniffles. "We missed you, too, amiga. If we're like this now, there's no hope for us next week."

"Hiya? Am I chopped liver, then?" Gordon calls.

Lila and Orion guffaw dramatically and rush their friend with bear hugs.

That leaves me and Dad. I stare at my white sandals. The arrivals board and the travel posters teasing trips to Spain and Costa Rica. Then my father's plane-scuffed face, his bleary blue eyes.

"You came," I say needlessly.

Dad adjusts his travel bag. "Was easy when I decided, same as you I suppose. With the Reyeses, it takes one call and they're already securing an extra wedding reception seat and a family dinner invitation. That whole-pig-roast affair and all."

It sounds so prodigal child. My heart beats a drum; I'm the lost daughter who exiled herself. But before I could crawl home on my own to beg for scraps, he came to me with a banquet.

I go, too, and fill my father's arms.

All the unresolved matters between my family and me cling like damp Miami as we load everyone into Elisa's Honda. They swarm around the dozens of quips and questions that Gordon and I field over our new relationship status. And when Gordon steers the van into the DoubleTree hotel for a quick luggage drop-off, the tension of unsaid things follows me into the room Dad and Orion are sharing.

Everyone freshens up, and Gordon finds me out on the balcony while the guys unpack. His arms snake around my middle as he pulls me into his chest. "Proof of life?" he asks in a sentimental nod to our "before."

"Good enough. But I need to tell them, Gordy." About the future plans I've made and shared with him the past few days. "We have loads of fun events before the wedding, and I feel I can't fully enjoy any of it until I'm completely honest."

"Tell them now, then," Gordon says. "Lila and I can wait in the lobby if you want it to just be your family."

I spin in his hold, shaking my head. "Lila *is* family. And you're . . . *you*." I breathe in and try something new. "Sit beside me while I do something hard?"

Gordon's reassuring smile is immediate; I stare at a face that's meant laughter and loyalty for years. Now there's everything more, and I see it all. "You've got this, Squiggs," he says before we clasp hands and enter Dad and Orion's room, settling on a small love seat in the corner.

"I need to tell you all something."

Dad and Orion turn from their various tasks, and Lila looks up from her phone. The next few seconds of silence are terrifying, but I can carry on. I will.

"Lila, I know you're dying to see your family, but this is important."

The trio consults one another for no more than a half second before bending their legs onto beds and chairs.

"It's about everything I'm doing next. I know now." I stretch to grab my Canon from my nearby tote and hold it up proudly. "This camera has become so much more than a hobby. It's what I want to do, for real. I want to take pictures." I start like that, getting real about my loss of self-trust, and what the camera was for a girl suffering a double-death loss. I end with what it is now. So much a part of the sunny and stormy life I have left. And the first real dream I've ever had. "I do want to talk to someone and get help. I want to learn to control my emotions and to not hide things or fight the world at every turn."

I scan three faces and see the open hearts behind them. The understanding that changes the angles of my family's posture. The loosening-up as they nod into my admission.

"I'm going to make a solid career with this camera. I'm still figuring out my specialization, but I've never been more sure." I turn to Orion now. "Here's the hardest part. You went to loads of trouble securing my university scholarship, and I'm so grateful—please don't think I'm throwing it away carelessly. It's just that I *know* a university path is not for me, and I don't need a degree to be a successful photographer."

My brother's leaning forward and actually . . . listening. I exhale a cleansing breath and go on.

"Whilst here, I couldn't stop thinking of Mum's piano and her wish to donate it as a legacy gift. So I want to give something meaningful, too. I'd like to ask the foundation to give my scholarship to another applicant who truly wants to attend uni. Someone who's always dreamt of that. And I didn't realize this at first, but I do now. In learning how to see myself better, I figured out how to compose the Greenly Center tribute. I know what to say."

Orion's unreadable for a few eternal seconds before he cracks a smile. Lila's already there. "I'm proud of you, Pink. I truly am," my brother says.

I take a moment with words that have seemed impossible for months, letting them fall into empty spaces. "I'm sorry for squandering opportunities and being unreliable. You and Dad have supported me even when I was at my worst. And now I want to support myself. I'll be paying for my photography classes and equipment on my own. I'll work extra hours at the shop. I know this might not be what you envisioned, but all I'm asking for—"

"God, you're so much like your mum," Dad says, his head bent low.

Air rushes from my lungs. "What do you mean?"

I don't expect the quick flutter of Dad's smile beneath a sheen of tears. "Did you know she dropped out of law school? You couldn't have. I realize I never told you or your brother about this. By the time you were old enough to appreciate the story, she'd already been diagnosed. And that's my fault. I tried to preserve us in the present, as long as possible. It hurt so much to look back over the past. We were so happy then. In longing and grieving for that time, I shut it out. Dementia took her memory, but it twisted mine."

And mine, I'm thinking. "It's okay, Dad. I understand. We do," I say, to my brother's affirming nod. "The diagnosis hurt all of us differently."

The room wears my truth like the warm things we know best. The tea we sell and England winter firelight. The beautiful cardigans my nan knits. Lila comforts her teary boyfriend, pulling him close as she blows me a kiss.

"Your mum left her program a year after we met," Dad continues. "You do know that there are generations of barristers and solicitors in her family. She was expected to join the ranks. But she had another dream, like yours. She wanted to marry a tea-shop owner and put her creativity into helping his dodgy new business grow. And it did—look at us now."

Dad gestures absently.

"The aesthetic and business model we currently use were all her doing." He sits up taller. "So let's find a way for you to use your creativity, too, and I trust you'll find the right program. Besides, we don't have a branding photographer yet, and we'll need that when we open in London and Oxford. You'd best get on it," he adds with a wink. "Like Mum."

And here is where I break, at one word, one woman who loved me for the brightest shooting-star amount of time. *Mum.* Gordon's there to catch me as my father's declaration settles in. Dad thinks I'm like my mother?

Wasn't she everything clever and kind and amazing? Her incredible heart is the real heirloom she left in our home. There's no way she could've been a better mum. But she fell in love and grabbed her dream, and she *did* better for herself and others. And so will I.

The next moments pass in a flurry of tissues and healing hugs. The air is cleared and new by the time Dad pops down to the lounge to return a call.

Lila holds up her phone. "Certain Cubans are getting impatient for their people. Mami told us to meet at Tío Carlos's house, and I can already smell the lechón."

"Qué rico el congrí y lechón asado." Gordon rubs his palms as he ducks out to join Orion on the terrace.

"Oh hey, now, Señor South Beach," Lila calls after him. When we're alone, she reaches into the pocket of her jeans. "I found something on your desk at home—promise I wasn't snooping." Her abuela's gold chain unravels from her palm.

I stare at the beautiful gift, shared across seas and families. "When I left, I didn't feel worthy of this. And I still haven't chosen the right charm for it."

Lila nods. "That's okay. I have a feeling you will soon. For now, you're set for sparkly things: photography, your adorable new novio, which we *will* be discussing later . . ."

"And my sister," I say. "Mi hermana."

She throws her arms around my shoulders, squeezing heartily. Then clasps the chain around my neck, where it belongs.

"Just in time," Gordon says when we join him and Orion outdoors. "This muppet was threatening to toss me over the balcony if I didn't agree to the rules of engagement for dating his sister."

Orion huffs in mock offense. "Come on, that's rubbish."

Lila shakes her head and goes to elbow Orion's shoulder, but he pulls a move, and she ends up in the tight circle of his arms.

I tuck myself into Gordon's side, and the four of us join the panorama of boats and skyscrapers and swaying palms.

Biscayne Bay glitters below, and I can't resist taking a selfie with my favorites. We huddle close with a city of hurricanes and heartbeats behind us. And in this uncropped frame, and all together, we're lightning.

EPILOGUE

OCTOBER

THE GREENLY CENTER
WINCHESTER, HAMPSHIRE, ENGLAND

"There are three things I'd like you to know about Evelyn Maxwell," I say after fumbling through my introduction and hopefully remembering to thank everyone.

I take a moment to scan the audience. Lenses and news cameras and blistering lights nearly eclipse my view of the front row. I need my people, and they're all here. My family and Gordon, all my friends. Even my Miami family, too. Elisa and Alan, Pilar and Ryan. This is one of those times when I must do something hard by myself. But still, I'm *not* alone.

"Rather," I continue, "here are three important lessons she taught me. Many of you know that I didn't have a lot of time with my mum. But I've realized that love and mothering work on their own timeline. And good mothers—well, they know things."

At least twenty pregnant teen mums sit in the audience. New mums with infants in their arms are here, too. "Good mothers know that sometimes the best thing you can do for your child is something that appears completely frivolous to anyone else." The audience chuckles. "Good mothers feed too many coins into supermarket gumball machines and buy the sprinkle cupcake when it's no one's birthday. They hold kitchen dance parties and let their little ones paint their nails and put glitter on places that never asked for it."

I tug at my hair.

"Secondly, to my fellow curly-haired friends—never ever scrunch. Evelyn Maxwell knew this. She taught me from her vanity mirror that perfect, un-frizzy curls demand loads of product worked into soaking wet hair. Not towel-dried. And we never use a brush on dry hair—the horror!" I gasp to the warmest laugher. "After sectioning off each curl and smoothing it down with gel, a good shake is all we need to get out the door for school. For work. For life."

I pause to find Gordon's reassuring face, and he blows me a kiss that flies into the center of my chest.

"And lastly, good mothers know that it's okay to change your mind. It's perfectly fine to get a new dream, to set out on a new path. To do something better and different and all your own. Evelyn Maxwell modeled that. And this was something that I didn't understand when I had her. When I was little. But she planted enough of it into this curly-wig head. Into a heart fed with pink and frivolous things. Good mothers do that—they give us small bits of what we'll need later on. They know we'll discover the most important lessons for ourselves, in time."

I exhale and smile over the crowd.

"The Greenly Center has her piano now. She was brilliant on those keys. And all my family asks is that you play it. Those of you who know how—please play it to bring a smile to others. And those of you who can't play a note, that's okay, too. Sit on the bench. Rest there when you're tired. Or excited. Or dreaming, and know that a daughter once sat there, with a mother. Evelyn Maxwell—a good mother."

ACKNOWLEDGMENTS

Dear readers, thank you for so faithfully and enthusiastically following me from the streets of Winchester, England, for Lila Reyes's story, back to Miami with Flora Maxwell. I'm so grateful to God, and to you, that I get to do this job and share my stories. I treasure each and every one of you.

To Alex Borbolla, thank you for knowing exactly what Flora and her story needed, and guiding me through every word with such kindness and brilliance. You're one of a kind.

To Sophia Jimenez, thank you for providing such wonderful insight, editing, and faithful support in getting *British Girl* from our computer screens onto bookshelves.

To my agent, Natascha Morris, you stand in countless gaps for me. Your dedication to me and my entire career is something I value more than I could ever express. Thank you will have to do.

To Lane Heymont, Stefanie Rossitto, and the entire team at The Tobias Literary Agency, thank you for your outstanding efforts and unwavering support. I appreciate you.

To my brilliant critique partners, Joan F. Smith and Allison

Bitz, this brightly colored book of mine would not be here without either of you. I'm so proud to call you my team, and my dearest friends.

To art director Karyn Lee and illustrator Andi Porretta, you did it again. The creativity, beauty, and whimsy you've added to the *Cuban Girl* world with this cover make me smile every time I look at it. It's a joy to have both of you creating such lovely things for my books.

To the entire Atheneum team, thank you for your dedicated efforts in bringing my story to bookshelves. Rebecca Vitkus, I am in awe of your talent and eagle eye. And many thanks to Clare McGlade, Tatyana Rosalia, and Morgan Maple for all your hard work.

To Crystal and the BookSparks team, I'm so thankful to have you in my book world.

To Jerry McCauley and James Bitz—two extraordinary photographers—thank you for making sure this author who can barely shoot a decent photo was able to write about the art and trade of photography with authenticity.

To Alexandra Overy, you're the finest British beta of all time. Thank you for making sure Flora and Gordon and the entire crew look and sound their very best.

To my amazing husband who navigated me around England so I could take in every corner, I love and appreciate you so much.

To my trusted group of author friends, I love you all. Thanks for making me laugh and feel not quite so alone in some of the stages of book publishing. It's an honor to work alongside you. A special thank you to Erin Hahn, Lillian Clark, and Kelly

Coon for helping me come up with this book title over too many Vegas mimosas, but never too many shenanigans.

To Ximena Avalos and Ashley Garcia, thank you for all your help with so many small details that make a huge difference.

To Mike Lasagna, Brittany Bunzey, Carmen Alvarez, Reese's Book Club, and countless other librarians, booksellers, and champions of diverse literature, thank you for supporting and inspiring me.

As I leave this book with the world, I do so as the mom of two children who are now in college, and so close to some of the challenges Flora faces in her story. I'm endlessly proud of both of you and thrilled that I get to watch you work toward everything you've ever dreamed.